MRLG

SO-AEE-340

The DRIFTER

Center Point
Large Print

Also by Lauran Paine and available from
Center Point Large Print:

Kansas Kid
Night of the Rustler's Moon
Wagon Train West
Six-Gun Crossroads
Dead Man's Cañon
Lightning Strike
Reckoning at Lansing's Ferry

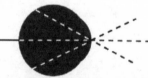

**This Large Print Book carries the
Seal of Approval of N.A.V.H.**

The DRIFTER

A Western Duo

Lauran Paine

CENTER POINT LARGE PRINT
THORNDIKE, MAINE

This Center Point Large Print edition
is published in the year 2018 by arrangement with
Golden West Literary Agency.

Copyright © 2012 by Mona Paine.

All rights reserved.

The text of this Large Print edition is unabridged.
In other aspects, this book may vary
from the original edition.
Printed in the United States of America
on permanent paper.
Set in 16-point Times New Roman type.

ISBN: 978-1-68324-661-9 (hardcover)
ISBN: 978-1-68324-665-7 (paperback)

Library of Congress Cataloging-in-Publication Data

Names: Paine, Lauran, author.
Title: The drifter : a western duo / Lauran Paine.
Description: Center Point Large Print edition. | Thorndike, Maine :
    Center Point Large Print, 2018.
Identifiers: LCCN 2017045628| ISBN 9781683246619
    (hardcover : alk. paper) | ISBN 9781683246657 (pbk. : alk. paper)
Subjects: LCSH: Large type books. | GSAFD: Western stories.
Classification: LCC PS3566.A34 D75 2018 | DDC 813/.54—dc23
LC record available at https://lccn.loc.gov/2017045628

TABLE OF CONTENTS

GUNNISON BUTTE

I

The man on the black horse left Lander four jumps in front of an irate Mormon posse with a bleak laugh on his lips and $4,000 wrapped in his bedroll.

He got well into the Wind River mountains, and although he slackened pace—he had to; these weren't just mountains, they were an adjunct of the awesome Continental Divide—he did not stop any longer than was required to favor the powerful black horse.

He left a southeasterly trail, but that was deliberate. Once he reached the desolation and cold wind around Rawlins, he changed course and headed west of the Medicine Bows toward Rock Springs, and from there on he still climbed an occasional peak to watch for sign on his back trail, but he scarcely expected to see any. Mormons were farmers, not horsemen. They were a narrow, bigoted, plodding, coarse people. They were also vindictive and pointlessly cruel, given the chance, but, as the man called Jasper had said with a sly wink, back up in Lander when they were planning their robbery of a payroll stage just south of Lander, Mormons were good at labor, good at being totally unimaginative, good at storing up those sheaves they were forever singing about.

From Rock Springs, where the man on the black horse lingered for two days, eating and sleeping, he headed directly toward the boundary line, and rode out of Wyoming and into Colorado, not far from Craig and the Yampa River.

He reached Steamboat Springs and the mountain cow range country beyond Rabbitear Pass, and there he slackened pace still more.

It was springtime, but in this north country that was no guarantee of much. The sun shone more, but it could be as cold as a storekeeper's heart during the day, and as icy as a schoolmarm's kiss at night. Winter lingered around the Steamboat Springs country far into summertime, some years, and *any* year the peaks roundabout, especially over in the direction of the mean little slatboard town of Kremling, never shed their coats of snow. A man could be riding through a lush meadow and get hit by a gust of wind straight off some eternal snow field that would be so cold it would curl his toes.

The outlaw had one hell of a ride ahead of him before reaching the Gunnison country, which was better than halfway down the full length of Colorado, but there was one consolation. It would be a sight warmer by the time he got down there.

There was another consolation; he had $4,000 in paper greenbacks squirreled up into his bedroll.

That was enough to buy a little corner of hell, and start a fire in it at both ends for quite a spell.

He went over to Meeker, then on down to Rifle, and at the latter place, when an old grizzled cowman offered him a riding job, he took it, put the black horse out to pasture, rode a string belonging to the cowman, and put in almost two full months helping at the gather, at the marking, and finally, when it was all taken care of, he also helped at a barn raising.

People liked him. He was an easy, affable man, with stone-steady blue eyes, a loose gait, and a lot of muscle packed inside a tough hide. He was one of those men of indeterminate years who could have been twenty-five or thirty-five years old. He was good with horses and knew cattle. He could have stayed in the Rifle country indefinitely; the old cowman offered him a permanent job as range boss. But although Rifle, Colorado, was a fair distance from the Mormon country up around Lander in Wyoming, it was still not far enough, so he finished at the barn raising, celebrated with the other range riders one night in town, and the following morning was long gone, headache and all, before the others went forth none too steadily to splash water into their faces.

They had known him as Jasper Littleton in the Rifle country. At Paonia on south a few leagues, when he put up his horse at a livery barn, he gave the name of Eli Morgan. His actual name

11

was Boone Helm, and, although he worked the northern ranges like a native, he had actually been born and partially reared down around old Tularosa, in New Mexico Territory.

That was why he kept on a southerly course; he had worked the high country for several years, but he had never become accustomed to so much cold, for such long periods of time. He had told that other range rider, the one he had only known two weeks when they decided to rob the pay stage, that, if he lived to be a hundred and fifty, he never would have thick enough blood to stand so much cold.

As a man rode south from Wyoming, the names all had a kind of raw newness to them. They were derived from earlier itinerants, such as Meeker, or they derived from functional things like rifles, or a spring with a boulder wedged in it so that it whistled like a steamboat. But the farther south a man traveled, the more he encountered a different derivation. The closer he got to the Colorado–New Mexico line, the more names cropped up with a Spanish twist to them. Below the Gunnison country, for example, there was a town named for an old Indian, Ouray, and after that the names were Del Norte, Monte Vista, Alamosa, Durango, Trinidad, and over the line there was Aztec.

Boone Helm knew every one of those places, south of Ouray, but more to the point, *he* was known down there. Not as an outlaw, but a man could never be sure those vindictive, bull-headed Mormons up north hadn't, somehow or other, picked up something about him they could trace, and Boone Helm had no idea of riding into Durango, for instance, where he'd worked the ranges for several years, only to ride into the iron embrace of some lawman's jailhouse.

He knew the Gunnison country fairly well. He'd summered there, but not as a rider, as a wild horse trapper, so, while he knew the country passably well, the people down there did not know Boone Helm, didn't know him by that or any other name. Furthermore, Gunnison was warmer than either Lander or Rawlins, or any of those other upland ranges.

Gunnison had been named for an Army officer who had been spying on both the early-day renegade Mormons and the Indians, in the guise of a surveyor. All that was ever known about the fate of Captain Gunnison was that his camp was found, plundered, with its occupants dead from lead poisoning. The Mormons said the Indians massacred the Gunnison party, and in fact some time later shiny surveyor's tools and instruments were found in the possession of Indians. But the Indians said the Mormons had killed Gunnison and his crew, and that was equally as probable. In either case, a town was named after him, and if that wasn't much solace to Captain Gunnison, at least it was a far better tribute than dozens of other equally as hardy and intrepid pioneers got, who succumbed to the same ailment.

By the time Boone Helm got down there, summer was upon the land, the grass was stirrup-high, the creeks were brimful from high-country run-off, the cattle were dark red with sassy-fat calves at their sides, and winter had been vanquished. It was a big country with mountains visible in almost any direction, with lower slopes in close, and with forested rims and lifts, like spiked humps of enormous supine animals, darkening the ranges where a man could ride for days without breaking free of forests.

Boone Helm hadn't been worrying about apprehension since shortly after leaving the Continental Divide behind, and by the time he got down into the Gunnison country, he had not one shred of doubt but that he had escaped clean. And he had. Providing he was prudent from here on, there was practically no danger at all.

He intended to be prudent. In fact, he intended to do even better than that; he intended to find a mountain meadow, set up camp, and live Indian-style for the remainder of the summer and maybe into the early autumn, which the Indians called The Time of Falling Leaves.

For four days he criss-crossed the country, staying well clear of the town, which was not much, actually, but was nevertheless a town. He had never cared much for towns even though he fully appreciated their convenience, and the necessity of them, especially in a sparsely settled cow country.

The place he ultimately settled in was what, up north, was called a park. It was southwest of Gunnison in the general direction of Ouray, but was not in fact within sight of either Ouray or Gunnison. It was upon a pine-shielded plateau where there was a brawling creek, a small lake, and half a dozen park-like areas as green as emeralds where the black horse could get as fat as a tick, if he wanted to, at least until first frost, then they'd have to go somewhere else.

He was prudent, too, about establishing his camp. He put it just within the fringe of trees, facing south and east so that he commanded a strategic sighting of all the most logical approaches for either game or mounted men. He needed the former to subsist, and while he did not especially fear the latter, the kind of men who would ride through in this hidden, hushed, and secret place could very easily be the kind of men who would back-shoot someone just to get his horse and saddle.

But that did not happen. For a week after setting up camp, Boone Helm fished the creek and the little fifty-acre lake, hunted, and loafed in the wonderfully benign sunlight. He told the black horse, one evening, when the animal came

15

close to the fire because he'd heard a cougar scream out in the darkness, that there should be a law requiring every man to take at least two weeks off each year and set up a loner's camp in a place like this.

Whatever the horse thought, if he thought of anything at all except that cougar back in the deeper hills, was not reflected in his face as he stood, sopping up heat from the firelight. He was a splendid animal in his prime, strong and deep-bodied with an endless amount of what range men called bottom, meaning endurance. He was also tractable and intelligent. He and Boone Helm had been together for three years now, so the black horse remembered no other owner. They got along better than a man and his wife.

In fact, for the length of time they were in their idyllic, solitary camp, the black horse was completely satisfied, and because he came to the whistle, and never wandered far, Boone never hobbled him even though he kept a pair of rawhide, plaited hobbles hanging upon a tree limb in the camp.

They both accepted life as it now came to them day by day. The horse thought no further than that. Boone occasionally thought further, both in retrospect and about their future, but he did it, usually, while waiting for a speckled trout to hit his improvised line at the creek, or while leaning his shoulders against a rough-barked old bull pine, staring into the supper fire, and without any sense of urgency at all.

It was a very good way for a horseman to spend his days.

II

The boy was an orphan. Not exactly, but close enough. He never knew his father and his mother had left when he was fourteen and he never saw her again. All he ever knew was that she had put on her fine dove-gray dress, her best button shoes, and the hat with the proud feather in it, and had driven off with the peddler from Chicago who owned the elegant team of chestnut geldings and the fresh-polished spring wagon with his sample cases in back.

He knew that much because he'd always been a light sleeper. When his mother had tried to close the door quietly, it had awakened him. He'd reared up in bed and had peered out the window. He'd seen her looking like a girl; he'd seen her smile up into the thick-featured face of the traveling man as she got into the buggy, and that was the last he ever saw of her.

When he arose and got dressed, the buggy was long gone in the rising sun of a New Mexico springtime morning. There was a faintly fragrant little skimpy lace handkerchief lying next to his head on the pillow with eleven silver dollars in it. That was all.

Fourteen wasn't old and it wasn't young, it was *both,* so the boy did not cry, exactly, but he stayed in the room for two days without turning up the lantern or going out to eat, and licked his wound, learning to live with the fact of abandonment. It was like being very ill but without the weakness of light-headedness.

Then he took his $11 down to Crampton's livery barn to buy a horse and maybe an old saddle with a blanket and bridle. Beyond that, all instinct told him to do was ride, to turn his back on Albuquerque and head upland into the clean air and emptiness of open country where he wouldn't have to meet another human being.

But $11, old man Crampton said, was about a third of what he needed. Just a halfway decent, using horse would cost twice that much. As for the saddle, blanket, and bridle, that would cost more than the horse by a damned sight. Then Crampton, with feigned sympathy, had said: "Yeah, I heard what she done to you, boy. Now I tell you what I'm going to do. You give me that eleven dollars and whatever else she left you . . . jewelry maybe? Her kind always got jewelry or fancy gewgaws . . . and I'll get you a stage ticket back East and maybe you can find her."

Instead, the boy waited until well past midnight, picked out a sleek, powerful dun horse, a saddle, and outfit, rigged himself out a mount, got across leather, and lit out northward, with old man Crampton's rubber-butted six-gun stuffed into the front of his waistband.

It was the first thing he had ever stolen, aside from some apples one time, and, another time, an Army compass made to resemble a pocket watch, which a drunk soldier had dropped as he staggered down the plank walk from a saloon in the Mexican part of Albuquerque. He'd never seen a compass before, and, anyway, he'd hated that cavalryman because he'd spied through the saloon side-wall window and had seen the soldier kiss his mother, who had worked in that saloon.

He had struck back at the soldier, and now, heading across the open country northwest of Albuquerque, he had struck back again. This time, not at Crampton the liveryman, particularly, or anyone else individually, but at everyone and *everything*.

He was tall for his age, almost six feet tall in fact, and he had dark curly hair and dark eyes. His skin was fair, his build willowy and wiry. Someday, obviously, he would fill out into a physically raw-boned, lanky, tough-muscled man, but that was a number of years in the future. Right now he was a boy who was balancing between childhood and manhood, but the farther he got from Albuquerque through the chilly early hours, the more he felt like a man. A horse thief at fourteen.

Before dawn arrived he left the dun gelding at the base of a brush knoll, went up there, and, Indian-like, squatted for nearly a half hour just watching. There was no sign of pursuit.

Later, with the morning half spent and with the uplands dead ahead where he'd be able to turn and twist in and out through the broken, hot country that lay below the rims of Barnanillo, he hid the horse and did the same thing again. This time, he saw dust far back, and while, of course, it could have been made by a posse looking for that most reviled of all Western outlaws, a horse thief, he thought it could also be one of those Army patrols that were forever criss-crossing New Mexico in search of reservation-jumping Apaches. In either case, he angled westerly, over in the direction of the massive, inert, dark, and mysterious mountains that lay a long distance on his left from Santa Fe. Over there, he could turn up almost any cañon and disappear in the vastness of those mountains. The trick, over there, was not to get caught by the Indians, but either way, Indians or posse men, he knew by instinct that his best hope was to keep moving.

He did; he stopped only to rest the dun horse. After three days the horse got a little tucked up, but he was as sound as new money and as tough as boiled owl.

The boy came over a brushy ridge the morning of his fourth day out, with one jack rabbit in three days to keep body and soul together, and saw the secret Indian camp where a family of hold-outs had thrown up a camouflaged brush shelter near a secret spring where some trees and grass grew.

He left the horse and sneaked down through the underbrush with Crampton's pistol sweat-slippery in his grimy paw, but the Apaches were gone, perhaps out hunting. He got up close enough to steal a Winchester saddle gun encased in a limber mule-skin sheath, and as many strips of fly-specked deer-meat jerky as he could stuff inside his shirt, then he fled back to the dun horse, climbed into the saddle, and struck out again with more fear in his heart than before, because the Apaches would be able to read his sign no matter what he did, far better than any posse men from distant Albuquerque. He had to use up a lot of space now; the only deterrent to an Apache was distance—and perhaps a town—but the boy did not find a town, did not in fact *try* to find one.

The jerky was good eating. It had been peppered to hell and back, which the Apaches had learned from the Mexicans, but when he found water, he'd wash as much of that off as he could, before eating the jerky.

Six days and he still worried about the Apaches—especially the one who had owned that Winchester—but he was by the sixth day almost as wild and wary and sly as the Indians also were, so he used every ruse that occurred to him, and in fact, although he thought, once, he'd seen two dumpy riders cross a ridge at a walk, and immediately altered course, if the Indians had followed him this far, he did not see them. At least, he did not see anything he could have recognized as an Indian.

He saw two towns, though, when he slanted back down out of the mountains to favor the dun horse, and crossed a lot of starved-out New Mexico wasteland. One was Española, and the other one, farther north, up where the land forms were changing, was Questa. He saw them off on his right from a considerable distance. He avoided them both, for although he was developing a craving for some kind of food other than dried deer meat, and although he probably could have ridden right up the full length of the main roadway of both places without being stopped, a week of flight—and fright—had made being wary and devious as a redskin second nature.

But one night under a two-thirds full moon he saw the dim and ghostly, hushed silhouette of ranch buildings, and, without even thinking against it, he left the horse again, stalked the ranch yard, found the hen house, and before two shaggy cow dogs even got his wind, he had

22

strangled a pair of hens and was running like the wind back to the horse. He laughed, this time, because the watchdogs only barked when he was back astride and, Apache-like, made a deliberate sashay in close so that those dogs would catch his scent and raise Cain.

This was the first time in a week he had smiled. What it signified was that he had found himself; he had discovered something he could do better than most other people, most other pale-eyed people anyway. He did not reflect—at fourteen—that there were hundreds of others, dark-eyed, dark-skinned people who could do the same thing and do it much better because it was both their heritage and their birthright, and that these dark people, for all their slyness and cleverness, were being ground into oblivion. All he thought, as he ran ahead of the morning sunlight with a pair of dead hens lashed to his saddle, was that he was master of this new world of hiding and coming out at night to strike, then fading away at high speed. It gave him a feeling of exhilaration nothing else ever had.

He cooked both hens over a dead-wood fire, which made almost no smoke, ate one down to the last bit of gristle, stuffed the other one inside his shirt, and rode until sunset, and some cliff-like serrated barrancas stopped him, or at least deterred him, until the following morning, then he turned westward and poked along through the superb desert country dawn until the sun was fully up, before those barrancas showed rents and faults that would allow a horseman to pass up through them to the plateau beyond.

It was all unfamiliar country, but he had been traveling through that kind of terrain for a week now. The difference was that where he now sat his horse, looking back, he was over the line into Colorado, which he had no inkling of, and wouldn't have cared even if he'd known.

There had been a way station on his route, which he had, as always, avoided with considerable wariness. It had been the village of Aztec, which he did not know and did not care. Aztec was the last town he saw after reaching the higher country.

It was cooler up here; the land was different. He could still look back hundreds of miles in the glass-clear air and see the endless drift and slant of desert, but on ahead there seemed to be more trees on the slopes, more promise of water and grass.

He lay over one day in among scented pines where grass waist-high to a tall buck Indian made the dun horse happy. And where a still pool lay in the bend of a mountain creek, he stripped raw, washed his filthy clothes, draped them over bushes in the sunlight of a little grass clearing to dry, then he eased down into that snow-water creek to bathe and could hardly catch his breath it was so cold.

Finally he divided his last chicken into three parts, postponed supper that night, and the following day ate the divided portions for breakfast, dinner, and supper. He hunted that day with the Apache saddle gun, but although he saw some elk, some deer, a lot of upland birds, he was never able too get close enough to shoot.

In the midafternoon he lay down in the warm grass of the tree-shielded meadow where the dun horse was drowsing, hip-shot, as full as a tick, and slept. He did not open his eyes again until the sun had set, shadows were slipping up around him throughout the forest, and mosquitoes half as big as small birds were swarming into his clearing from their dark daylong hiding places.

He usually slept with the saddle blanket beneath him, between him and the ground. This night, he slept with the sweat-stiff, smelly blanket over him, and that baffled all but the most persistent mosquitoes.

The next morning he had lumps where he'd lost blood to the little insects, but when the sun returned, they went back to their dark places to hide, and the boy arose with the same gnawing in his gut he'd learned to live with this past week.

He would have liked to have been able to stay in this delightful, serene, and hospitable place longer. In fact, as he told the dun horse while he was saddling up, he'd like to find a place like this where they could both simply eat enough, and do nothing, for the rest of the summertime. Then he struck out northward again.

There were more towns, once he got near the edge of vast cow country grassland again. One of them was called Del Norte, he knew, because someone had painted that name, and the distance to it, upon a great gray stone on the east side of the stage road.

He did as always; he went far out and around Del Norte as though he were an old wolf, or a reservation jumper, and, when the way was uncluttered, he headed northward again. Slightly westward, but always northward.

Into his second week now, the boy, whose name was George Alden Morgan, rarely looked back, rarely thought back, and sat straight upon his dun horse. Under some circumstances a boy of fourteen could make the transition to an early manhood fast. Those circumstances, patently, had to do with the total and absolute necessity for such a lad to *make* that transition. George Alden Morgan had made it.

III

Any experienced outlaw, but especially an experienced horse thief with the prospect of uninterrupted flight ahead of him, would have made dead certain of one thing in particular before he saddled someone else's animal and began his run for life. This thought would have occurred to any mature man who was stealing a horse for the first time, but there were more reasons than simply youth and inexperience that had inhibited George Alden Morgan back in Albuquerque. The shock of finding that his mother could do what she had done had been one reason. Another had been the feeling of near helplessness that had all but overwhelmed him afterward. But as he rode eastward between two Colorado towns, Ouray and Gunnison, after several weeks of riding across abrasive stone and sand and flinty gravel, the fatal oversight appeared when the loyal, strong, and durable dun horse began to limp, began to favor his front end with an increasing soreness. He was not shod.

For the boy the horse had become a lot more than simply his mount, his way of escaping posses and Indians. The horse had become a friend, a confidant, a companion, a substitute for friends and even for his family. He could have left him tied in some trees somewhere near one of the cow outfits in this upland grassland country, and gone down in the small hours of pitchblende night to steal a fresh horse from a ranch corral or a cow camp remuda. A *shod* horse, this time, and perhaps that is what he should have done. But human beings are complicated critters, even relatively unscarred, fourteen-year-old ones, so he would not abandon the dun horse. They were friends; a man never abandoned friends, no matter what.

He rested the horse all day, killed and cooked and ate a cock pheasant he'd managed to blow to bits with the Winchester, and in the late midday he screwed up his courage and against every instinct headed straight up the stage road to Gunnison, in search of a blacksmith. He waited until midafternoon because, as even some thin shadows arrived, they were welcome. He was beginning to think the way most night riders did, that darkness was his ally. He wanted to reach that yonder town when most folks had finished whatever it was they had been doing for the day, but he wanted to reach it before the blacksmith closed up shop for the day. That was how he timed his entrance to Gunnison. But he still could not force himself to ride boldly into town, so he skirted around the place like a scouting marauder, and entered from the southeast, after he had figured out which of all those buildings would be the smithy.

The place was quiet. It was too early for supper, yet, and too late for fresh daily enterprises, so, as the boy had speculated, Gunnison was quiet. The blacksmith was banking his forge fire when the boy rode to his doorway and peered in. The blacksmith, a burly, bearded, black-eyed man, peered back. The boy looked thin and sun-blasted, ragged, and with a constantly moving, half-wild slant to his pale eyes. These things did not, in the older man's view, mesh with the well-bred, valuable horse the boy was riding. Still, the blacksmith, a fortyish man, was prudent. He strolled out as the boy swung down, glanced at the worn-down hoofs, and said: "Shoes all around?"

The boy nodded. "Yes, sir. How much?"

"Dollar," replied the blacksmith matter-of-factly. "Two bits a foot. Offsaddle him and fetch him inside to the cross-ties." As the blacksmith turned back to coax fresh life into his forge fire and stir the coals, he watched the lad. Obviously the horse meant a lot to him, and just as obviously the horse liked the boy. Well, one thing the world west of the Missouri River had its share of was runaway kids. If this one had in fact actually stolen that valuable dun gelding, let the damned nosy law make something out of it—he shod horses for a living.

There was almost no rasping to be done on the dun's feet, and each frog was worn smooth, too, so about all the blacksmith had to do before fitting and nailing shoes was gouge out on both sides of the frog and insure the fit of his blanks at the forge and anvil. All this was entirely satisfactory to a horse shoer who had, near the end of the day, already turned out a dozen other shod horses and who had also hammered a buggy axle straight, after some damned fool had tried to straddle a boulder off the roadway.

He watched the boy from the corner of his eye, and just before he dunked the first shoe into the filthy wooden bucket to cool, he said: "Yonder's the café, and next to it's the general store. If a feller was hungry, he'd make out right well at either of them places."

The boy went, and the blacksmith stood back in the cool, sooty gloom of his shop, watching. The boy crossed over with a lithe, springy step, but always watching. Sure as hell he was a runaway, and sure as hell he'd stolen this good dun horse. The blacksmith went to work. A lot of years earlier he'd done as bad; he'd deserted the Army and had ridden off on a neck-brained cavalry horse. Only luck had looked after him; subsequently he'd discovered just how thorough the Army was at tracking down horse-stealing deserters. It hadn't caught him, but that was only because of a fool's great good fortune. He started nailing, clinching, and rasping. By the time George Alden Morgan got back, he had two shoes on and was finishing up on the third hoof.

The boy had a bundle of food tucked under one arm, a new shirt, and a fleshed-out look to his middle. The blacksmith smiled to himself, said nothing, and went on working. Sooner or later, the lad was going to run head-on into trouble. The blacksmith wished he knew how to advise him, but he didn't know, so he kept all his thoughts private, and, when he finished up and tossed the tools back into his tray, he shoved out a thick, dirty paw.

The boy dropped a silver cartwheel into the man's hand, led his horse out to be watered, first, then he saddled him, and, as the bearded, impassive man watched, he tied his food-bundle aft of the cantle, and mounted. The boy turned, cast a fleeting smile back, the blacksmith gravely inclined his head, and the boy turned off to his left between the shoeing shed and the next building, heading for open country. He wouldn't have ridden up the full length of the main roadway if his life had depended upon it. He'd had nerves crawling like writhing snakes under his hide, as it was, all the time he'd been in Gunnison, and now he had to control a powerful urge to bust out the dun horse and run like the wind to get away from that place.

The bearded man went over to bank his forge

fire for the second time. It was quitting time now, finally. He looked up only when a thick, slightly swaggering man walked in from out in the dying day and said: "Hey, Fred, who was that skinny kid riding the dun horse?"

The blacksmith gazed with an expression in his dark eyes of restrained dislike as he answered: "Never seen him before, Jack."

"Have his horse shod, did he?"

"Yeah."

"Paid you?"

"Yeah."

"Well, I seen him eatin' like a wolf cub over across the road. Didn't look to me like he'd et a square meal in days. Looked to me like he'd been on the road a spell, too, dirty as a Siwash Indian. Then I seen him get on that dun horse a few minutes ago. You know, Fred, that was one hell of a horse."

"Nice animal," conceded the blacksmith, finishing at the forge and turning to put up his tools before leaving for the evening.

The man called Jack snorted. "*Nice* horse, hell, that animal's worth maybe as much as a hunnert dollars."

The blacksmith turned slowly. Every town had at least one man such as Jack Davis; they lied, cheated, stole, did everything that skirted close to breaking laws, without ever breaking any law that would land them in serious trouble. To the blacksmith they were more contemptible than a real gun-swinging renegade. He said: "What's on your mind, Jack?"

The thickly built man answered promptly. "That was a runaway kid on someone's good horse, sure as I'm a foot tall."

"What of that?"

"Maybe no one wants the damned kid back, Fred, but I'll bet you money someone'd pay twenty, maybe even fifty dollars to get his horse back."

Fred leaned upon an anvil. "You have in mind going after the kid?"

"Wouldn't you, for maybe fifty dollars? Hell, I can overhaul him in camp tonight and fetch him back here by sunup to be locked up until we can find out who he is and where he went and stoled that dun horse."

"No, I wouldn't go after him," responded the bearded man. "Did you see that Colt pistol shoved down the front of his pants, and that Apache saddle boot over his Winchester?"

"What of it?"

"That boy's come though a lot of country, Jack. Apache country. And no damned reservation jumper gave him that saddle gun and sheath. You just might get one hell of a surprise if you went stalkin' after him. Want some advice? Forget it. Leave the boy alone."

"The hell I will," snarled the burly man. "You

make it sound like some teen-age punk of a horse thief could get the best of me." Jack's coarse features changed subtly. "Maybe no one'd ever claim that dun horse." They looked at one another a moment or two longer, then the burly man turned on his heel, lightly for a man of his thickness and heft, then went briskly striding up in the direction of the livery barn.

The blacksmith went to the doorway to watch. Afterward, he ranged a thoughtful glance along the edge of the horizon, and decided that the boy would reach the uplands well ahead of Jack Davis. If he managed that, the blacksmith had a fair idea Jack would not catch him. He *hoped* Jack would not catch him.

Fred went back into the shop to finish sorting things out for the day, and later, when he went up front to push the sagging old doors close and bolt them, he saw the distant figure of a mounted man heading northwest on the trail of the boy. For a while he stood gazing out there, in the middle distance, thinking to himself that Jack Davis was the kind of a man who might start out with something in mind such as he had mentioned in the shop, catching the boy and fetching him back as a runaway for the reward on the horse, but who might end up burying the boy in order to claim the dun horse for himself.

The blacksmith's bearded lips moved in soundless profanity. He slammed home the bolt on his shop door, then stepped to a nearby trough to sluice off his hands and arms and face, and after that he strode up in the direction of the livery barn. Like a number of other local people, he kept a horse boarded up there.

After he had wordlessly saddled up in the gloaming, the blacksmith rode back to his small house across town from the shoeing shop, buckled a Winchester under his saddle fender, settled a shell belt and holstered Colt around his thick, strong middle, got back astride, and, still irritated with both himself and Jack Davis, walked his big bay horse for a mile beyond town, northwesterly, until the animal had warmed out, then he booted him over into a lope.

He had an advantage over both the lad and Davis; by now it was murky enough so that neither of them would be able to see him coming. Maybe, earlier, the boy, if he was as wary as Fred thought he probably was, had seen Jack trailing him. Fred hoped so. But just in case he hadn't, or just in case he got a little careless and that damned louse of a Davis got close enough, Fred intended to be there. Not because he meant to prevent Davis from returning to town with the lad and the dun horse, but to make damned certain that is what happened, instead of maybe something a hell of a lot worse.

It wasn't his affair, but still few men, thinking the kind of thoughts the blacksmith was thinking, wouldn't have decided to intervene. No matter what a half-starved kid had done—and at that lad's age it couldn't have been anything too terrible—he deserved better than to run afoul of a man as completely unprincipled as Jack Davis. But Fred was still mad at himself for getting involved. He'd been eleven years in Gunnison, minding his own business, doing honest work, and now this. . . .

IV

For George Alden Morgan the escape from Gunnison was an empty triumph, for when he finally halted in tree cover and hunkered at the knees of his horse, watching all that land back down there, it was as empty as the face of the moon. Still, he felt an enormous relief, even when he told himself he hadn't actually had anything to fear down there. The trouble was, he could only half make himself believe this to be true. Even when he tried to shake off the deviousness, the sly and wary watchfulness long enough to tell himself he was getting as bad as an Indian, in his thoughts as well as his actions, it was not altogether convincing.

He climbed back to the saddle, set a ranging course toward the high country, opened a can of sardines as he rode, and for the first time since leaving Albuquerque he had a comfortable gut, and ample confidence as he allowed the dun horse to pick its own gait and game trail. It was that ample confidence, as any older, more seasoned outlaw could have told him, which was the forerunner of disaster. A man who had stolen a horse could never, as long as he lived, let down very much, and especially for as long as he straddled the stolen animal.

The evening settled in slowly, the way it usually did in early summertime. That was perhaps all that saved the boy. It was still light enough, even in among the giant pines and fir trees, when he decided to make a final last reconnoiter before heading deep through the uplands in search of a place for his night camp.

He left the horse tied and walked back a short distance where there had been a slight rocky escarpment where no trees grew and that offered a fair sighting of all the land below and off in the direction of Gunnison—and saw the thick-bodied shape of a bulky man riding a close-coupled dark horse, just before the thick-bodied man's horse crossed up off the grasslands into the trees.

He did not have much of a glimpse. The man was already too close to the forest to be in view long, but the boy saw enough. He had no idea who that burly man was, wouldn't have known him in any case, but there was a better than even chance the man was on the boy's trail. It wasn't that bushy-faced blacksmith back in town; this man was thicker and he was also beardless, but beyond that the boy could make out nothing.

He went back to the dun horse, untied him, piled aboard, and, instead of following their earlier gradual ascent, he turned off almost due westerly, and, although he did not like doing it to the dun horse, he pointed him straight into the deepest, higher segments of the forest. He was not trying to widen the distance between himself and the oncoming man so much as he was seeking to choose a trail the follower would not expect him to take, while at the same time getting as far into the darkening forest as he could.

But luck has a habit of helping those in dire need up to a point, then blithely abandoning them. The boy stopped twice to listen. Both times he heard shod hoofs grate over shale rock dead behind him. How that man had followed the sign so well in the settling dusk was worth wondering about—some other time. The boy changed course again, heading on a skirting course around the massive haunch of a slope, and it dawned on him only when the dun horse loosened a scatter of shale rock how the burly man was keeping track of him. Then, he swore at the new horseshoes; a bare-footed horse wouldn't have made a third as much noise.

He finally dismounted, near a break in the rising slope beyond which he thought there would be a grassy park or a meadow, because he could see through the treetops where they thinned out, and he very carefully led the dun horse up toward that meadow. Up there, at least, with matted grass underfoot, the horse wouldn't make a sound.

The oncoming rider never seemed to falter, which was both eerie and frightening. He never pushed his horse; he never quartered to pick up the sign; he simply kept right on coming. The boy had a taste of panic, for a moment, until he finally got up across a spongy, ancient carpet of pine needles, and debouched upon the twilight-lit park. It looked to be no more than perhaps forty or fifty acres in size, completely girt with bull pines and enormous bristle-topped fir trees, and, as he had expected, it was thickly overgrown with grass and flourishing weeds, as well as small flowers.

He stopped stockstill to listen. The burly man was no longer making a sound. That might have been reassuring except for one thing. If the boy had had enough sense to dismount and lead his animal soundlessly, so, in all probability, had the burly man. The boy turned, squinted through the dusky gloom, decided to head northwest toward the nearest tree fringe, and moved very cautiously with the obedient dun horse close behind.

They almost made it. In fact, the boy was probing ahead where he felt certain they would be able to find good protection, when a horse whinnied somewhere behind him out over the meadow, and it did not matter that this was not the dun, because that sound carried well through the stillness of twilight. Without a doubt, the burly man had heard it, and regardless of whether it was the dun or not, he would probably infer that it was, and be guided to the meadow. The boy would have cursed if he'd been able to; instead, he froze in fright, and before trying to see where that strange animal was, out there somewhere in the grass, he thought he heard footfalls, faint as though made by moccasins, ahead in the direction he had meant to go to hide.

He pulled the six-gun out of his waistband, turned the horse, and led him on an angling course toward the more northerly fringe of trees, thinking that if that had been someone stalking him along the fringe of forest, then at least he would take his chance on this new adversary, and with any luck settle with him before the burly man reached the meadow and also came hunting him.

He reached the trees, stepped through into pitch darkness, balanced the Colt, straining in cold fear to see if there was indeed someone ahead of him, as well as behind, and when he neither saw anything nor heard another sound of skulking, careful footfalls, he pushed on through into the deeper darkness. Then he turned, held a hand lightly across the dun's nose to prevent his horse from making a sound, and waited until the burly man appeared.

It was quite a wait. The man arrived, eventually, upon the far rim of the meadow, but he was being extremely careful and until he moved silently forward, stalking the boy with a carbine in both hands, he was not really discernible in the poor light. But once he got away from the background of trees he was easily visible. If there had ever been much doubt about this stranger being on the boy's trail, there certainly was none now. Nor did that Winchester, nor the holstered Colt on the man's right hip, suggest that he had anything very peaceful in mind.

The boy could have shot him. At least he could have shot at him when the burly man came as silently as an Indian across through the failing twilight where there was at least some light. He did not try. In fact, he did not even cock the Colt, although he tracked the man's silhouette as steadily as he could. Without any reason that the boy could discern, the burly man suddenly halted, listened a long while, then grounded his carbine, and, twisting from the waist, peered back the way he had come. The boy heard nothing. Clearly, though, the burly man had not only heard something, but was positive enough of this that he now turned fully, facing in the opposite direction. He remained that way for almost five full minutes, before suddenly whipping back around facing the trees, and moving swiftly toward them. He didn't quite make it.

Back down where the burly man had emerged afoot onto the meadow, a man's gruff voice called ahead softly: "Jack! Come on back here!"

It did not sound to the boy as a threat, or even a very strong order. It almost sounded as though that hidden man down there in the trees was simply annoyed and disgusted.

The burly man stopped in mid-stride, close enough for George Alden Morgan to see his face, and grimaced. Then he turned. "That you, Fred? What the hell do you think you're doing?"

"Going back to town with you," growled the blacksmith. "Now come on back here."

"You damned fool," responded the burly man, holding his voice low. "He's bound to have heard you and commenced to run again."

The invisible man down in the trees said: "Let him go."

"What!"

"I said . . . let the kid go."

"Damn you, Fred. He's a horse thief."

"You don't know that, you're only sayin' it. Now, get your tail back down here. We're goin' back to town."

The burly man called Jack looked downright astounded. For a moment he glowered in silence, but eventually he spoke again.

"What in the hell has got into you, Fred? This

ain't none of your affair. You damned idiot, you're a blacksmith. Go on back to your forge and anvil, and leave other things to . . ."

"Jack," interrupted the blacksmith, still using the same quiet, deep tone, "I've got you fair in my sights, and you don't even know for sure which tree I'm behind. Now, god damn it, I'm not going to stay up here all night arguin'. You come down here and you damned well do it right now!"

The burly man held his silence again, as astonished as before. He looked to the boy like a person who, having been confident about the behavior of another person, could not believe his ears. Then the real surprise arrived. From southward, to the boy's right, down in the fringe of trees, a man said: "Jack, you better do what Fred just told you. Otherwise, I'm coming out there and split your skull plumb down the middle. And, Jack, you drop those guns before you take a step."

The boy stiffened; so there had been someone ahead of him, pacing him up through the dark forest where he'd initially thought of going to hide. It did not cross his mind that the same luck that had deserted him an hour and a half before had now come back. He was no longer caught between two invisible armed men, but the burly man was, sure as April.

For a while Jack did nothing. He was, evidently,

along with being a bull-built individual, very bull-headed. He looked over his shoulder, then he looked southeastward, down where Fred the blacksmith was hiding, or at least was not discernible.

The man off on the lad's right spoke again. "Jack, I'm sort of like the feller yonder in the trees. I'm not going to stand around here all night waiting for you to make up your mind. If you figure to use that gun in your hands, you'd better start firing, because I'm only going to wait another five seconds, then I'm going to start firing *at you.*"

Jack opened his hands slowly. The Winchester fell soundlessly into the grass.

The man close to the boy said: "That's very good, Jack. Now the pistol."

Jack obeyed. He did not search the rearward trees for the man who had done this to him; he was glaring in a rage back down where the blacksmith had not said a word throughout all this. "You simpleton!" he called. "Now you satisfied? Now you happy with what you've gone and done?"

Fred did not answer, but the man in the nearer fringe of forest spoke up. "Jack, start walking back the way you came. When you get back to your horse, you get onto him, and, if you've got a lick of sense, you won't even look back until you're in Gunnison. Go on now, and take Fred

44

with you. I'm going to shag the pair of you down to the range land. So help me, if either one of you so much as even *looks* back, I'll let all the air out of you from back to front. Now get the hell going!"

Jack started trudging back down in the direction of the blacksmith, his face twisted with an expression of murderous rage.

V

The boy's quandary was understandable. In his anxiety to escape the man named Jack, he had managed to run into some other man who had been camping on that little hidden meadow the boy had stumbled upon. In the boy's urgency he had eluded one stranger, and had been rescued by another stranger, even though all he'd wanted right from the moment he'd left Gunnison was to return to his secret, elusive, and solitary life.

He thought momentarily of mounting and fleeing up through the forest darkness, but, as he stood there procrastinating, the invisible stranger did not walk up where the boy could see him, yet he was there nevertheless because he spoke from back a yard or two among the black-barked fir trees.

"Who was that one with the carbine, boy, and what did he want?"

It was answering a talking tree. All the boy could do was look in the direction from which the man's voice had come. "I never saw him before in my life," George Alden Morgan replied. "I'd guess him to be after my horse."

"Put that pistol back into your waistband," ordered the voice, and after the boy had obeyed, a compactly built, lithe-moving man came out from among the trees with an almost silent step, looked briefly at the boy, then looked longest at the dun horse. Finally he nodded. "Maybe he was after your horse at that. He looks to be a right fine animal even in the dark." The stranger came closer, tipped back his hat, enabling the boy to make out a little more of him, and said: "What's your name?"

The boy swallowed. "George."

"George what?"

". . . Smith."

The man considered. "Is that a fact? Well, that's strange. My name's Smith, too."

The boy took this sarcasm with a shifting glance. "George Alden Morgan," he said, still avoiding the man's blue, stone-steady look.

"All right, George Alden Morgan . . . but that's a plumb mouthful so I'll just call you George. Now tell me something, George, about that dun horse."

"He's mine, and we been on the trail for a long time. I had him shod in Gunnison, and that first feller started shagging me from back down there. I never saw him before in my life, like I told you. I think maybe the other one that never walked out of the trees was the blacksmith from town."

"The horse, George, the horse. I really don't care much about those other two. At least for a while yet I won't care about them. George, how old are you?"

"Sixteen."

"How old?"

". . . Fourteen."

The man sighed. "We been standing here talking for maybe ten minutes and you've tried two lies. George, let me tell you something. Don't even try to run an inside straight on me again. I never liked horse beaters, kicking mules, or biting dogs, but most of all I never liked liars. Now, about the dun horse . . . ?"

The boy shot a look back at the man, jumped his eyes away quickly, then, after a moment of thought, turned back again. "I stole him."

The cowboy's teeth shone in the gloom. "Where? Hereabouts?"

"No. Down in Albuquerque."

The man pondered that for a moment before speaking again, and from this point on he did not mention the dun horse again, except to make one comment. He said: "Well, let's offsaddle him and set him loose on the meadow. He'll get along and I'd say from the looks of him, he could stand a night's feed and rest. Then we'll go on over to my camp and have some grub."

The man had not mentioned his own name, but as he moved closer to help offsaddle the dun horse, he seemed relaxed and affable. Even if the boy hadn't owed him a debt, and even if he wasn't glad for the company, which he had not thought he would be, he still could not have ridden off. At least he did not think he could have, so he did as the cowboy suggested, then, with his rigging carefully suspended from a tree limb where salt-hungry varmints couldn't get at it, he accompanied the man back through the trees to another, smaller grass clearing where the man's camp was, and they sat down with the first strong light of a rusty old summertime moon brightening the uplands a little.

The man made a tiny fire, set a dented little old coffee pot upon some flat stones above the fire, then tossed aside his hat, leaned back against a tree, and studied the boy for a full minute before saying: "George, are you a runaway?"

In a sense he was. In another sense he wasn't. He couldn't have answered, truthfully anyway, by saying either yes or no, so he explained why he had taken the horse, even though bringing this all out again inevitably resurrected the old ache.

The cowboy listened, rolled a cigarette, sat over there without moving, and when it had all been told, he filled two cups and leaned to hand

48

George one of them, still without commenting. Then he tasted his coffee, found it exactly as it was—not very good, but better than no coffee at all to a confirmed coffee drinker—and spoke: "Well, first thing in the morning we'll have to move camp. That feller with the carbine might not give up, and of course we've got another little problem. If he figures you might have stolen that horse, why then the next time he might come riding up here with the law and a posse."

George said: "He couldn't know I stole the horse."

The cowboy smiled. "Sure he could, George. I never saw either one of you before, and then I've only seen you in the dark, and I figured that out when I first saw you sneaking across the meadow. You're too damned young to have saved up money for an animal like that. You're pretty ragged and hungry-looking, even with that new shirt. The dun is worth good money, more money in fact than most range riders and bums like that feller with the carbine would have." The cowboy's smile lingered, soft and amiable, lacking in cupidity or deceit. It was almost a lazily confident smile. "Well," he said, "I was getting ready to hunt up another meadow anyway. I've been loafing around this one until the fish don't bite much any more, and most of the game's got my scent, so hunting's not too good either. By the way, George, where were you heading?"

That was the easiest answer of all. "Nowhere. Just northward I guess. Just riding is all."

The cowboy accepted that, finished his coffee, and flung the dregs away. "You like to fish?" he asked. "There's good fishing in these mountains. Good hunting, too. In fact, if a feller doesn't have to be somewhere, and if his horse could stand a month of filling the pleats out of his gut, this isn't bad country to spend the summer in."

George didn't know a thing about fishing, and he'd already proved to his own satisfaction that in order to be a successful hunter you had to know a lot more than he knew; instinct alone was not enough. "I guess I like to fish," he replied, and reddened at the cowboy's stare. "Well, I never did any," he added defensively.

"Your paw didn't show you?"

"He's dead. I never saw him. My maw said he died back East somewhere."

"Yeah. Well, you better fetch your saddle blanket for a ground cloth, and take one of these Army blankets, and make up your bed. We'll move camp about sunup, before Mister Winchester decides to try again."

George remembered something. "He's a real tracker. I don't know how he did it, except that my horse would hit a rock now and then with those new shoes, but he never lost me even after it commenced getting dark. And I sure tried to lose him."

The cowboy took this oblique warning with an expression of indifference. "I didn't come down in the last rain, either," he said drolly. "Now go back and fetch your gatherings and let's turn in. It'll start getting cold directly."

George arose obediently and headed back in the direction of the meadow. The cowboy killed his cigarette, scratched his head, then gave it a big shake as of resignation, and strained to listen. Now, at last, the boy had his chance to rig up and ride on. The cowboy was interested in whether he'd do this or not, so he sat and listened, and later, when he should have heard a horse passing through the night, and he did not hear any such sounds, he propped himself against his fir tree again, both hands behind his head, wondering what he had got himself into now. All he'd wanted to do this summer was lots of nothing. Already, he had to strike camp and find a more distant and less accessible place. Interesting thing about life and whatever it was—whoever it was—that controlled life, and living, and a man's destiny, just when it seemed plain as day that a man was sole arbiter of his own doings, something like this happened, over which he had no control, and about which he could do little. Once, his second year on his own, he'd wintered with some Utes, and one night around a tip fire, he heard an old man say that maybe, with the exception of Apaches, everyone else was wise enough to know for a fact that there was a guiding Great Spirit.

George returned, lugging not only his saddle blanket, but also his bundle of food. He put the bundle over on the cowboy's side of the fire ring of stones, then turned and made up his pallet. When he turned back, the cowboy was watching him, so the lad said: "Tinned stuff I got down in Gunnison. Sardines and peaches and prunes, and some tinned meat, too."

The cowboy nodded. "No luck hunting, George?"

"No."

"Well, maybe you never learned much about that, either."

"I went hunting a couple of times, when I was a little kid."

The cowboy soberly accepted this without showing more than the faintest twinkle in his eyes. "When you were a little kid," he murmured. "Well, we'll find a new camp where the hunting is better, and maybe your luck will change." He sighed. "You know, two things a man misses up in here, whiskey and noise."

George, who had tasted whiskey twice and had recoiled with mild nausea both times, offered no comment on that. As for the noise, he'd had a week of the kind of depthless silence a person encounters in the primeval places, and he learned to use it the same way Indians used it, as a background against which sound would strike and echo. He had got so that every sound had significance, had meaning for him. He liked the silence and said so.

The cowboy did not pursue this, instead he said: "You made any plans, George? I mean, have you figured out what you're going to do? You can't just go on riding all over hell's countryside forever, can you? Someday you'll have to put on a tin beak and get down and scratch with all the other chickens. Be a cowboy maybe, or a horse breaker, something like that?"

George had once, a couple of years back, seen some volunteer firemen in their shiny black leather helmets and their handsome red coats, clinging to a horse-drawn pumper wagon racing up a roadway. Afterward he had told his mother when he was large enough, he wanted to be like that. But now, that didn't seem to be what the cowboy meant at all, and, otherwise, George hadn't really thought very much about things of this kind, so he simply finished making up his pallet, then sank down upon it, cross-legged, and said: "Maybe a cowboy, like you say."

"Naw, not what I say," responded the cowboy. "What you think. Anyway, cowboying isn't something a man had ought to make a career out of, because, once you start getting a little gray

53

in your hair, cow outfits begin finding excuses why they don't need you . . . and the same day they hire a younger feller out of a saloon, maybe. Well, we don't have to fix that tonight anyway, do we?"

The cowboy went to his bedroll, kicked off his boots, removed his gun belt, carefully rolled it, and placed it so that the saw handle of his six-gun was within inches of where he'd be lying, then crawled under his blankets, rolled up onto his side, and said: "Good night, George."

The boy answered, wormed his way beneath the Army blanket, settled flat out on his back, and stared straight up through the bristly tops of the tall trees where he could see a slash of open sky above the center of their little clearing, and thought back. He had piled a lot of living into the last two weeks. He had also piled up a store of memories, but just before he closed his eyes, he asked Whoever Was Up There to be kind to his mother, to look after her, and make things good for her. Then he slept like a stone.

VI

They were riding upon an elk trail three miles northwest of their previous camp when the sun finally arrived to lend light to their world, and to warm most of the kinks out of their backs. They had ridden one mile up a creekbed, and another time they had crossed a hair-raising slick-rock ledge where even steel horseshoes could not make an impression. After that they paralleled game trails without leaving a single shod-horse imprint in the dust of any of those trails.

By high noon the cowboy pointed to a break against the blue skyline, and without speaking set his course in that direction. George was impressed; the cowboy did a lot of things that were pretty obvious, after they had been done, like losing their sign in the creek water, and like angling across that slick-rock ledge with a thousand-foot drop-off on their left, not only further to lose their trail but also to challenge anyone who might be following.

Now, as their horses humped up the last fifty feet of a deadfall-littered pine slope, they came out atop a grassy fringe that bordered a blue-water lake, so blue that even the sky overhead looked pale by comparison.

They set up camp. The cowboy never appeared to move in haste, and he never seemed to waste a motion. It took them the balance of the day to get things organized, and, as the sun sank, the cowboy pointed to circular ripples upon the lake's surface where a fish had floated up to snatch some kind of an unwary bug. "Looks promising," he said, and went around gathering rocks for their fire ring.

He accepted George as though they had been partnering on the trail for at least a year. He made him laugh a little, and sometimes he'd look down his nose at him.

It was a good time; George would remember it as long as he lived. Over the next ten days he learned more from the cowboy than he'd ever learned from any schoolmarm. None of it had much to do with reading and writing and ciphering, but it had a lot to do with things such as reading sign, outthinking upland game, figuring the weather a day or two in advance, and how to think as animals thought.

The cowboy said his name was Boone. He did not say whether that was his first name or his second name. Nor did it matter in the slightest.

They even made a tree-limb rack, dug a pit, lined it with stones, and, using green wood, smoked some of their fish. They caught too many to eat, and, as Boone said, it was a sin to waste things that were put here to keep a man alive, so they had smoked trout, fried trout, even baked trout rolled in big leaves and cooked under the ground by heating rocks and putting them into the pit, and covering the whole thing.

They also had grouse and mountain quail. They saw wapiti, elk, and deer, but Boone did not think they had ought to have to lug too much around with them when they moved camp. For that kind of living, he told George, a man really needed a good pack mule, which was better than a pack horse.

They stayed at this nameless lake for almost three weeks. The dun horse had gotten back his sleek glow, and his tucked-up gut had filled out again. He and Boone's black gelding formed an enduring friendship. Neither horse was flighty or particularly demonstrative, but, if one got out of sight of the other among the trees, there would be some nickering back and forth.

Boone spent three afternoons showing the boy how to use a lariat. He also said the boy had ought to have brought along a jacket and some blankets, when he'd left New Mexico, but sooner or later they'd find a town and that deficiency could be remedied.

Once a heavy upland rainfall caught them. Their camp wasn't rainproof at all, and for the two ensuing days they had to put just about everything they owned to dry in the hot sunshine; otherwise, it would have begun to rot, particularly their clothing and saddle blankets and bedding.

Finally, one evening at the fire when George was lying with his head propped upon an open hand watching the little fire, Boone said: "Well, nothing lasts forever. Directly now you'll see the leaves start turning." He tilted his head to wrinkle his nose. "It's up there, just beyond the northward peaks, and, when you hold your head just right, you can smell it. Autumn, George, and after that, winter."

There were some things a person could sense with as much strong certainty as though he had read them written out in big black letters. George did not lift his eyes from the fire, but he knew by instinct that something in his life was about to change. He said: "Where do you go in the winter, Boone?"

The cowboy thought a moment. "I used to head down into New Mexico. Maybe this year I'll head southwest, over into Arizona. Main thing is that a man's got to be where the sun still shines by the time this country up here is under a foot of snow." Boone gazed steadily at the lad. "You?"

The boy continued to stare into the little fire. "Arizona, too." He looked up at the cowboy. "Sure are a lot of places I've never seen."

Boone, cross-legged, leaned thoughtfully to build a cigarette. If the boy had been eighteen or nineteen—but fourteen was far too young to start out being a saddle tramp. He might still end up being one, the land was full of men who had just given up trying to reach an apex, but it sure was wrong to help a boy start out being a drifter. Boone lit up, gazed out upon the moonlit, still surface of the placid lake, and sorted through a half dozen alternatives to abandoning George, and later, after they had doused their fire and rolled in, he lay on his side of the stone ring, thinking.

The best alternative he could come up with would require him to ride southward into New Mexico, which he did not much want to do, but if he did, indeed, head southwest over into Arizona, where he knew no one, didn't even know the countryside, there wouldn't be much chance of fitting the boy—easing the boy—into a place where boys like him belonged.

The following morning as they were frying grouse and making coffee, Boone said: "Tell you what I figure we'd better do. Head out and around, southward. Ride west of the Chaco River . . . you know where that is?"

"No."

"Well, the Chaco's down in New Mexico." At the sudden tightening of the boy's face, Boone then said: "Don't fret. The Chaco's west of that big stand of mountains you came up through into Colorado. It's one hell of a distance from Albuquerque. We'll ride out and around those mountains over close to the Arizona line, and, when we get down by Gallup, maybe we'll lie over for a few days. But there's a place called Zuñi farther down. It's a sort of Indian town, but with everything worth owning held by cattlemen. They even own most of the buildings in the town. Zuñi is a damned long way from Albuquerque."

George frowned. "But I thought you said we'd be going over into Arizona."

Boone had an answer. "Zuñi is so close to the line you could shoot a cannon at Zuñi, and the ball'd land in Arizona." That was true, but that was not why he had mentioned Zuñi. Nor did he allow George a lot of time to reflect, not right then anyway. "I figure, if we start striking camp today, we can take the trail ahead of sunrise in the morning."

George nodded. "All right. Boone, why does everybody always want to start doing things before sunrise?"

Boone laughed. "Damned if I know. That's how I learned, and I reckon that's how most range men learned. But if you sit and think on it, it is sort of funny, isn't it? A man could get up two hours later in summertime, and he'd still have two hours more of working daylight at the other end of the day, wouldn't he?"

In a tone of mild bewilderment George said: "There sure are a lot of things that need changing, aren't there?"

Boone's smile came up quickly. "You know, I was just a little bit older than you are when I first had that same thought. Now, well, I'll sure agree that things could stand having some slack yanked out of them, but I don't know as I'd expect most folks to know where to begin, or even to really make the changes, if they knew how."

They began dismantling their camp. It was something neither of them liked doing, not just the manual work of striking a camp, but getting ready to abandon this place that had been so pleasant in a golden, lazy, uncluttered, and peaceful way.

They bedded down that night with their gatherings rolled and ready to be secured to saddle leather. In the morning when George opened his eyes, Boone was already cooking breakfast with his hat shoved far back on his head, and with a thoughtful expression puckering the outer edges of his eyes.

They ate, brought in the horses, got everything cinched up and lashed down, then Boone gestured for George to lead off. "Pick us a gradual southward trail and keep your eyes open. There'll be an elk or buck run yonder somewhere leading to the grasslands. Take it, and with any decent kind of luck we'd ought to be maybe twenty, thirty miles west of Gunnison."

George did as ordered. Always before Boone had done the trailblazing. This time, obviously, he meant for George to gather a little more savvy. Boone was a good teacher—of range-country lessons, anyway.

They did not get out of the mountains upon the cow range until the sun was steadily soaring toward its zenith, and, although George winced every time they saw a rider small in the distance, and would have much preferred making this crossing after sunset, he had the kind of faith in Boone that ameliorated his dread to a large degree.

They did not see Gunnison but George guessed about where it would be, and when he thought they were roughly parallel to it, he said: "I wonder if that feller with the carbine who trailed me up to our first camp got into a fight with the blacksmith who wanted him to go back?"

Boone had no idea, but he said: "There aren't too many blacksmiths I'd want to tussle with. Anyway, we've got *our* end of all that, and they've got *their* end of it. They'll never know what became of us, so I reckon that'll work both ways."

They had to cut eastward a few miles below their paralleling course with Gunnison because some cow outfit was moving a thousand head and they had no wish to meet either the cowboys, or all that bad-tasting dust. This new course put them within sight of the north-south stage road, and George did not like that very much, either, but by midafternoon the ramrod-stiffness was leaving his backbone, and by sundown he was loose and easy again in the saddle, while Boone told him some anecdotes set in the rough cow camps Boone had worked in. It was the most natural thing in the world for George to believe Boone was exactly what he looked, acted, and talked, like, an everyday cowboy. Maybe a little better than that, maybe a top hand or a sometime range boss, but in any event a professional range man.

Dusk came slowly, as usual, and lingered well along into what should have been nighttime. They drifted more inland, more westerly, after they were well away from that miles-wide drift of cattle, and eventually lost sight of the stage road altogether. They should have quartered the countryside for a decent campsite, but, instead, they kept riding. Boone understood his companion's uneasiness, and favored it until just before darkness arrived, when he decided they had better find their campsite, and it was then too late.

They had to make a dry camp, which was nothing disastrous, except that it was better to have water at hand to wash by, to use for making their java, and for the animals. Boone scolded himself for being too lenient and getting them into this fix by pointing out to George that a man should always start getting ready to quit for the day when the sun was still high enough to allow him to find a good place to toss down his bedroll.

The following morning they had been two hours on the trail before locating a creek. There, they spent half a day loafing, then rode on again, heading on an angling course that was more southerly than westerly. From here on, Boone

Helm knew the land forms. He told George they would slide over to the west side of those huge mountains, as he'd explained back at their lakeside camp, and from there they would not only be back in New Mexico, they would be on a steady course for Gallup, and lower down, the next place, which was their destination: Zuñi.

VII

They never reached Zuñi. That is, Boone Helm eventually reached Zuñi, but George Morgan never did.

They were well down into New Mexico, west of the humpbacked, huge-hulking mountains, which lay on their right, and were well in view of the immense sweep and almost limitless run of empty country around Gallup and beyond it, over in the direction of the stone forest and, beyond that, the painted desert with all its awesome strata of differently colored sand and stone, when Boone's roving glance picked up something between them and Gallup. It was still not in their view, although Boone knew exactly where it was upon the horizon. He stopped the black horse and sat like stone for a full minute without speaking.

His bronzed face was solemn-set, so George held back his question, and tried to make out whatever it was that had made this abrupt change in Boone. George did not see anything until Boone had already turned and pointed. "Make for those rocks yonder," he snapped, and led off in a fast walk.

George saw something, finally, a loose band of horsemen coming inland and upland from above where Gallup lay, heading straight for the mountains. He asked who they were and got a chilling answer.

"Break-outs. Reservation-jumping renegade bucks on a raid."

George leaned to ease his horse into a lope. Boone scowled. "Walk. You run that horse now and it'll be like sending up a flag telling them we're over here. Apaches can read more into a stand of dust than you and I can read out of a book. Walk your horse."

George rode, twisting to peer rearward. He could only make out the riders because he could follow down below their rising dust and see movement that came and went, that shone then faded in the brilliant, clear sunlight. As he settled forward, gauging the distance they had to cover to find a place of concealment, he said: "Where's the Army? It's supposed to be around, isn't it?"

Boone's lips pulled slightly downward. "Yeah. There'll be patrols buzzing like honey bees, but, if we're not almighty lucky, all they'll find will be where we did our best." He looked over. George's face was flushed, but that could have been from the heat. He was excited, very naturally, and he acted apprehensive, which was also normal, but he did not seem to be badly frightened. Maybe that was because he had never seen what bloody-handed bronco Apache bucks did to people they caught.

Boone said: "We'll make it into the foothills, nothing to worry about there. Whether they'll come this far north and see our tracks is something else."

George's response was candid. "How did you figure out it wasn't just a bunch of range riders, Boone?"

"Wrong time of year for cowmen to be heading for these mountains. The cattle have all been drifted down out of here a month back. And those riders are punishing their horses. Only men who do that, this kind of weather, are ones on the run." Boone looked ahead toward the broken country. "Flush an Apache in open country and he'll head for the mountains every time. Somewhere behind them are soldiers or cowmen loaded for bear. That may be what'll save our bacon, George. If they by-pass us, that'll be just fine. If they don't and if they cut our sign, why then we'd better pray hard whoever's keeping them riding that hard is pretty close behind."

They got to the nearest broken country. There were no trees but there was a seemingly endless variety of flourishing, wiry, spiked undergrowth, all of it overlaid with dust, so that each time they brushed through, gray powder touched them in layers.

There was no time to hide their tracks; there was only enough time to find a good place where they could not be crept up on from behind. Boone led them to just such a hide-out, stepped from his saddle, dragging forth the saddle gun from its boot as he reached the ground, and George imitated everything he did, even to taking their horses back deeper into the underbrush where they would be hidden, and in the hot shade.

Then they moved back outward again, carbines in hand.

The dust was so much closer George was surprised. The last time he'd looked it had seemed that the renegade Apaches were miles distant. Now they were plainly visible as horsemen, and even as he hunkered beside Boone Helm in the parched, hot, and breathless fold of a side hill they had chosen as their place of concealment, he could make out individual riders. They *were* Apaches. That fact, driven home finally, made fear rise inside him like an icicle. He tore his eyes away only when Boone laid a hand lightly upon his arm and softly said: "They're going up the next cañon. Damned good thing we didn't pick that one, but, even so, they're going to pass too close. You go back and mind the horses. Don't let them make a sound." Boone turned, saw George's growing paleness, squeezed his arm, and smiled. "We're going to make it. Just you make sure our hairy friends back there don't turn out to be Indian lovers. Go on."

George turned and ducked back and forth through the heat and thorny bushes.

The Indians were slowing a little, not to favor their badly used-up mounts, but because they wanted to mill momentarily and have a long rearward look before running up into the cañon. Boone had a good look at them. There were eleven Apaches, all young bucks, all armed with pistols, knives, and Winchesters. Most of them had plunder tied either to their saddles or to themselves. Obviously they had been on a raid.

They were big-headed, barrel-chested, bronzed men with bandy legs too short and spindly for their upper torsos, and they wore *n'deh b'keh* moccasins, which, in Boone Helm's view, meant they were hold-outs, or what the Army called "blanket-Indians," Indians who hated everything white civilization had brought, including boots. They were bloody-hand broncos, no question about that. Suicidal raiders so full of fury and defiance that probably none of them would be alive five years hence.

George could see them, not well because of the tall stand of intervening brush, but he saw enough to feel that icy terror all the way out to his nerve ends. Now, finally, he was petrified with fear.

It was the first time in his life he'd ever seen death no farther away than four or five hundred yards. It was a debilitating experience. He stood with the horses, scarcely breathing, with sweat running under his clothes, and with his Apache carbine clutched in one hand.

A head-banded buck riding a head-hung fine bay horse gave forth with a guttural complaint that ended as a sort of shout so that his farthest companions could hear, then he turned, ranged a look along the cañons ahead, and gave his exhausted horse a savage kick. The animal responded, the buck passed from sight, all the other Apaches streamed beyond sight up the cañon, and George leaned against his horse, head to one side, straining to hear those eleven riders rattling over stones and tearing at the underbrush as they made their way steadily ahead.

Boone straightened up, squeezed off sweat with a limp shirt sleeve, got up to his feet, and started to turn back. Motion at the corner of his eye froze him in place. An Indian came back down out of the cañon riding bent forward, eyes fixed to the ground. He had a carbine in his right hand, the single rein of his war bridle in the other hand. He turned northward, staring intently at the ground, and Boone eased back into the underbrush and sank silently to one knee. George saw the Winchester raise very slowly to Boone's shoulder, and forgot to breathe. There wasn't even time to wonder how that bronco buck had guessed they were around here, somewhere. The Indian stopped dead still where he crossed their fresh tracks, suddenly yanked straight up, swinging his head toward their cañon. Boone fired.

The Apache's horse sprang sideward in total astonishment. The buck hit the ground like a sack of wet grain.

Boone ran back, yanked his black horse half around, and sprang across the saddle. He looked at George and said: "Ride!"

They broke out of the cañon in a flat-out run. The dead Indian was lying where he had taken the bullet, but his bewildered, sweated-out stolen horse, no longer under hand control and not knowing what to do or which direction to go in, attached himself to Boone and George. As they raced belly-down away from the slope, the riderless horse raced with them.

George looked back. There were Indians half-way up the slope in the far cañon who were sitting their horses, looking outward, backward, and downward. They could guess what had happened now, with those two fleeing horsemen in plain sight, but as the distance widened almost dramatically, George's terror began to settle into a kind of desperate estimate of the gambling odds. His horse and Boone's black were fresh and strong. The used-up mounts under those bronco bucks wouldn't have enough left in them to overtake the fleeing horsemen, and still bear them back into the relative safety of their secret place in the mountains, not with strong pursuit somewhere along their back trail. In the end, George faced forward and simply concentrated upon riding.

The Indians did not pursue them. They did not even go back for their dead companion, which they would have done under normal circumstances. They had the best of all reasons for turning their backs and kicking their spent horses on up through the mountains.

Boone slackened pace, after a little more than two miles, gave his black its head in a slogging walk, and sat half turned with one hand on the cantle, studying the rearward country for a long while before he said: "You know, it's close calls like that, that could make a man get gray-headed." When he turned to face the boy, he was smiling. "I don't think they'd have all come back down to finish us off even if that lone bronco had started a fight with us. They've got a long way yet to go, and damned poor stock to do it on." Boone studied George for a moment, then added: "Might as well put up the carbine."

George did not even remember having the thing in his hand. As he sheathed it, he said: "Were you scairt, Boone?"

"Scairt silly," replied the older man soberly. "You?"

George wiped a soggy palm down the side of his trousers as he replied: "Not at first. Only when they stopped out there and looked back, and I could see 'em plain as day. I had a magazine once that showed them killing folks . . . when they stopped out there, I was never so scairt in my life. Then that one you shot came back . . . how did he know we were around?"

"Scent," replied Helm. "Horse scent I'd guess, but he wasn't very clever. Whatever they were running from had the others too busy keeping up, to do what that one did. He wasted time and took an unnecessary chance . . . and now he knows something we don't know, doesn't he?"

They were another mile and a half away from their breathless, dusty hide-out when Boone picked up another sighting and pointed. "This time they're riding different, aren't they?"

That was true, this time the oncoming horsemen, who looked to be about twice the number of the bronco bucks, were riding in a kind of loose order. There were six men flung wide ahead of the main body out across the desert. They signaled with heliograph mirrors, which George had never seen done before, the moment they saw two horsemen coming toward them, and at once the main party picked up their gait and galloped ahead to where the skirmish-line of scouts sat still and waited.

"Soldiers," said George.

Boone was quiet, right up until the soldiers were close enough to make out their red-bronzed faces, their sweaty blue shirts, and their bristling dragoon mustaches. Even then he did not speak until the strung-out, long-legged, lean-flanked cavalry officer hailed him. Then Boone raised a hand, palm forward, and rode on up to the officer to speak.

Those bronco bucks had laid waste a five mile stretch of cow country, burning buildings, shooting solitary and unexpecting riders, killing cattle and horses on sight, and in three different places they had stalked ranches in the predawn and attacked with a whirlwind's ferocity leaving behind nothing but charred and mutilated bodies.

The lieutenant did not linger long. He asked Boone to turn off north of Gallup and go out to the Red Rock Ranch and tell them out there that soldiers had killed four, that Boone had killed one, and that the soldiers were heading up into the mountains to kill the remaining ten, even if they had to run them down to their *ranchería* and take on the whole band.

Boone agreed, then the soldiers rode stiffly ahead in a mile-eating jog that would save their horses and still allow them to catch up with the broncos, perhaps about midnight, or maybe in the wee hours, tomorrow.

VIII

They met a freighter on the Gallup road, northward, who told them where Red Rock Ranch was. He knew the place, he informed Boone, because years ago he'd toted in seven wagonloads of kiln-dried bricks, and that was something damned few buildings in the towns were made of, let alone any of the ranch buildings.

"Red as Alabama clay," stated the grizzled freighter. "That's the damnedest contract I ever had. Takes a heap of money to import building bricks in this here country, partner. Seemed like an awful waste of money to me, when there's a million acres of mud around here a man could make adobe bricks out of for his house."

Red Rock Ranch lay inland, toward the heat-hazed mountains, with its range spilling outward and slightly downward so that, when a man passed through the mighty stone markers on each side of the entranceway, where the wagon ruts went, all he had to do was look out and around and see in all directions for hundreds of miles. On up that rutted road where lazy dust puffed to life under their horses' hoofs, the ranch house stood upon an even higher elevation, back a couple of miles where the slow-rising land gradually swept to a flat-topped broad plateau. Up there, trees stood, and green growth showed, but otherwise, this time of year, the Red Rock range was burned pale with every stalk of grass standing cured on the stem.

Boone finished studying the onward set of buildings, the great log barns, two of them, the bunkhouse and shoeing shed and open-fronted wagon and buggy and workshop building, and finally reached up to scratch his head. "No cattle and no horses," he said. He dropped his hand to the saddle horn and began faintly to scowl. "No riders."

George had an inkling that this carried with it a significance that he did not really fathom, beyond realizing that a vast cow outfit just simply had to have range men and cattle. He said nothing. Up ahead, that two-storied, proud brick house standing amid its grassy place and trees, with its awesome wide white-painted verandah with the curlicued iron scrollwork, held him in silent awe. It didn't look like the pictures he'd seen of the President's mansion in Washington, but for some reason he was put in mind of that other house; his reaction was the same as it would have been in Washington. He rode on up beside Boone feeling as though he had no business here, as though at any minute a big dragoon would stalk out and order them away, or something like that.

But no one appeared. They tied up out front of

75

the brick house, dismounted, and Boone turned slowly to take the measure of the vast ranch yard. Not a sound carried over to them from anywhere, except for a door at the log bunkhouse swinging faintly on its dry hinges in a slight, hot breeze.

The hair arose along the base of George's neck. He shot a look at Boone. That soldier who'd asked them to come out here and carry the message—maybe this was why he'd wanted them to do that. Maybe, somehow or other, there was a connection between those bloody hands and this magnificent house, this huge, ghostly ranch.

Boone cleared his throat, lifted off his hat, re-settled it, then jerked his head and led the way to that white-painted verandah. There were chairs out there, and at one corner a swing hung suspended several feet from the floor by great chains going upward into the underside of the upstairs gallery. Boone balled his fist and rattled the door with his knocking. He did that four times, and each time they heard echoes chasing themselves in a big room beyond. Finally the door opened. A raw-boned, gray-haired Mexican woman with fine, slightly hawkish features looked steadily out at them—over the ten-inch barrel of a huge old Dragoon revolver that was cocked.

Boone eyed the woman, eyed the gun, and said: "Ma'am, we ran into some Apaches southeast of here over against the mountains. Some soldiers came up. One of them, an officer, asked us to come by and tell someone out here that they had killed four, and that my partner here and I killed one. The soldiers are still on their trail."

The angular woman lowered her gun but did not ease off the hammer. Soundlessly she stepped back. "Please, *señores* . . ." She inclined her head ever so slightly.

Boone and George entered. It was ten degrees cooler inside than it was outside. The house had large rooms, immaculately kept, with shiny flag-rock floors and dark draperies over lace curtains at each window. The woman took them through a large parlor, through a banquet-hall-size dining room, furnished with silver pieces and magnificent mahogany pieces, down a cool, gloomy hallway to a low-ceilinged bedroom near the rear of the house, and there she knocked very softly, then slid the door open as she said: "*Coronel*, here are two men . . . here is a man and a child . . . who have talked with the soldiers." She stepped aside.

The man had white hair, a faintly ruddy face with a strong jaw, a lipless mouth, and, when he glanced up at the man and the boy in the doorway, his eyes were a very dark shade of blue, so dark in fact that in the shadowy, cool interior of that room with the low ceiling they looked brown. He was no more than average in height, but because he also happened to be fine-boned and thin, when he arose to face the doorway, he seemed considerably taller.

He said nothing although he nodded to his guests. Boone repeated what he had told the man's housekeeper, or whatever that Mexican woman was, and afterward the white-headed man said: "I'm Fitzhugh Bonner." He did not cross to the doorway, nor offer his hand as he said this. "I'm grateful to you for riding out here." Fitzhugh Bonner stared toward the door a moment before speaking again. "It must have been out of your way. That was very kind of you, especially this time of year."

Boone acted a little embarrassed. "You're plumb welcome, it wasn't much. If we could put up our horses down at the barn overnight . . ."

The white-headed, erect, older man finally moved. "By all means," he said, and strode toward the door. "It will be nice to have horses in the barn again. There's an empty bunkhouse, too, gentlemen, but of course when María rings the supper bell you will dine with me."

He took them rather briskly across the yard to the nearest large log barn, which happened to be a horse barn complete with box-and-tie stalls as well as a harness room and a place for grain. When they entered this barn, blessed coolness washed over them again, probably if not entirely because of those immense, shading trees outside, along with the patch of green grass over in front

78

of the colonel's brick mansion, and the well-watered flowerbeds.

They watered their tired animals, washed them down, stalled them, and forked down a big bait of hay for each horse. Throughout this somewhat lengthy chore, they kept up a running conversation with the white-headed man. He seemed, for some bizarre reason, to become more verbal, more immediately concerned when he was outside his magnificent red brick house. Up there, seated in the soft gloom of that little low-ceilinged room at the back of his house, he seemed detached, disinterested; he seemed to consider anything that came to his attention up there an intrusion. At least this was Boone's and George's impression.

At the barn he was quite different. He explained that the reason the dragoon officer had asked them to come by Red Rock Ranch was because those Apaches had attacked his home place day before yesterday, had run off the last of his breeding horses, had killed the last of his *vaqueros*. There had only been three left, every one of them almost as old as the white-headed man himself; they had been riding for Red Rock Ranch ever since its owner had founded it twenty-seven years earlier—and the dragoon lieutenant had been both understanding and sympathetic when the white-headed man had told him that this latest raid had finished him.

Boone listened, and, when they were done caring for the dun and the black, he walked out front where late-day shadows were mingling with the fragrant shade, and rolled himself a smoke as he said: "You don't run cattle, Mister Bonner?"

The older man's lipless wide mouth widened still more in a hapless half smile. "Red Rock Ranch hasn't run cattle in some years. I still kept a few blooded horses from which I raised some fine cow horses. Those are the animals the Apaches ran off. They probably shot them, too."

Bonner considered George, his expression clearly showing curiosity, but he said nothing about the lad.

Boone lit up, rolled his eyes out over the immense range, blew smoke, and settled more comfortably against the smooth barn logs. "Kind of a big ranch, Mister Bonner, not to have anything on it eating the grass."

The white-headed man fixed Boone with a direct stare. "Are you familiar with this part of the country?" he asked. "If you aren't, I'll tell you something. It's not just Apaches. There are also marauders from over the line, down in Mexico. They ride the full distance up here to Gallup to raid. And there are bands of rustlers, horse thieves, gunmen, the scum of the Southwest, over in those same mountains the Apaches ran back into. I have fought them all for almost thirty years . . . my wife died last year.

That was also the year cattle thieves ran off the best of my cattle. I sold what remained before they got them, too. Then, day before yesterday, the Apaches came again. This time, my men were out with the horses. Now, I have nothing. Just my buildings, my land. Did you tell me your name?"

Boone looked at the older man. "Helm. Boone Helm."

"Mister Helm, I am an old man. I've been fighting one way or another all my life. In the Confederate Army, out here against Indians, marauders, horse thieves, and cattle rustlers. I've buried my wife and a good many men who rode for me. Day before yesterday when I lost the last of my horses and my *vaqueros* . . ." The older man turned solemn eyes toward the empty miles of his range land. "I was sitting in there thinking, when you arrived, that now the thing for me to do is leave . . . go back to Virginia, and spend my last days in peace in a civilized country."

Boone dropped his glance to George, who was being as quiet as stone, watching the old patrician. Boone said: "You were a colonel in the Rebel Army?"

The very dark blue eyes came around. "I was a colonel in the *Confederate* Army."

Boone took the rebuke in stride. "How long did Red Rock Ranch pay its way, Colonel?"

The thin shoulders rose and fell. "Most of the time. Twenty years or so. Why?"

"Kind of a shame to abandon something that's given a man pleasure, and the kind of a living that would allow him to import red brick into this adobe country and make a regular Virginia-style estate out in the middle of the New Mexico cow country."

Colonel Bonner said: "Mister Helm, you are a young man. When you are older, you'll realize that men only function well when they have personal reasons for doing so. My wife and I worked hard to create Red Rock Ranch. She loved it as much as I did. We overcame obstacles and laughed at them. Twice, she forted up with the *vaqueros* and me right here, in that barn you're leaning upon, and fought off Mexican marauders. Well, Mister Helm, she is buried out in our private cemetery over yonder in that grove of trees behind the house. That was all I had, that and the livestock, and my *vaqueros*. None of them remain, and, as I said, I'm an old man. For the past thirty years, I've worked, planned, fought, and prospered. Thirty years, I suppose, is about all any one man is supposed to have things his own way. After that, he should move aside for the next generation."

From the house, the angular, gray-haired Mexican woman came to the edge of the verandah and waved a white cloth, then she pointed. Colonel Bonner turned slowly to gaze out over the countryside.

Boone saw them first. "Horsemen riding in from the east," he said, and pointed. Then he turned toward George. "Make them out?"

George made them out very well. "Six," he replied. "White men, riding slow and bunched up."

Boone grinned. "You're dead right." Neither he nor George was very concerned right then, but as Colonel Bonner finished his study of those approaching horsemen and turned back, his comment, and the depth of genuine bitterness in his voice, made Boone and George look up again.

"Carter Thompson and his contemptibles. Gentlemen, we had best step inside the barn. It never rains but what it pours."

IX

George and Boone followed the colonel into his barn where they stood a moment, silently appraising those approaching horsemen. Then George asked who they were and, before replying, Colonel Bonner gazed at the lad again, as he'd done earlier, out in front of the barn. He seemed interested; at least he seemed curious about a gangling youngster riding through hostile country like this.

Then Bonner said: "Carter Thompson is a

free-graze cowman. He's been running cattle south and west, mostly, but because he owns no land, and because cowmen out here don't build fences, Thompson's herds can be found almost anywhere. He keeps twelve riders, every one of them a killer. He's the only cowman in this entire countryside that no one seems to bother very much. Last year he hanged four Mexican marauders in sight of Gallup, so the local *peones* would tell their friends and relations over the line in old Mexico what happened to men who raided Thompson herds." The colonel loosened his cloth coat, and for the first time his companions saw the very business-like, sheathed six-gun. Bonner went on speaking, all this while, gauging the distance as the oncoming riders came closer to the shade of his ranch yard.

"Carter Thompson has grazed his cattle on my land for the last two years, and when I've ordered him off, he's laughed at me. Early this spring he came right up into the yard, and told me that unless I expected to be buried here, I'd ought to abandon the ranch and go back where I came from."

Boone peered ahead, picked out the man in the lead of those slow-riding horsemen, and said: "Is that Thompson, out front, the big feller with the black hair and the swarthy hide?"

Bonner nodded. "That's Carter Thompson." He turned. "Gentlemen, be prepared for anything,

84

but whatever you do, be very careful. He'll know I no longer have any *vaqueros*."

Boone thought a moment then said: "We'll just sort of step back into the shadows, Colonel." He turned, took George with him, and went over where their saddles were draped. There, Boone lifted out his carbine, nodded as George did the same, then the two of them walked over to the opposite side of the log barn where they commanded the best view of the yard. When they were standing motionlessly there, invisible to riders in the yard, Boone looked around at George and said: "You know, partner, it's beginning to seem to me that one or the other of us always, somehow, manages to bring bad luck to the other one." He smiled. "You're not jinxed by any chance?"

George smiled back. Regardless of who those men were, just now riding into the yard out front, George had seen Boone Helm in action. George leaned upon his carbine in emulation of the older man as he replied: "It might be me. Sometimes lately my luck hasn't been very good."

Boone slapped the boy lightly upon the shoulder. "Your luck's plenty good. You rode away from eleven bronco Apaches. Not many folks can say they've ever done that." At the sound of shod hoofs crossing through the late-day gloom toward the front of the barn, Boone softly spoke to George as he lifted his carbine and faced forward: "Don't do anything until I do something, then do exactly as I do. Understand?"

George understood. "Sure," he answered, and lifted his carbine, holding it across his body two-handed, exactly as Boone Helm was doing.

The horsemen rode up to the front of the barn, halted, and sat their saddles, gazing at the white-headed man in the barn opening. They were unable to see into the barn very far, not altogether because it was murky in there, this late in the day, but also because what little daylight remained was in their eyes.

The swarthy, squarely massive man Bonner had identified for Boone said: "Too bad you lost your horses, Colonel. We seen them red devils runnin' them off." Thompson glanced toward the bunkhouse, where the door still sagged open. "Where are your *vaqueros*?"

"Dead," replied Bonner shortly. "The Apaches also caught them away from the ranch, out on the range."

Thompson's black eyes came back to rest upon the man in the barn doorway with mock pity. "That's sure too bad, Colonel. Plumb too bad. Well, an old man without no wife, no cattle, no horses, and not even any greaser cowboys . . . no point in you stayin' out here, now, is there?"

Colonel Bonner answered shortly again: "I'll make that decision, Thompson, when I'm good and ready."

The square-built man's expression changed subtly. "It's already been made for you," he told Fitzhugh Bonner. "You better clear out, Colonel." The swarthy, sweat-shiny face was cold-set. "You know what could happen any night now, Colonel. Them Apaches could come back and riddle you in your bed."

"They very seldom attack at night," replied Bonner, and the swarthy man came right back with a savage answer. "Yeah, you and me know that, but when they find your dead carcass, folks'll say they killed you maybe in the mornin' or the afternoon. But one thing you can count on, folks'll swear up and down it was the Apaches. And it won't have been done by them at all. Colonel, you're a wise man. You've been goin' downhill for several years. You're too old to come back again. I'm doin' you a favor lettin' you pack up and clear out. Take some good advice and go back East or wherever you come from. Otherwise, you're goin' to get killed."

Bonner moved his right elbow slightly, to brush back the right side of his cloth coat and expose the holstered six-gun.

Carter Thompson did not move, probably because he knew this was not a threat, but behind him and slightly to his left a Mexican cowboy with a pockmarked face went for his gun—and from inside the barn a carbine made its flat, stunningly sharp report, and the Mexican dropped out of his saddle without even a grunt.

Some of the horses flinched when that gunshot exploded inside the barn, but neither Carter Thompson nor any of his riders shied. They had been caught unprepared. Now they alternately glanced at the dead Mexican, and toward the dark interior of the barn.

For a while no one said a word. Eventually a savage-eyed, narrow-faced man, younger than any of Thompson's other riders, kneed his horse closer to the front of the barn, his body masking the right hand he had upon his holstered Colt.

Thompson said: "That's far enough, Sandy."

Colonel Bonner, just as erect and defiant as before, nodded approval of Thompson's admonition. "Good advice, Thompson. Now pick up your Mexican and get off my land."

Thompson did not act as though he had even heard. Looking blackly and impassively down into the barn, he said: "Colonel, you just made one hell of a bad mistake. You just bought yourself a bullet. Who you got inside the barn? Hirin' a gunfighter ain't goin' to save your lousy damned hide." Thompson leaned as though to alight. Evidently, instead of being deterred by the killing of his Mexican, Carter Thompson had been icily enraged. Instead of leaving, he was going to dismount and start a real fight.

Bonner caught him before he'd kicked his

right boot clear of the stirrup. "Stay up there, Thompson. You step down and you'll be next."

The black-eyed free-grazer did not straighten back, but he hung there without dismounting, either. He looked contemptuously at Bonner. "You silly old damned fool, what chance have you and some idiot with a carbine behind you got against all of us?"

Boone fired again. Carter Thompson's hat left his head as though borne by wings, and sailed backward several yards, then fell in the dust.

A second Winchester bullet sang close to a man on Thompson's right. So close in fact, the man's horse winced and the man threw himself down low with a squawk.

Thompson very slowly hauled himself back upright in the saddle. "How many in there?" he asked, without seeming to be very mindful of how close a bullet had come to his upper head. "God damn you, Colonel. If you think you can . . ."

"Ride," ordered Boone Helm, from back in the gloom. "Turn that horse, mister, pick up your dead greaser, and ride out."

Carter Thompson's low, broad forehead creased. He continued to gaze ahead, over Colonel Bonner's head. But instead of speaking, he turned, motioned for someone to hoist his dead rider across the saddle, and as he prudently raised his rein hand to depart, Thompson demonstrated his clear conviction that he was indeed facing someone inside that log barn who could, and who most certainly would, kill him unless he obeyed that man's edict. Without having any inkling who Boone Helm was, Carter Thompson understood him precisely; he understood men like Boone Helm a lot better than he understood a redoubtable patrician like old Colonel Fitzhugh Bonner.

Without a word, Thompson turned his horse, leaned to accept his ragged, bullet-torn hat from one of his companions, and led the withdrawal that followed. The last horse to leave the yard was the one carrying the dead man, belly-down, tied across his saddle.

Boone and George walked forward. George eased down the hammer of his carbine, wiped a flood of sweat off his face although it was not that hot inside the log barn. When Boone and the colonel walked out into the yard to make certain Carter Thompson was still riding, George followed along, carrying his Winchester in the crook of one bent arm, exactly the same way Boone was carrying his weapon.

Finally Fitzhugh Bonner said: "Mister Helm, I'm right obliged. That's the first time I've been able to get the best of Carter Thompson since he first showed up around here, four or five years back. Him, and his crew of gunmen and cutthroats." Bonner turned, saw George, saw the boy's carbine, and said: "You fired, son?"

George nodded,

"Good lad," said the colonel, and smiled. "How old are you?"

George saw Boone's head come around. George had been teetering between saying sixteen and seventeen. Instead, he did not answer at all; he turned and walked back to the front of the barn the way he'd seen Boone do when he chose not to speak on some subject.

The Mexican woman came forth with a hand bell and gently rang it. Colonel Bonner waved back and the woman disappeared through a doorway. Boone, thinking back, said: "Colonel, I didn't do you any favor when that Mex went for his pistol. Even if Thompson had been someone else and not a free-graze renegade, he wouldn't have taken the loss of a rider without harboring a grudge. He'll be back, and next time I'd judge he won't just ride up into the yard. Maybe he wasn't just talking when he mentioned you getting riddled in your bed."

Colonel Bonner, strolling toward the house with the other two, answered Boone's observation calmly and without a trace of fear. "Mister Helm, I've been expecting someone to try that for a couple of years. All my men have been expecting someone to assassinate them. There really are very few killers in New Mexico Territory who will stand up and face you. Everyone out here kills from cover, if they can.

As for that man you shot . . . he invited his own killing."

Boone brushed that aside. "I'm sure even Thompson realizes that, Colonel, but what I'm getting at is that Carter Thompson struck me as someone who wants something, and today he sure as hell got his nose rubbed in it around here, which will make him ten times more determined. Colonel, about what you mentioned concerning moving back to Virginia . . ."

"No," replied the older man, stepping up onto the verandah and reaching to hold the door open for his guests. "As I told Thompson, Mister Helm, if I go, it will not be because anyone has scared me off. If I go at all, it will be because I have decided it is time for me to go. Well now, gentlemen, if you will follow me, I'll show you where you can wash up. And maybe if you left those Winchesters here, behind the door . . . ?"

The graying Mexican woman passed soundlessly through on her way out of the handsome big parlor. She turned, crossed glances with George, and smiled. He smiled back. She was the first woman he had smiled at in several months.

X

They did not stay overnight in the red brick house but went down to the log bunkhouse, which was south of the horse barn. They looked in on their horses first, then strolled back to the dark little porch of the bunkhouse and sat a while, for as long as was required for Boone to smoke a cigarette, then they turned in. It had been not just a long and eventful day for both of them, it had also been a very long, tiring one.

Boone had already washed, shaved, and forked feed to the horses by the time George went out back of the bunkhouse to wash and comb his hair. In fact, Boone had arisen ahead of the sun, which was his custom, and since then he'd made a rather thorough examination of all the buildings, of the corrals, even of the little cemetery within its iron fence that lay behind the colonel's house, out a few hundred yards where a number of immense trees cast perpetual shade.

He came back, and met the lad out behind the barn where George had gone, after he'd discovered their horses had been fed. They exchanged a greeting, then George said: "That town you talked about, Zuñi, how far is it from here?"

Boone answered as they slowly retraced their steps up through toward the front of the barn.

"Not far. There's a river south of Gallup . . . a big boulder wash, more than a river . . . and Zuñi's just beyond the south bank." Boone looked at the boy. "Are you worrying?"

George was. "They'll come back, won't they?" he asked, without having to define who "they" were.

Boone halted out where the new daylight was turning all that vast emptiness into a rose-colored paradise. The air was fresh and fragrant and cool, visibility was practically unlimited, and there was an unmistakable sense of something everlasting, where they stood, looking toward the distant mountains. Boone answered the boy in a quiet way: "Thompson'll come back. He just about has to. A man like that lives on force and pride. We played hell with both of them for him yesterday. You can't ever humble a man, even a little, and not have him remember it. Yeah, he'll probably be back." Boone looked at the lad. "You worrying?"

George was essentially honest, so he nodded his head. At the same moment the gray-headed Mexican woman came out upon the verandah, over at the main house, and rang her little bell. Then she beckoned to them, and, as they started forward, she stood watching. When they got close, she nodded at Boone, but smiled at George. Then she led them inside to the large dining room, and left them.

Colonel Bonner appeared within moments, his attire fresh and immaculate. He looked more like some patrician laird than a Southwestern cowman, and as they sat down to breakfast he acted differently than when they had first met him in this same house. Evidently he had been busy with his thoughts last night, because he said: "If those soldiers caught up with the reservation jumpers, they may bring back my horses. Unless of course the Indians have killed them. But in either case, what you said yesterday, Mister Boone, is quite true. A ranch this size needs livestock on it." He smiled over his morning steak and fried potatoes. "Otherwise, Carter Thompson may be right. If a man isn't going to operate his land, and doesn't mean to protect it, he might as well abandon it, eh?"

Boone gave a cautious reply to this kind of talk. "Colonel, if Thompson's got his heart set on moving into your brick house and taking over Red Rock Ranch, maybe what's at stake isn't just running livestock."

The older man said: "It never was just running livestock, Mister Boone. Since my wife died, it's been whether I wanted to keep on. Several days ago, when the Apaches struck, and the last of what I'd built up over the years was wiped out, it appeared to me that I was finished."

Boone studied the older man. "And today it doesn't look that way, Colonel?"

Bonner's bright, steady gaze lingered on Boone. "That depends, Mister Helm. I've made money over the years. I've lost some, too, in the form of cattle and horses, and I'd be foolish to consider re-stocking Red Rock Ranch now, under these circumstances, with Thompson and the Apaches running amuck, unless I had a fair idea I could survive, wouldn't I?"

Boone said: "What makes you think you can survive, now, Colonel?"

"You. You and George," replied the older man, watching Boone closely. "I'm too old, the lad's too young, but there have to be men somewhere around who'd hire on at Red Rock Ranch. You can do the hiring and firing. I'll buy the cattle."

George stopped eating and looked at both the older men. Boone, prepared to give Fitzhugh Bonner a short answer to what he was suggesting, saw the boy's alert, hopeful expression, and checked his answer until he'd drained the coffee cup in front of him. Meanwhile, Colonel Bonner went on speaking.

"Start out with two hundred head of cows and five or six bulls, Mister Helm, and, if things work out, go on from there, building up the herd."

Boone finally said: "Thompson . . . ?"

Bonner's answer was cryptic. "That would depend upon the men we can hire, wouldn't it?" Boone looked rueful, so the colonel spread his hands. "Mister Helm, if this is the new order of things, and if Red Rock Ranch is to start functioning again as a proper cow outfit, why then we'll have to abide by the new rules, won't we?"

Boone finished his breakfast and leaned back. "Exactly what did you have in mind?" he asked pointblank.

"You as range boss," stated Bonner, without adding another word to it.

Boone arose. He knew George was watching him, was waiting for his reply. So was Fitzhugh Bonner. Boone said: "Colonel, my partner and I were on our way down to Zuñi. Seems to me we'd better just keep on riding." At the looks of disappointment across the table from him, Boone sighed. Then he temporized by saying: "Well, George and I'll talk it over down at the barn."

That's what they did, talked it over down at the barn, and when Boone pointed out that Carter Thompson was no one to take lightly, the boy said: "Neither was that man back on the meadow above Gunnison."

There was a world of difference between that man and a man like Thompson, but Boone did not point this out. He said: "You want to stay on here, George? You want to cattle ranch?"

The answer to that was in the radiant eyes of the boy and in his quick smile even before he spoke. "It's the best chance I've ever had," he replied, and Boone understood the depth of real meaning behind those words. It was the best chance George Morgan had ever had to belong somewhere.

Boone went out front, rolled a smoke, studied the blue-blurry distant mountains where the heat was beginning to accumulate, and made his own, personal decision. Maybe he couldn't bring it off, but maybe he *could,* and if he did bring it off, George would have something to build a life upon when Boone rode on. If a man had to fragment his existence, it was better to do it this way, probably, than just drifting here and there, from the mountains to the prairies, not really contributing anything, and once in a while, like robbing that stage up north, doing a little harm.

George spoke from just back inside the barn: "Boone, you see those horsemen yonder?"

It was like being plunged into cold water on a hot day, the way those words hit Boone Helm. The last time he'd seen riders approaching like that, in a slow-walking band, it had been a prelude to serious trouble. He scanned the land, saw them better than a mile out coming from the northeast on an angling course, and, without taking his eyes off them, he said: "Better go fetch our carbines, George."

As the boy moved to obey, he squinted hard, then said: "Would he come back again today?"

Boone reiterated his earlier order without

answering the question. "Go get our carbines, George."

After the boy had departed, Boone stepped into the doorless barn doorway, loosened the Colt in his hip holster, and hardly more than glanced around when Colonel Bonner came striding across the yard from the direction of the main house.

The colonel stopped, made a long, silent study of the band of riders, slowly shook his head as though satisfied these men were not the ones he expected, then he said: "Who are they, Mister Helm?"

Boone did not answer until he had puzzled out something. Whoever they were, they were riding bunched up around one of their number, and that man was hanging limply in his saddle. It was too early for that man to be drunk, and there were no towns back in the direction they were coming from, so the sagging horseman had to be injured.

Boone said: "Colonel, I'd guess they saw your buildings and headed over this way because they've got a hurt man with them."

Boone was right. About the time George came back with the Winchesters, the horsemen reached the first shade at the far side of the ranch yard. By then it was obvious to Boone, Colonel Bonner, and George Morgan that one of them was injured.

There were five of them, not counting the injured man. As they came closer and saw the watchers at the horse barn, they angled over there. When they pulled up, a bronze-faced lean man looked down gravely.

"Had a little trouble back on a mountain side last evening, gents, and my friend here picked up a bullet in the collar bone. I was wondering, if you had the space, could we sort of settle him down in your bunkhouse? He's in pretty bad shape."

Colonel Bonner pointed. "Over there, that log house. Take any unoccupied bunk. I'll fetch my satchel and join you down there in a few minutes. Mister Helm, maybe you and George could lend a hand?"

Boone put aside his carbine, as did George. They went with the travel-stained range men over to the bunkhouse, got the injured man out of his saddle, and carried inside. They got him comfortable on a lower bunk, and stripped him to the waist. His shoulder was terribly swollen and discolored. Boone saw George's color drain away leaving the boy's face looking like old putty. He said: "Go get us some hot water from the main house, George."

After the lad had gone, Boone looked up at the bronzed man. "He's fourteen years old." The lanky cowboy nodded understanding. He and his companions stood around the bunk, saying nothing. They were all seasoned, scarred men; none was young and none was old. When

Colonel Bonner arrived, carrying a black bag in his hands, and shouldered everyone aside before leaning down to examine the injured cowboy, they all stood back a little to give him room, then watched the older man work. It struck Boone Helm at once that Fitzhugh Bonner was an experienced healer; he wondered if the colonel hadn't picked up some of this knowledge back during the war.

That bronzed man raised his head, when he was satisfied old Bonner was good at what he was now doing, doctoring the injured man, and said: "Better care for the horses, fellers." At once, the other range riders turned and left the bunkhouse. Then the bronzed man walked as far as the front porch with Boone Helm, and said: "Damned bunch of broncos riding used-up horses hit us out of nowhere on the side of a lousy mountain northeast of here. They tried hard to get our animals. That's how Jamie got shot. They might have got the horses, at that, but . . . just like in the stories . . . the cavalry come charging up. Mister, it got pretty damned hot around for about a half hour, before them damned Indians turned tail and ran for it, with the dragoons right after them."

Boone said: "You get any of them?"

"Yeah, three. They left 'em lying."

"That white-headed man inside, Colonel Bonner, will be right glad to hear you got three. My partner and I got one yesterday. Those break-outs ran off the colonel's horses and killed his riders." Boone extended a hand. "Boone Helm."

The bronzed man shook. "Russ Petrie. Me 'n' my friends finished the season up north and were heading down toward the border to stay warm next winter, and maybe run a few mustangs. Last damned thing we expected was to run into a band of damned hostiles. We thought the Army had them all corralled by now."

"They're corralled all right," explained Boone. "But that don't keep a few strong hearts from busting out to raise the yell every now and then."

Down in front of the horse barn it looked as though Red Rock Ranch were a genuine cattle outfit again. There were riders down there, sluicing off at the trough, caring for their horses, talking back and forth in the cool shade, and the idea suddenly occurred to Boone, so he asked Russ Petrie if his friends figured on lying over until their injured companion could travel. Petrie's answer was almost automatic, it was so casual. "We'd sure admire to. We can work for our keep. Not a man amongst us hasn't been a top hand up north with the cow outfits." Petrie studied Boone a moment. "You the range boss, by any chance?"

Boone smiled, then shrugged. "I'm supposed to be, I guess."

XI

Colonel Bonner and Boone Helm stood in the pewter night with moonlight softening all the harsh contours roundabout, gazing back down in the direction of the lively and lit bunkhouse where Russ Petrie and his companions had settled in, and Bonner said: "I dug out the slug. It must have hit something first, before it hit Jamie. The thing was pretty well spent, and it was also slightly flattened. It broke his collar bone, but at that he could have come off much worse."

Boone said: "How long before he can ride, Colonel?"

Bonner looked skeptical in the moonlight. "He won't even be able to get off that bunk for a week, Mister Helm. After that, it's my guess he won't be strong enough to sit a saddle for another month."

Boone smiled quietly. "Good. This afternoon that ruddy-faced one, Russ Petrie, offered to stay on, the lot of them, and work for their keep until Jamie can ride again." Boone turned slowly. "Strange how things work out sometimes, isn't it? Red Rock Ranch just acquired a full, experienced riding crew. Isn't that what we were talking about at breakfast this morning?"

Colonel Bonner kept staring at Boone. "Stay

on, and work? That's almost a miracle, Mister Helm. Did you hire them?"

Boone smiled again. "Well, Petrie asked if I was Red Rock's range boss, and I told him maybe I was, but I didn't take up his offer. Wanted to talk to you first."

Bonner said: "You do the hiring and firing. I told you that this morning." The colonel straightened up off the corral stringer he'd been leaning against. "Well, I'll be busy down in Gallup tomorrow, Mister Helm, so I'd better turn in early tonight." As he started away, Boone sighed, but if the colonel heard that, or guessed at its implication, he neither spoke nor turned back.

George came out of the bunkhouse in search of Boone. When they met out at the corrals, George told Boone that the cowboys were in the bunkhouse playing blackjack, and that they treated him as though he were one of them. It was clear, even by moonlight, that George was as happy as he had ever been. That was understandable to Boone, so he let the boy talk, let him say whatever he felt like saying, without once interrupting, and later, when George headed for the horse barn to look in on the dun horse, which was something Boone had taught him to do—always look in on his animals just before bedding down—Boone lit a smoke and ran a searching glance up along the star field overhead, making his own, private decision about staying.

He strolled back, eventually, to the bunkhouse, and was met upon the little porch by Russ Petrie, who was cocked back with his feet upon a railing, his chair precariously balanced. Petrie was hatless, and somewhere along the way he had also shed his spurs and gun belt. Boone said: "Mister Petrie, we had a little trouble around here yesterday with a free-grazer named Carter Thompson. I shot a Mex cowboy of his over there in front of the horse barn. If I were you, I'd wear my gun, even after supper."

Petrie tilted back his head to look up where Boone leaned upon a porch upright. "We sort of gathered, from listening to George, that the old gentleman's had his share of grief over the past couple of years. George told us about what happened over there yesterday. Sort of too bad folks living in a country as big as this one is can't try to get along, ain't it?"

Boone nodded. "Yeah. But everywhere I've ever been seems to me there's at least one Carter Thompson, Mister Petrie."

The bronzed man said: "Just plain Russ'll do fine."

Boone accepted that. "What I was leading up to, Russ, is that you and the others rode in at a bad time. We could rig out one of the wagons in the shed and haul your friend down to Gallup. You fellers could put up down there, and not have to sit in on whatever happens around here."

Petrie's tough eyes studied Boone. "Are you staying on?"

"Yeah. But I've got a reason."

Petrie's gaze did not waver. "The boy? You're looking for a decent place to settle the boy?"

That surprised Boone. "You're pretty good at reading sign, Russ."

"Naw," said the range man, "not really. George told us about his maw pulling out on him, about meeting you, and you sort of saving his bacon over a horse, then fetching him along with you. Mister Helm, we all of us, one time or another, run across one or two of those runaway lads. Just not very many of us do what you're trying to do for them. I reckon we'll stay on, Mister Helm."

Boone smiled. "In that case, my first name's Boone."

Russ accepted that and asked: "Any relation to old Dan'l Boone, by any chance?"

Boone had been asked this before and he gave the same answer now. "Not that I know of, and I kind of doubt it since I don't like walking, and seems to me he walked just about everywhere he went."

Russ yawned and stretched, and eased the tipped-back chair forward very carefully, then he arose, stepped to the porch railing, studied the high sky, the darkened big flow of range land in the direction of the invisible mountains, and said: "Wonder what luck those soldiers had?"

Boone did not reply. Someone inside must have made a killing at the twenty-one table because a man's jubilant crowing erupted. Russ turned, smiling.

"We all rode for the Hatchet cow outfit up in Wyoming. Got to be pretty good friends, the six of us, so, when the drive was finished down to rail's end, we just drew our time and headed south. Every man in there is a good hand . . . for money, whiskey, or bullets, Boone."

This was Russ Petrie's guarantee, and Boone accepted it on Petrie's judgment. He said: "I think the colonel's going down to Gallup in the morning to buy cattle and start up again."

Petrie turned and eased down upon the railing. "Good idea. We're likely to be ranch-bound for a few weeks, and none of us'd want to live off the old gentlemen without earning our keep. If he'll fetch back the cattle, we'll work 'em for him. As for that other thing, that trouble with this feller Thompson, if it don't get too bad, why I reckon we'll just get along all right." Russ Petrie smiled a little in the porch gloom. "If Mister Thompson is just plain dead set on being ornery, well, then I reckon the bunch of us'll just have to learn him where the boundary line lies, won't we?"

They entered the bunkhouse, which was warmer than the yonder night, and which was finally beginning to smell and look like a bunkhouse.

Aside from the horse sweat and leather scent in there, Petrie's men had hung spare shirts, as well as booted Winchesters, upon the walls where they had selected bunks. There was a strong odor of equally as strong tobacco, too. Later, when they all turned in, and the last one down doused the lamp, Boone lay back thinking that this, really, was his true environment; that loafing away a full summer had been pleasant. He had enjoyed every day of it, but loafing could be a lot more tedious than working, and he was glad to be among stockmen again, in a bunkhouse that had the old, familiar smells and sounds again. He looked over at George's bunk. The rangy, long-legged lad was already dead to the world. Maybe, for a boy like that, there were better environments, somewhere, but Boone was unfamiliar with them, and anyway, there was absolutely nothing wrong with being a stockman. If George learned the range man's trade, and learned to be good at it, he'd have as fine a trade as any man who could stand up on his hind legs, and a heap better trade than an awful lot of them.

Boone rolled onto his side and went to sleep.

When the predawn chill arrived, he awakened, heard someone's cadenced snoring nearby, rolled out soundlessly, got dressed, and was heading out back to shave and wash when the wounded man stopped him with a whispered request for water. Boone got a glassful and stood beside the bunk while Jamie emptied the glass, then he asked: "Feeling any better?"

Jamie, who was young and tough-looking, smiled crookedly. "Mister, I'd have to perk up one hell of a lot just to feel well enough to die."

Boone grinned. "You'll do, Jamie. Next time keep down."

"I *was* down," stated the wounded cowboy. "That bastard got me some way, by slithering up along the ground through the brush like a snake." Jamie sighed. "Sure played hell, didn't I? We was all going down across the desert and find us some mustangs."

"You can still do it, but not for maybe a month," stated Boone. "If I can rustle a bottle of whiskey around the ranch somewhere, I'll fetch it along."

Jamie said: "Thanks, range boss, I'd sure appreciate that."

As Boone continued on out back to the wash rack, he decided that these riders held nothing back among themselves; they had already figured out everything they had to know while they were at Red Rock Ranch.

When Boone went down to fork feed to the horses, he saw that one of the buggies was already gone from the shed, and that a set of harness was missing from its peg inside the saddle room. The colonel was also an early riser, evidently.

He finished up at the barn and headed for the brick house. There were seven ambulatory men, and one flat out on his back, who would need breakfast. He did not know whether the colonel had said anything about this to María; he didn't even know whether María, who worked at the main house, would feed hired riders, but one way or another he was going to have to make certain they got fed, even if he had to get the grub up there, and return to the bunkhouse with it.

There was a bright light in the back of the main house so Boone went around back, hat in hand, and rolled thick knuckles across the rear door. María came out, saw him, motioned for him to enter, and he smelled the cooking food at once. As he trailed her to the big kitchen, he passed a doorless passageway and saw a big, long cook shack that was what range riders called the dining room. The table had been set. There were already two big pots of hot coffee ready, and, when Boone faced forward again, the gray-headed woman said: "You worried whether I could cook for so many, *señor*?"

He smiled at the hard, black eyes. "No ma'am. I worried whether you *would* cook for so many. I never doubted that you could."

The black eyes, set in the aquiline, hard face, showed just a hint of humor and appreciation. "Are they up yet, *señor*?"

"Probably they're stirring by now, ma'am. Want me to go get them?"

"I'll ring the bell," said María, and kept gazing

steadily at Boone. "The colonel left very early. *Señor*, I am grateful for you staying here. I have been watching him shrivel up for so long now. It hurts the heart to watch something like that. I have prayed, *señor*. Do you believe that prayers are answered?"

Boone considered the inside of his hat. The last time he had prayed had been as a small child. "I suppose they get answered, ma'am," he murmured.

María changed the subject. "That boy . . . he is too big for your son, no?"

"We're not related. I just found him, and sort of brought him along."

María seemed to have already guessed as much. "He is big and someday he'll be strong. When there are things you can't do for him, *señor*, send him to me."

Boone smiled slowly. María, however she had acted at their first meeting, was different now. "I'll send him to you," he promised. "His mother abandoned him for some feller in a fancy buggy."

"His father?"

"Who knows, *señora*?"

The black eyes asked the question before María framed it into words. "*Señor*, why are people like that?"

Boone had no answer. "I wish I knew. Pretty lousy damned way to treat kids, isn't it?"

"*Sí, señor*, a pretty lousy . . . damned . . . way

111

to treat them. But I think that will change, won't it?"

"I hope so."

María finally smiled candidly at Boone. "I'll go ring the breakfast bell now," she said, and left him standing in the fragrant, warm kitchen, gazing after her. She was a good woman, wise and strong and good. That would help an awful lot, too.

XII

Three of the riders were over at the shoeing shed, another one was at the bunkhouse with Jamie, and Russ Petrie was down at the corrals with Boone and George, when one of the men across the yard at the shed made a high, warning, whistling sound. Everyone raised up. Boone saw the riders and pointed them out to Russ. It looked like a large body of them. They made considerable dust, and even though they seemed to be miles away to the southwest, their angling course was obviously toward the ranch.

No one speculated out aloud, but it was a sure bet those range riders were doing a lot of private speculating. Then George, with the youngest eyes among them all, said: "It's soldiers and they're driving some loose horses ahead of them."

He was right. The older men could begin to

make out the same blueness of all those lazy-riding horsemen when the distance had closed up to about a mile and a half. Boone had no idea how many horses the Apaches had taken from Bonner's ranch, but he counted eighteen animals being driven ahead of the troopers.

Russ Petrie went over to open some corral gates. His companions, without a word from anyone, went up to block the north end of the ranch yard so that, when the horses trotted in, they would be unable to trot on through, but would have to turn in through those opened gates.

The sun was directly overhead; there were dancing waves of summertime, midday heat in all directions, and the peculiar haze that lingered in this huge country from midmorning until sunset made it very hard to correctly estimate distances, including the distance between those oncoming cavalrymen and the yard.

Russ strolled over to Boone without taking his eyes off the soldiers. "Looks like they got a piece of those damned broncos, don't it?"

Boone nodded, and as the troopers herded the loose stock into the yard, the horses suddenly dropped off to a head-hung walk, their leaders going straight for the corrals. Of course, those animals knew exactly where they were to go because they had been reared here. The men who had prudently taken up a position at the north end of the yard began drifting back as the soldiers, in cool shade for a change, drooped in their saddles and headed for the stone water trough.

Boone went up where the officer was dismounting. The lieutenant looked dehydrated; he looked ten pounds thinner than when Boone had last seen him, but he smiled, showing strong white teeth in his sun-blasted face, and pulled off a gauntlet as he said: "We got that many horses back for Mister Bonner. It's not the thirty head he lost, but it's better'n none of them." The lieutenant's hard, moving eyes came back to Boone and stayed on him. "I didn't figure you'd still be in the country," he said.

Boone's answer was quietly thoughtful. "No big hurry, Lieutenant. Where did you catch the broncos?"

"They made a bad strategical mistake. They tried to jump a bunch of cowboys for their horses. That slowed them down just enough, so that when they broke off that fight, we were too close for them to avoid us. We caught them atop some sagebrush rims. There wasn't much decent cover for them, and damned little for us when we came down out of the chaparral. They put up a hell of a fight, at that." The lieutenant smiled. "They'd been whittled down to six or seven men. We buried them up there on the rims, rounded up their horses, gathered up their guns, and turned back. Now, as soon as the horses have been watered, we've got to push along. I'd like to make the post below Gallup before nightfall."

Boone offered to feed the troopers but the officer, very clearly a man who drove himself as hard as he drove his men, declined. They had eaten upon the rims about dawn, and he said his men were a picked troop especially trained for the kind of privation and hardship that was required, not only for chasing renegades, but running them down; he did not want to break that training.

A half hour later the dragoons were back astride, jogging southward out of the shade toward the immense, long sweep of empty land southward. One of the cowboys slowly shook his head.

"I'd sure hate like hell to have to serve under that officer."

The others agreed, one way or another, then they went out to look at the corralled horses. Someone spoke out in a condemnatory tone of voice.

"Lousy damned Indians. They got no feeling for animals at all. Look at them horses, tucked up, rid down, cut and bruised . . . half dead. It's a god-damned shame."

Russ turned a good-natured smile upon the man who had said that. "Got any solutions, Charley?"

Evidently Charley did have, because he turned indignantly and stalked toward the horse barn where there was a shelf of salve and curative powders. A couple of the other men went along to lend a hand. Russ looked a little apologetically at Boone.

"Didn't mean to sound like a boss."

Boone brushed that aside. "The main thing is to doctor the horses." He gazed thoughtfully at Russ. "But you were a range boss, somewhere," he said.

Petrie conceded that. "Yeah, a couple of places up north. Hell, a man don't get as many lumps and scars as I've got at this trade without, once in a while, running into a boss' job. Personally I'd as leave be just a top hand. You can get drunk Saturday nights and not have to worry about things."

Colonel Bonner returned about sunset. Boone met him at the barn and helped unharness the horse and push the top buggy over to the shed. Over there, they leaned in the shade and quiet as Bonner reported the results of his trip to Gallup.

"There are a few men down in town . . . older men, like me . . . who usually have a few head of good stock to sell. I put together two hundred head from three different ranches. They'll push them up to Red Rock in a day or two." Bonner looked over where the corrals were. "Whose horses are those?"

"Yours. The cavalry brought them back. The lieutenant said you'd lost thirty head. There's eighteen head over yonder. Like the lieutenant said, Colonel, it's not all you lost, but it's a hell of a lot better than getting none back at all."

Bonner continued to lean in the warm shade, gazing across toward the corrals. "Getting back to the cattle. We'll have to do some work on the corrals. There has been no stock in them in over a year, so some of the posts and stringers will probably have to be re-set. Then we'll have to organize the men into roping pairs. We'll have to vent every brand and put on the Red Rock mark. The irons are in the harness room at the barn."

Boone already knew this. He had found, and had examined, those irons the first evening he'd been on the ranch.

Colonel Bonner gravely fished forth two cigars from inside his cotton coat and handed one to Boone. Then he just as gravely struck the match and held it. After they had both lit up, he savored the smoke and seemed to settle more comfortably where he was leaning upon the top buggy. "My last shot," he said quietly.

Boone understood the inference perfectly. He thought, rolled the cigar in his fingers, and after a while he spoke. "I reckon even doing something wrong is better than not doing anything at all, isn't it, Colonel?"

Bonner's leaned, lined face creased into a smile. "You're a man it's easy to be around, Mister Helm. Considering you're no older than you are, I'd guess that you've lived a little."

Boone let all that pass and said: "Colonel, I got to thinking about something today."

Bonner did as Russ Petrie had also done. He surprised Helm by his next statement: "The boy, Mister Helm?"

"Yeah, the boy. He thinks this is the greatest spot on earth, and he thinks those range men are the best men on earth."

Bonner's lingering, gentle smile persevered. "He could possibly be correct in both cases, Mister Helm. Go on."

"Well, Colonel, I'm going to be riding on one of these days. You and I both understand that. But the boy deserves better than to be a saddle bum. He's willing and he's pretty smart, for being only fourteen and all." Boone raised his eyes to the older man's face. "Colonel, if you'll keep him, help him grow into a man, I'll set him up with a few head of cattle so's his keep won't cost you anything."

Fitzhugh Bonner pulled in a big gust of smoke and trickled it out slowly. Then he said: "Mister Helm, I've thought about the boy the last couple of days. My wife and I never had children. One of those things folks don't appear to have much control over. I got to thinking, on the drive back this afternoon . . . maybe the boy would like to stay on, and, if he would, maybe, if he turned out to be the kind of a man both you and I would be proud to know, well then, Mister Helm, he could become like a son to me. As for you setting him up . . . I can do that."

Boone conceded. "Sure you can, Colonel. But with me it's something I *want* to do." He reached inside his shirt, untied something in there, and pulled out a cloth money belt. He held it out, and, when old Bonner did not move, Boone said: "Colonel, you take the boy on my terms or he goes south when I ride on."

Bonner accepted the money belt. "For a few cows," he murmured.

Boone smiled. "More than just a few. There's four thousand dollars in there. That ought to get him a pretty nice size herd. With you managing it and making George do every damned bit of the work, he'd ought to be fairly well set up by the time's he's twenty or so."

Old Bonner gazed from the belt he was holding to Boone Helm. "Four thousand dollars . . . ?"

"You can count it over in the main house, Colonel. It's all there. I won't say a thing about this to the lad. You won't, either, I figure."

"But, Mister Helm . . . four thousand dollars is twice as much as he's going to need to get a . . ."

"No, Colonel, he's fourteen. That's not so young when you figure how slow cows calve out enough heifers to hold back for more seed stock." Boone tapped ash from the cigar. "My terms, Colonel, remember?"

Bonner slowly folded the money belt and

stuffed it into a pocket. "Mister Helm, come up to the main house with me and have supper."

Boone almost declined. His place was in the bunkhouse with the riding crew. But, too, there was more to be talked out, so he accepted, and as they started trudging across the yard in the late-day coolness, the colonel asked about Jamie. Boone said he was looking much better, then he remembered his promise to fetch along a bottle of whiskey, and asked if there was any at the main house.

The colonel said: "Brandy, Mister Helm. The finest drink of all for a man with a bullet hole in him. French brandy. It doesn't anger the blood like cowtown whiskey. I'll give you a bottle for Jamie right after supper."

They talked cattle, then, and range, and feed, water, marking, culling, all the basic essentials all stockmen eventually get around to, no matter what else might be on their minds, and later, when they had washed up for supper and María came to smile a welcome home to Colonel Bonner, the old man surprised Boone with an almost casual statement.

"Her husband was my *mayordomo*, my range boss for eighteen years. He was one of the men those Apaches caught out alone and killed."

That, then, accounted for the cocked pistol in María's hand when she'd first opened the door to Boone and George, and it undoubtedly also accounted for her grim, bleak expression, right up until this morning, when she had smiled.

When she came to serve them supper in the main dining room, Boone looked up and smiled. María looked back and smiled. The colonel did not seem very tired, even though he had unquestionably put in a very hot and arduous day. Boone got the impression that the old man had dredged up a fresh supply of strength and will within the past twenty-four hours.

During the course of their cowmens' conversation over supper Colonel Bonner continued to refer to Boone as "Mister Helm," until eventually the younger man said: "Colonel, my first name is Boone . . . and I don't think that I'm related to old Dan'l Boone."

The older man accepted this with a very slight nod of the head. He said: "All right. And do you expect we can have those corrals ready by the time the cattle arrive, Boone?"

XIII

It was the day the cattle arrived, being driven by six or seven riders from three different ranches down closer to Gallup, that the colonel asked Boone to let the others go out and take delivery on the range. George went with Russ Petrie and the riders. Boone watched them go from out back of the barn. They were to make the count, and if all the cattle where accounted for, Russ was to sign the receipt, then they were to bring the cattle on in and corral them so that the following day they could be run through the working corrals.

Colonel Bonner stood out there with Boone, and, as the riders loped away, Bonner said: "That boy rides like he was born to the saddle."

Boone said nothing. He was thinking how the boy had acquired that muscular, bred dun horse, but if anyone were to explain to the colonel how the lad had got that animal, it was going to be up to the boy.

Then Colonel Bonner mentioned the subject that had been on his mind, the subject he'd wanted to talk over with his range boss. "Boone, that's a damned good riding crew we've got. I can't remember when I've had as many real top hands at one time. I've been thinking. I understand their feelings about being loyal to their wounded friend, and I certainly can appreciate how they feel about earning their keep while they're staying at Red Rock Ranch, but doesn't it seem more nearly reasonable to you that I hire them all on and pay them riders wages? You see, I aim to pick up a few hundred more head of cattle, as I find the kinds I want, and that means I'll have need for a good crew. If I let these men work for nothing, they'd pull up stakes as soon as Jamie can ride, then I'd have to go around trying to find half as good a crew as I've already got."

Boone didn't need all that justification for paying the riders. His comment was succinct. "Like you say, Colonel, you probably couldn't hire this good a bunch of men. Yeah, I agree with you. Hire 'em on and they'll probably stay. That talk about running wild horses is what they all say at the end of the riding season, when they're ready to head south. But professional stockmen just naturally want to do ranch work. Want me to mention hiring them on?"

"I'd appreciate that," stated the colonel. "Now, I've got to go up to the house and re-open my books and bring them current." He smiled. "It's a good feeling, Boone, being back in the cow business again. Gives a man a reason to look forward to tomorrow."

As the colonel strode across the yard, Boone watched him, then told himself that it was strange how a few head of cows, a wounded man in the bunkhouse, a young boy full of eagerness, and a riding crew could make so much difference in a man.

They returned with the cattle in midafternoon, got them corralled in spite of the resistance of a few sly old corral-wise cows, and afterward, as the men were putting up their horses and washing in preparation for supper, Boone took Russ aside and told him what the colonel had said.

Russ thought about it for as long as was required to roll and light a cigarette, then he told Boone he'd bring it up that night in the bunkhouse. He said: "If they want to hire on, I'll stay." He glanced over where the cattle were milling in the corrals. "Hell of a note to crave the smell and sound of anything as dumb as cow brutes, ain't it?"

They laughed together. Russ handed over a copy of the signed receipt, said they'd visited a little with those Mexican *vaqueros* who had delivered the herd, and during the course of that visit the Red Rock riders had been told that the Army was beefing up its territorial posts and there was a rumor that the reservations were going to be put under around-the-clock patrol. Then Russ said: "Not that that'll make a heap of difference to bronco bucks. That's part of the challenge, trying to see if they can't slip around the soldiers and get clear of them to raid, but if they get down here again, it won't be so easy next time. Not with all of the fellers around to ruffle their feathers a little."

That last remark was a clue as to how Russ Petrie was beginning to think. Not as an itinerant rider, but as a man who was deciding to remain where he was.

Boone went up to the main house to hand Colonel Bonner the receipt and to report a full count on the cattle. He lingered to have a cup of whiskey-laced coffee and to discuss other matters, including the very strong possibility that Petrie and his men would stay on. They were still in the ranch office when María came to the door to say there were three horsemen approaching from the southwest, which was in the direction of Gallup.

The colonel grabbed up his hat and led the way to the front verandah. Out there, his hat brim shading his eyes, he stood without speaking for a long while, studying the oncoming riders.

Boone did not know the strangers, but then, even if they proved to be local cowmen, he would not have known them anyway. One thing he was confident about was that, whoever they were, it was very improbable that they would prove hostile. No three men bent on trouble would ride into the yard of a ranch with a full riding crew between the barn and the bunkhouse, if they were in their right minds.

Bonner grunted, finally, and said: "That one in the middle wearing the dark hat is Tevis Franklyn. He runs cattle southeast of us. I don't know the other two."

As it developed, the other pair of horsemen were Tevis Franklyn's range boss, a man named Burns, and his horsebreaker whose name was Aurelio Rodriguez. When Franklyn reached the yard and saw Bonner over at the main house, he rode right on up. Bonner and Boone Helm

125

walked out into the yard to meet Franklyn, and when the hand-shaking was finished Franklyn, standing at the head of his horse, rawhide reins in his hand, said: "I heard down in town you were buying again, Colonel. Figured I'd ride out and see if you were, because I've got three hundred head of bred cows I'm going to get rid of." Franklyn turned slowly at the sound of someone flattening a horseshoe on an anvil, and for a moment he let whatever else he'd been about to say hang in abeyance. He looked over where Petrie and another man were putting some tools into a wagon, and where another couple of men were lining up horses to be shod out front of the shoeing shed. When he turned back, Franklyn had a puzzled expression on his face. "I heard a couple of days ago in town you was fixing to quit, Colonel. I heard the Apaches cleaned out the last of your horses and shot your men. This morning someone said you were buying cows. I guess you could say I really rode up here to see which it was . . . going or staying."

Bonner said: "Staying. Mister Helm here is my range boss. That's my crew down there in the yard. About those three hundred cows, Tevis . . . why don't you and I step inside?"

Boone took the other two strangers down in the direction of the barn to care for their animals, and the horsebreaker's black eyes missed very little of the activity as they walked along. Eventually he left the others, and Boone did not catch sight of him again until he and Franklyn's range boss strolled toward the bunkhouse. Aurelio Rodriguez was out back of the main house in conversation with María. No doubt they would be speaking Spanish, the native language for them both.

Franklyn's range boss was an amiable man who looked completely capable. As they were crossing toward the bunkhouse, he said: "Mister Franklyn's quitting. He's gone and leased the ranch to a couple of neighbors. Now all he's got to do is sell the cattle and get rid of the horses. Hell of a note. I've been riding for him for six years. Sort of got a feeling for the place."

Boone was interested. "Why is he quitting?"

"We lost a full hunnert head to Indians and rustlers so far this year, and it ain't even autumn yet. We also had two riders shot out on the range by them damned reservation jumpers. He says he's going over to Albuquerque and quit bucking the odds for a few years. Sure hate to see him go, and worst of all, there's some free-graze men encroaching to beat hell down in our country. Mister Franklyn says to hell with it . . . if it's not rustlers or Apaches, it's Mex raiders or free-grazers, and if it ain't them things, when he's ready to ship, the price of beef goes all to hell."

They reached the bunkhouse, stopped on the porch when they both saw Tevis Franklyn and Fitzhugh Bonner come forth, over at the main house, strolling along side-by-side in quiet conversation. As Franklyn walked along, he was pulling on a pair of buckskin rider's gloves. His range boss sighed.

"Well, looks like they come to an agreement. If they did, I'll be ramrodding the drive that'll deliver them three hunnert cows up here within the next few days. Now, reckon I'd better round up Aurelio and head for the barn." The range boss offered his hand, and afterward turned to step off the porch in the direction of the horse barn.

Colonel Bonner went down with Franklyn, waited until he and his two riders were in the saddle, then he looked around, saw Boone, and came over to report that he had, indeed, agreed upon the purchase price, and that Franklyn's riders would drift the three hundred cows north within the next few days, depending upon how long it took to make the gather.

The colonel squinted over at Boone. "That's more nearly the number of head we need to make expenses." He looked out where those three horsemen were heading back southward. "Damnedest thing . . . just last week I had no livestock, no riding crew, no range boss, and no intention or incentive to go on with Red Rock Ranch." Bonner laughed. "This week I'm up to my hocks in cattle and cowboys again." After a moment, Colonel Bonner said something else, something Tevis Franklyn's range boss had mentioned in passing. He said: "They're having a little trouble with the free-graze outfits on the south range. It seems to me that with Franklyn quitting, maybe that will help him, but it certainly won't help the other ranchers down there. Franklyn employs seven riders. With him gone, that's seven less men to help hold back the free-grazers."

Over at the shoeing shed an abrupt outburst of rough laughter captured Boone's attention. Over there, a man was sitting flat on the ground, both arms straight to the ground behind him. In front stood a short-backed seal-brown horse solemnly gazing back at the seated man. It was obvious what had happened; in the course of that cowboy's raising a hind leg of the seal-brown to nail on a shoe, he had been kicked down by the horse. The other men were delighted. The man on the ground wasn't, and when he arose he looked around for something to throw, and, finding nothing suitable, he put both hands on his hips and blessed that short-backed horse for a full minute and a half without once repeating himself. It was a masterful performance. Colonel Bonner chuckled, then stepped off the porch. María hadn't rung her little bell yet, but it was almost time for her to do so.

Boone, fishing in a pocket for the makings, saw George emerge from the barn, heading for the bunkhouse. Boone had his cigarette rolled and lit by the time George reached him at the bunkhouse. Boone told the boy about the additional three hundred cows, and George was pleased. "Charley said that's what we needed, to make it work, three or four hundred more cows and another sprinkling of bulls." George stepped up onto the porch, twisted a little to watch the colonel on his way across the center of the yard, and, when the gunshot came and the colonel went down, George's mouth dropped open, his eyes mirroring stunned disbelief. Although his reflexes were better than those of any other man on the ranch, there were cowboys running from the shoeing shed, even from the barn and the corrals, before George finally overcame his total astonishment and began running.

Boone was the first one there. He did not look up and around, although obviously the assassin who had shot Fitzhugh Bonner still had to be somewhere around. Only after Boone had opened the colonel's cotton coat and seen the bloody wound did he raise his head, and even then he did not look around. He said: "Doesn't look too bad . . . the bullet grazed him good, though. Russ, rig us out some horses. Four of 'em. And pick which two of the men you and I'll want with us." As Petrie started swiftly back toward the barn, Boone saw George coming, and said: "Stay with the colonel. Charley, you stay with the boy and the colonel. Whoever he was, I doubt like hell that he'll try again, but you and George keep both eyes wide open." Boone stood up. "Couple of you fellers pack the colonel on up to the main house and hand him over to María." No one asked questions; in fact, no one said anything at all, and the main reason they did not was because of the strained look on Boone's face as he turned on his heel, hiking swiftly toward the bunkhouse, where his booted carbine was hanging.

XIV

The pair of cowboys who left the ranch with Boone and Russ Petrie were both sun-blasted, dehydrated, rawhide-tough men. Wherever that bushwhacker was, he had an unyielding foursome on his back trail, and the first mistake he made, after the actual shooting, was to be riding a barefoot horse, because the moment they found where he had been lying in underbrush with his saddle animal nearby, to make his murder attempt, they also found that while the horse had indeed been barefoot, obviously to make anyone who found the tracks believe the bushwhacker was a reservation jumper, the horse's shoes had been pulled off only a very short while earlier—and there were visible nail holes in the powdery dust where the shoes had been clinched to the hoof. The pale-haired cowboy called Rube, who made the ground study while Boone and the others sat their saddles, waiting, finished reading sign and accepted the reins to his mount before reporting.

"White man," he said, stepping gracefully across leather and reining around to pick up the trail. "But he wants us to believe it was an Apache shot Colonel Bonner."

That was all the pale-haired man said. He led the way slowly, at first, and a half hour later, studying the distant outfall of land, he booted his horse over into a steady lope. The others kept up. They had a fair amount of daylight left even though it was late in the afternoon. There was an off possibility that they might even run their man to earth before nightfall, but as Russ said, when they finally slackened a little, if they did find their bushwhacker ahead of sundown, it would be a miracle, because in all this open country he could see them trailing him. There was no thought of slackening off in their manhunt or of turning back, and in all probability they would have trailed that bushwhacker just as far and for as long as their horses could stand the pace, but when they finally saw the direction of his tracks, Boone said: "That's Gallup down there on the right. I reckon that clinches it. He sure as hell was no Indian."

They reached the outskirts of the town just ahead of sunset. Because Gallup had been the main town of this vast desert empire for many years, and also because it had always had a large Mexican population, as well as an Indian community where the silent, impassive, dark natives came and went from month to month, Gallup was one of the most unique towns in all the Southwest. It had every kind of architecture, but adobe predominated. It also had several streets to its business district, and although there were no military posts very close, it also always seemed to have a large number of cavalrymen striding its roadways, and Army wagons upon its streets.

Boone as well as the men with him had all been in Gallup before, but since none of them was a townsman, when they rode in through the quiet late evening, when most people were at supper, the cowboy called Rube said: "That bastard is going to be like a needle in a haystack in this town. Any of you fellers know the place very well? I sure as hell don't. All I remember about Gallup is that it used to have a big Mex for a constable. He was big enough to throw a saddle on. That was six, seven years back."

Boone had been very quiet on the ride. He did not open up a whole lot now, as they walked their horses down a main thoroughfare. The town seemed almost deserted, it was so quiet and empty-looking at suppertime.

They found a livery barn, and next to it the

usual public corral. They entered the livery barn, offsaddled, ordered grain and hay and a rub-down for their animals, and Boone asked the hostler about the blacksmith shop. After he received instructions on how to find the shop, and was told that the smith lived out back in a small cottage across an alleyway from his shop, they went out front to confer.

It was Boone's opinion that their bushwhacker would not have had the shoes pulled off his horse in town. It was also his opinion that the man who had shot Colonel Bonner was one of those vengeance-seeking free-graze gunmen. Russ Petrie thought they ought to find the free-graze camp and ride out there, but neither Petrie nor any of the other Red Rock riding crew knew how many men Carter Thompson had working for him, nor the kind of men they were. Boone knew, though. He said: "If we end up hunting a free-grazer, we're going to need an awful lot of luck. Their leader, a feller named Carter Thompson, is mean to the bone, and he's got a dozen gunmen who are just as ornery. We've got to be damned careful. I've got a feeling shooting folks in the back comes natural to that whole bunch. For the time being, let's split up and start visiting the saloons. We want to know if any free-grazers are in town this evening, and, if they are, we've got to know how many and where. But don't ask straight out. Those men will have a favorite saloon. If they spend much money there, they'll have friends behind the bar. We'll meet back here in front of the livery barn in an hour. All right?"

Russ had a suggestion. "If it's likely to be that bad, maybe we'd do better to go in pairs. Pretty hard to slip a knife into a feller's back if he's with someone."

They paired off. Russ and one of the men crossed the road heading south, Boone and the other rider, the one named Rube, remained on the west side of the empty roadway, and began strolling northward. Gallup had its share of saloons. The only part of town where there was not even one saloon was down where the Indians camped. There would have been one down there, too, but for two things. The most important thing was that Indians rarely had any money, and the second reason there was no saloon was because there was a law against selling liquor to Indians. This law never prevented Indians from getting whiskey, but at least in a town the size of Gallup where there was not only a constable's office but also a deputy U.S. marshal, since the money to be made peddling liquor to the Indians was not commensurate with the troubles likely to go along with it, and also because the legal traffic in hard drink quite adequately soaked up all the available liquor, no one made any real effort to sell whiskey in Indian town. In Mex town, where there were at least a dozen *cantinas*, all operated by natives, liquor flowed like water, and, although it was never very wise for a solitary *gringo* to visit those Mexican saloons after dusk, two armed *gringo* range riders were something else. One kind of *gringo* in particular was thoroughly hated, but completely left alone in Mex town: Texans. For generations Mexicans on both sides of the line had suffered at the hands of what was called *Tejano pistoleros*—gunfighting Texans. Even when one such a man appeared in the *cantinas*, unless the place was full of Mexicans he was safe from attack—usually—and the first *cantina* Boone and Rube visited had only a sprinkling of dark-skinned patrons, with none of them looking as though they wanted trouble.

In fact, Boone and Rube visited three *cantinas* before they met any armed *vaqueros*, and even then, when Boone's companion exchanged a greeting with one particular *vaquero*, all the other armed Mexican cowboys in the place seemed tolerant. That particular *vaquero* had been on the drive north when that first two hundred head of cattle had been delivered to Red Rock Ranch. He was a burly, swarthy, black-eyed man with a wide smile and an easy affability.

Boone shook his hand, bought a round of drinks, and when he and the *vaquero* were leaning side-by-side at the bar, Boone engaged him in an easy range men's conversation. The Mexican eventually said it was a terrible thing what those

Apaches had done at Red Rock Ranch. One of the Red Rock *vaqueros* who had been caught out alone and shot to death had been his cousin. The Mexican smiled at Boone with his black eyes showing a depth of deadly cruelty. "Someday I will make that right, *señor*. Someday I will catch an Apache out like that, and when I do . . ." The *vaquero* made a slow hand motion of twisting a knife as he pushed it into someone's flesh, then he downed his fiery tequila and shrugged thick shoulders. "But there is a rumor down here, *señor*. A *gringo* gave those Indians guns and ammunition, and promised them good horses, if they would make that raid." The black eyes came up, hooded like the black eyes of a puma. "No one says any such thing to the law in Gallup." The *vaquero* shrugged. "In this part of town, no one likes the *gringo* law." The black eyes smiled mockingly. "*Gringo* law is not for these people in Mex town."

Boone ignored this last remark. "What white man?" he asked, and the *vaquero* studied Boone for a long time before speaking again.

"*Señor*, there are only two of you. Me? I am only one more. That is not enough at all. The man they say helped those raiders did it for a good reason. Already one cowman is quitting . . . *Señor* Franklyn. Do you know him?"

Boone nodded. "We've met. Forget *Señor* Franklyn and tell me who . . ."

"Do you know the walls have ears?" asked the Mexican. "All over this town, the walls have ears, *señor*. A man can wake up somewhere else because his throat is slit from ear to ear." The Mexican nodded at a tall, hawk-faced *vaquero* who strolled past without smiling, then hunched over his empty glass again as he said. "Tell me why you want to know so much?"

"A bushwhacker shot Colonel Bonner this afternoon. We tracked him to Gallup . . . on a barefoot horse."

The *vaquero*'s head came up. "Killed the *coronel*, today?"

"No, didn't kill him. The bullet broke a couple of ribs, though, and plowed a hell of a gash along his left side, but he'll live through that." Boone shook his head when the paunchy barman came padding along to see about refills, then padded away again as Boone said: "The next time he may shoot straighter, *amigo*. For that reason I want to make damned sure he doesn't get a second chance."

The Mexican settled back thoughtfully against the bar for a moment, then he said: "A barefoot horse . . . that would be an *Indio*. But no *Indio* who is out shooting people would come to Gallup, would he? *Señor*, who would shoot *Coronel* Bonner?"

"The same man," stated Boone quietly, "who would make life so miserable for Tevis Franklyn that he'd want to quit and leave the country."

The *vaquero* looked around. "You think so?"

"I think so. Because I was in the barn at Bonner's ranch when that man threatened the colonel, told him he'd better abandon his ranch, or he might not live to get away."

The Mexican said: *"Ahhhh."* Then he flagged for a refill and said no more until the barman had come and gone. Even then he said nothing until he had upended the glass to drop that almost paralyzing amount of pure tequila straight down, but afterward, wiping his lips on a soiled sleeve, the *vaquero* said—"Come with me, *amigo*."—and led the way out into the bland night.

They strolled past dark adobe buildings, past a place where a young man was serenading a girl with only his soft, sad song indicating what was taking place, for neither he nor the girl was in sight. They walked all the way down to the center, and there the *vaquero* lit a thin cigar, looked all around very casually, and finally said: "Do you know Carter Thompson, *señor*?"

Boone knew Thompson as well as he wanted to know him. "We've met. He's the man who told Colonel Bonner to leave or he might get killed."

"Well then, *amigo*, if you know that much, it is enough, no? That is the same man I was talking about in the *cantina*. But you must be very careful. He has many friends down here in Mex town, and up there in *gringo* town." The *vaquero* studied Boone's face in the pale starlight as he inhaled smoke, then exhaled it. "I will warn you, *señor*, Carter Thompson hires Texas gunmen." The age-old fear and dread was in those words. "And he has at least a dozen such men working for him. *Señor*, it is common knowledge around Gallup that one day Carter Thompson will control all the range. He is the only man who can use the Apaches. To fight such a man would be like fighting Satan himself." The Mexican showed perfect white teeth in a deadly smile. "You will have no help, but if you happened to kill *Señor Satán*, then of course many people would become your friend. That is always how it is, no?"

Boone's interest in this kind of conversation was minimal. "Where is Thompson's camp?" he asked, and at once the Mexican's expression underwent still another change. He stared at Boone with obvious sadness.

"East of here about six miles, *señor*. It is very easy to find." The Mexican's thick shoulders rose and fell again. "They do not make any secret of their camp. Six miles east, toward those foothills where the Indians come from. *Señor*, you will never get there. But if you do, you will never get back."

Boone smiled, and looked up as Rube came

walking soundlessly up to them. "*Gracias*," he said to the *vaquero*, and turned to walk away with Rube. The Mexican watched until they were lost to sight, then he sighed, wagged his head, and finished his little cigar.

XV

Boone had no intention of riding out to the free-graze camp. He did not entirely trust the *vaquero*, either, even though he had seemed sympathetic and approving. When he met the others back in front of the livery barn, he outlined an idea he and Rube had discussed, and which had nothing to do with riding to the camp of Carter Thompson. There was just one thing wrong with Boone's idea—unless that bushwhacker actually had come from the free-graze camp, the Red Rock men were going to waste a lot of time. No one mentioned this possibility, any more than they mentioned going to the law, which was convenient, being available in two separate places in Gallup. This was a range men's affair and range men would settle it. They would settle it their own way, without the law, and in their own good time.

Rube and the other cowboy were left at the livery barn. They were to get something to eat, then get some rest. Boone and Russ Petrie had something to do yet, before they also got some rest. They went up through *gringo* town, visiting the saloons. Nobody knew them even though they both worked for one of the largest, best-known ranches in the country. If this being unknown was an advantage, it was also a disadvantage, for neither of them knew anyone else, practically no one else at any rate. Boone saw Tevis Franklyn's range boss in the second saloon they visited, who he had spoken the day Franklyn had arrived at Red Rock Ranch to discuss selling bred cows. But Boone did not go near the him. He and Russ had a particular purpose; tonight, they were cultivating bartenders.

It could be a risky business in more ways than one, to stand the drinks in order to have a few words with a barman. The way Boone and Russ Petrie managed it was simple. Boone would ask pointblank where he could find someone who rode for Carter Thompson, and Russ, who would be standing as far up or down the bar as he could get so that they did not appear to be together, would then wait and watch, but his particular part of the little plot was to pay no real attention until Boone left the saloon. Russ was then to see who followed him, if anyone at all did follow Boone.

They had had no success at all until they reached the third saloon, and even there it did not happen as they had anticipated. No one actually followed Boone out of the saloon. He had already given up in there after having two beers, and also after receiving a cool if not actually hostile series of answers from the bartender, and left the saloon to pace along the roadway, waiting for Russ to catch up. Evidently the man who detached himself from the darkness in a recessed doorway and began trailing Boone Helm after Boone had walked out of the third saloon was someone who had picked up the information at either the first or second saloon that someone was looking for a Thompson partisan. The mistake this man made was precisely the mistake Boone and Russ had hoped someone would make; he began following Boone—and a dozen yards back Russ Petrie began following *him*.

Boone did not realize he was being followed. He heard someone back there, and because he was becoming discouraged as well as dog-tired he just naturally assumed that it was Russ coming up behind him. Until he heard the gun cock. Boone slowed to a gradual halt, then turned back very slowly, making a particular point of keeping his right hand clear of his right hip.

The stranger was slight and wiry. It was difficult to tell much else about him in the darkness, and he had his hat tipped down in front, further concealing his face. Boone saw Russ Petrie stop deadstill back down the plank walk. Then Russ slid sideways and disappeared down between two buildings on his right. Boone said:

"Well, *amigo*, what's it going to be . . . shoot or shut the window?"

The gunman finished his study and replied: "Who are you, mister, and why are you goin' around town askin' about someone who rides for Carter Thompson?"

"Might want to hook up," murmured Boone, speaking slowly and taking his time. "Are you a Thompson man?" It was an unnecessary question; Boone had to keep this going until Russ got closer.

The wiry man said: "Yeah, I'm a Thompson man. There's a lot of us, and it ain't wise to go around Gallup askin', like you been doin'. Who are you?"

"I'll save that for Carter Thompson," replied Boone. "I've heard he's well on the way to controlling all this cow country. That sounds like the kind of a man to hook up with. What does a feller have to do to meet him?"

The wiry man seemed to be having trouble making up his mind about Boone, but he got some assistance. Slightly behind him, on his right, where a pair of warped wood fronts met their side walls, which were solid adobe, Russ Petrie said: "Hey, partner, you better lower that damned gun and ease off the hammer, unless you want a hole blown in your back big enough to drive a six-horse hitch through."

The wiry man did not move or speak. He

continued to cover Boone with his cocked Colt. For a long moment he stood like that, then Russ spoke again.

"You got one second to make up your mind."

The wiry man lowered his gun, easing off the hammer, and turned loose where he stood, shoulders slumping as Russ came over, took the gun from the man's hand, then holstered his own weapon and reached with a powerful hand to pull the wiry man over into the full darkness of a doorway and push his back against the locked door.

"What's your name?" Russ asked, and smiled a little at his own question.

He got back a predictable reply. "John Smith."

Boone strolled over to stand, thumbs hooked in his shell belt, gazing at their prisoner. He gave his head a little dolorous wag. "I was hoping we'd do better than catch Thompson's horse holder."

The wiry man stiffened, then flared out at Boone. "Horse holder, your tail."

Boone continued to stand contemptuously. "There's not enough to you, mister, to be much else."

"If your partner hadn't caught me from behind, I'd have showed the pair of you," snapped the wiry man. "I'll take you both at the same time in the middle of the road."

Russ made an exaggerated look of terror. "Billy

the Kid!" he exclaimed, doing exactly as Boone was doing. "Dead-Eye Dick. Which one are you, Mister Smith?"

The wiry man balled both hands into fists. Obviously he was not only bad-tempered, but was also hair-triggered. It was conceivable, too, that being slight of build and not overly tall, he had long ago developed a compulsion to prove himself. He said: "Just let me have a gun, you god-damned cowboys. Just let me have a gun for two minutes."

Boone shrugged. "I've got a better idea. You walk down to the livery barn with us, Mister Smith, where we've got some friends, and the lot of us'll sit down and talk a little."

"Like hell," snarled the wiry man. "I won't tell you a damned thing."

"No one asked you to tell us anything," stated Boone.

The wiry man fixed Boone with a shadowy look of lethal fury. "You're lawmen. You're a pair of god-damned lousy lawmen."

Boone slowly shook his head. "Nope. Care to try again?"

The wiry man said nothing, but he continued to glare, so Russ reached, caught him by the shoulder, dragged him from the doorway, and aimed him southward.

"Walk," Russ ordered. "Head for the livery barn at the lower end of town, and cross the road when you get down there, and, Mister Smith, if you sprint for it, I'll kill you. Now walk."

The wiry man walked, stiffly and angrily with a stamping tread, but he obeyed, and, when they finally started across the road down by the barn, he said, speaking over his shoulder: "You better have a whole damned army with you." That was all he said until they took him deep inside the cool, old, lamp-lit livery barn and up a ladder to the loft where their companions were. After the other two men had awakened and sat up to shake chaff off and stare, the captive's lip curled and he said: "Four? Is that all you got, four men?" He snorted in a derisive way. "You're going to get killed. You don't stand the chance of a . . ."

Boone reached, leaned hard, and shoved the wiry man down upon the hay. Then Boone, standing over him, said: "How come you didn't go back to Thompson's camp tonight?"

The wiry man looked up. "Go back . . . ? Who says I had to go back?"

Boone did not reply to the question. He tried another tack. "Who did Thompson send up north to kill Colonel Bonner at Red Rock Ranch?"

This time the wiry man's twisted expression smoothed out very gradually. They all saw this change in the poorly lit hayloft. The wiry man said: "That's who you are. You're from Bonner's spread. We heard he'd hired on some riders."

Boone drew his six-gun, kneeled, and pushed

it gently against the prisoner's side. "One more time, partner, then we'll dump your carcass on the road to Thompson's camp. Who did Thompson send up there to shoot Bonner?"

The wiry man did not take his eyes off Boone's face. Just once did his gaze flicker. That was when Boone eased back the hammer of his Colt and the little abrasive sound carried throughout the hushed hayloft.

Russ spoke in a half-whisper to Boone: "Go ahead. It'll just be one less worthless bastard. If you shove the barrel hard enough against him, it'll muffle the sound."

The wiry man suddenly squirted words out. "No. Wait a minute. The feller Carter sent up there is called Tombstone. I don't know him by any other name. I met him here in town, gave him my horse, and he dusted it for camp."

"Why did you trade horses?"

"His animal was tenderfooted."

Boone raised his eyes to Russ. The only way John Smith, or whatever his real name was, could have known about the bushwhacker's horse being tenderfooted was if he had actually met the man. Obviously John Smith was telling the truth.

Boone said: "How do we get our hands on Tombstone?" Boone shoved the gun barrel forward a little to remind John Smith he was a long way from being out of the woods yet.

"How?" gasped the wiry man. "I don't know how."

Russ smiled into the man's face. "You'd better know how."

For three or four seconds the wiry man looked from face to face. There was not a shred of sympathy visible. He looked up at Boone again. "He might come into town tomorrow. There's nothin' much doin' right now. We're just waitin' for a feller named Franklyn to make a gather."

Rube said dryly: "Yeah, three hundred cows, so's you bastards can raid his holding ground."

The wiry man looked at Rube briefly, then faced Boone again. "All right. You fellers know more'n I thought. Anyway, until Franklyn makes his gather, we got nothin' much to do. Tombstone drinks hard. He gets into town every day. Him and some of the other men." John Smith thought a moment, then reiterated an earlier statement. "You four don't have a chance. Not a chance in hell."

Boone ignored this last statement. "What does Tombstone look like?"

John Smith thought, then shrugged thin shoulders. "Like everyone else, as far as I can see. He wears a big Mex sombrero. He won it in a card game one night and ever since he's been wearin' the silly thing."

Boone eased back his six-gun, let the hammer down very gently, and leathered the weapon.

Then he considered John Smith. "What'll we do with you?" he murmured, and, when John Smith started to speak, Russ growled him into silence as Rube said: "Cut his lousy throat." The other cowboy seconded that: "Someone give me the knife, I'll do it right here."

John Smith was probably a brave enough man, and he was undoubtedly both tough and resourceful. No other kind of men lived as long as John Smith had lived in the troubled Southwest, but neither John Smith nor most other men could remain completely detached when they knew very well they were just one blink of an eyelid away from death. He said: "Listen, fellers, I helped you. I told you everything you wanted to know. That's sure as hell worth *something*."

Rube agreed. "Sure is, friend. That's worth a quick bullet through the head instead of a slow knife in the guts."

Boone looked across the top of Smith's head at Russ. "No sense in handing him over to the law, so let's tie him up and dump him out back in the alley somewhere."

Russ nodded and reached to pull John Smith up to his feet. The wiry man co-operated without a complaint. He avoided looking at Rube again, as all four of his captors stood up, heading for the ladder down out of the loft.

XVI

Disposing of the gunman calling himself John Smith was easier than Boone had anticipated. They got ropes from the livery barn harness room, without interrupting the deep slumber of the night man, but when they went out back where Rube was watching their prisoner, Rube pointed to a shed across the alleyway.

"There's a big fir snubbing post in there, with a log chain embedded in it. Somebody must have owned an awful mean big horse sometime."

They took John Smith over there, found the chains and snubbing post exactly as Rube had said, and even Russ smiled as they gagged Smith, tied him like a turkey, then chained him at the ankles and around the neck. The only way John Smith could get loose, even if he somehow managed to slip out of the ropes, would be if someone came along; otherwise, there was no way one person, by himself, could work those chains loose.

They returned to the livery barn, held a council, then leisurely got their Winchesters and split up, walking casually through the small hours of the quiet, darkened town. By the time dawn arrived the four of them were in four strategic positions. Rube and the other Red Rock rider were at opposite ends of the main thoroughfare. They could catch sight of everyone entering, or leaving, Gallup. Boone was across from their particular livery barn, and Russ Petrie was up near the second saloon they had visited the night before. If anyone wearing a Mexican sombrero arrived in town this morning, and providing he was not a Mexican, he was going to be detected at once and tracked to his destination.

Boone, like the others, had plenty of time to think while he waited. It disturbed him to reflect upon the chance that the bushwhacker called Tombstone might ride in with half a dozen other gunmen from the free-graze camp. It did not disturb him from the standpoint of what could happen if there were gunshots, because the gunmen neither knew there were four armed men waiting, nor because he did not have full confidence in his companions. What worried him was that if Tombstone brought along half or two-thirds of the free-graze men, some of *his* men might get cut down. He did not believe there was a gunman in the free-graze camp worth that price.

The heat came slowly, that morning, as it usually did in the early daytime, but, once it began accumulating, it kept right on building up until by ten o'clock it was downright hot. That was when Boone saw Russ turn almost casually, up by the saloon where he had received the signal from the north entrance into town, and remove his hat, hold it aloft while he pretended to wipe sweat from his face, then drop the hat down upon his head again. Tombstone was coming!

Boone repeated the signal for the benefit of the man south of him. Then he stepped out very casually to the edge of the plank walk and peered southward. The Red Rock man down there hove into sight. Boone gestured for him to start northward, up closer. The man obeyed at once, carrying his carbine in his left hand, which brought a few stares from sidewalk loafers. Men did not as a rule walk the streets of a town carrying Winchesters. They did not need long-range weapons for town shooting.

Boone saw the riders enter town up the north roadway. He picked out the man wearing the Mexican hat immediately. Tombstone was a chunky, squatty, unshaven man. He didn't only wear that Mexican sombrero, he also rode a splendid, silver-edged Mexican saddle, complete with box *tapaderos* and a rawhide reata secured behind the cantle on the right side. Tombstone almost looked Mexican, from that distance. He even had the dumpy build of most *mestizo* horsemen.

There were four riders with him, all weathered men, at home in the saddle, armed with Colts as well as carbines, all riding good horses. Even from that distance, Boone could see that those five men rode arrogantly. They clearly feared nothing and were ready to challenge anyone who crossed them. A particular rider held Boone's attention. He had only seen Carter Thompson once before, but that had been a good, long look. Thompson was riding between two other men, and the bushwhacker called Tombstone was on the far side of the man on Thompson's right.

Boone had not bargained for this. He'd had some idea that since Tombstone was a hard drinker, he might come almost furtively into town by himself. Like a lot of other people, range men drank, but scorned drunks. Evidently Tombstone was either not yet a drunkard, or else what John Smith had meant was that Tombstone drank hard, but not habitually. In any case, there he was, walking his horse down the roadway with four other free-graze men.

Boone saw how people on the plank walks on both sides of the road looked up, then quickly looked away again, except for a few of the ingratiating variety, who smiled and waved in a fawning way. The Red Rock rider, walking up from the lower end of town carrying his Winchester, was still well south of Boone when those slouching, completely oblivious free-graze riders turned in up in front of the saloon where Russ Petrie was. Apparently this was their favorite bar.

Boone saw Rube coming down from the upper

end of town, also carrying his carbine. He looked for Russ, saw Petrie amble to the edge of the plank walk from back in overhang shade out front of a harness shop, and pause out to study the position of the sun, the distance between himself and the free-graze men who were now dismounting. Finally Russ turned, looked down where Boone was, and nodded gently. Boone stepped out into roadway dust and joined the other two Red Rock men who were converging.

Still, Carter Thompson and his men suspected nothing. They looped their reins, stepped to the boardwalk, milled together briefly, then walked ahead toward the spindle doors of the saloon. They never passed through them.

Boone called from near the center of the road. From up north, Rube sang out, too. Thompson paused and turned, looking at Boone, who he did not know. He still did not act concerned, but when the other three free-graze riders saw Rube walking toward them with a Winchester in his left hand, they stopped dead still in their tracks.

Carter Thompson, watching Boone approach, seemed very gradually to become aware of something offkey. He eased his right hand down toward the Colt on his hip.

Russ called him about that: "You better make it damned fast, Thompson!"

The free-graze leader's head jerked a little. He had not even seen Russ until this moment. Now, he knew, they all knew, what was coming, but it had happened so swiftly and so unexpectedly more time was required before all of them could adjust to it. They might have got that time, except that two jaunty *vaqueros* came jogging down into town from the north, and the killer called Tombstone saw, or thought he saw, Rube's head turn a little at the sound of horsemen coming up behind him. Tombstone went for his six-gun. Russ moved and so did Boone Helm. Two gunshots exploded almost simultaneously. Those two jaunty *vaqueros* yanked back so fast their horses reared. The *vaqueros* did not even pause to see what was happening; they hauled around, sank in the spurs, and fled wildly back up the roadway.

That Red Rock rider who had been walking northward from the lower end of town did not step out into the roadway at all. He kneeled, took a long rest upon an upright post with his Winchester, and fired. Rube, upon the opposite side of those bunched-up men out front of the saloon, also used a Winchester instead of a Colt. He held it low in both hands and levered, then fired, without aiming.

Boone was watching the man in the Mexican sombrero, but Carter Thompson partially screened Tombstone, so Boone was watching when Thompson ducked down, swinging from the waist toward Boone as he streaked for his holster.

Boone fired twice, saw Thompson's knees buckle forward, and drove in a third bullet. Thompson's gun fell; he put forth his left hand to brace against the nearest wall, could not reach that far, and, as Tombstone jumped ahead and half turned to face Boone, Carter Thompson went down in a heap, one outstretched hand hanging in the dirt, over the edge of the plank walk.

A Winchester made its flat, harsh sound from behind Boone and to his right. Tombstone was offbalance when that little waspish bullet reached him. The impact knocked him against the swinging doors of the saloon. Boone fired, Russ fired, and back down the roadway that Winchester cut loose again. Tombstone went over backward through the batwing doors flat on his back with his boots showing from below the doors, soles outward and toes up.

One free-graze man fell and hung there on all fours like a gut-shot bear. The remaining two men, trying to back-peddle toward the hitch rack, suddenly threw down their guns and yelled out that they had had enough. The man down on all fours very gently eased forward until he was overbalanced, then dropped face down and did not move again. The roadway was completely empty its full length, and long after the last shot had been fired and the last echo had died, the roadway remained empty.

Boone walked, reloading. Russ stood there,

doing the same thing. Rube was keeping the pair of unarmed free-graze cowboys covered with his cocked Winchester, and back down the south roadway that other Red Rock rider was striding up toward the saloon, carrying his Winchester, two-handed and ready.

Boone stepped up, peered at Tombstone's boot soles, which had not moved, then saw where the bushwhacker's Mexican sombrero had fallen. Russ strolled over and leaned to retrieve the Colt from Carter Thompson's hand. As he straightened up, he said—"Souvenir."—and toed the leader of the free-graze riding crew over onto his back. "He's got enough lead in him to sink a ship, Boone." Russ looked around. "Two lousy prisoners. Now what the hell are we going to do with them?"

Boone did not answer. He waited until the rider from the south roadway came up, then he called to Rube. The last thing he did was point to the tethered horses and gaze coldly at the frightened, beaten free-grazers. "You sons-of-bitches get mounted," he said softly, "and don't even get down for a drink of water until you're out of New Mexico. Ride!"

Those two men scuttled to their mounts, clambered aboard, sank in their hooks, and did exactly as they had been ordered to do. They raced southward down through town without once looking back. Boone turned, saw Russ gazing at him, and jerked his head. "Now it's our turn . . . let's get the horses and head for Red Rock, before the lousy law shows up."

Russ obeyed, as did Rube and the other cowboy. Those last two talked a little as they hastened down to saddle up, and afterward, when the four of them were loping out of Gallup to the east, but Russ said nothing at all. From time to time he'd shoot a sidelong glance at Boone, but he kept silent until they were angling northward, in the direction of Red Rock Ranch. Even then, though, he kept silent until he and Boone were a dozen or so yards out front of the others. Finally he drew his horse down to a walk, looked at Boone, and said: "Mind if I ask a personal question?"

Boone smiled a little. "Go ahead."

Russ cleared his throat. ". . . You had a reason for not wanting to hang around back there until the law showed up?"

Boone's little smile lingered. "Yup, I had a reason. And I still have it."

Neither of them touched upon this subject again, not even when they got back to the ranch in the late night with a moon that was slightly fuller tonight, casting a ghostly light earthward. But later, when they had cared for their horses and the other two riders headed for the bunkhouse, Boone called Russ back. They stood out front of the barn in the thick, dark shadows.

Russ said: "Something on your mind?"

"Two things," replied Boone. "I'm leaving, and the other thing is . . . will you and your friends stay on? The colonel needs you, and so does the lad."

Russ settled back against the smooth front of the horse barn. "Yeah, we talked it over. We'll stay on. This is good country, the old man's fair to work for." Russ gazed at Boone. "You'd better tell the boy good bye. I can't do that for you. No one else can, either. . . . How far back are they on your trail?"

Boone did not believe they were still on his trail at all, but a thing like that gunfight in Gallup today would fill up a lot of newspaper columns from California to Montana, and eventually the law was going to ride up to Red Rock and ask questions, and, from that, there was always a possibility someone might fit some pieces together.

"I don't know how close they are," he told Russ. "Probably not close at all. But I just don't like the risk."

Russ nodded. "Yeah, you goin' to talk to the boy?"

Boone nodded, then shoved out his hand. They shook, and Boone turned away.

XVII

The bunkhouse had a light burning when Boone entered. Jamie and the pair of men who had been in the fight down in town were talking. Two other men, both in their bunks, were listening. One of them really wasn't a man although he was as tall as any man in the room. Boone went there and grinned as George smiled upward as he said: "Sure glad you got back."

Boone shifted his weight from one foot to the other one. The door opened, he saw Russ enter, and he eased down upon the bunk across from the boy. "I want you to promise me something," he told the boy. "I want your word you'll stay here with the colonel for at least one full year."

George's smile faded slowly. His eyes widened with enquiry, first, then, a little later, they reflected apprehension. Boone did not allow him much chance to speak, right at first.

"You stay with the colonel, George, and you learn all you can from Russ and Rube and Charley, and the others. Get up when they do in the morning and bed down when they do at night. You like this life, so it ought to come easy to you. Someday, I expect, Colonel Bonner'll have a talk with you."

"What about, Boone?"

"Well, about you, and your future, you and him. That's for him to say, not me." Boone arose and held out his hand. "Good luck, George."

The boy sat up and stared at the extended hand. Then he took it and they shook, once, before Boone drew his hand away.

George said: "Boone . . . you're going away?"

"Yeah. But you're not, you're staying here where you belong. Where you're going to earn your way and learn your trade."

The boy looked steadily upward. His lips flattened, hard, but that was the only show of feeling he allowed himself, and Boone appreciated this, so he smiled as he said: "We'll meet up again, George. Someday, and when we do, you make damned certain you can look me plumb in the eye. All right?"

"Yes," the boy said shortly, and closed his lips tightly afterward.

Boone understood, or thought he understood; this was the second time someone George wanted to be with, and depend upon, was abandoning him. There was no other way, not in the world of men, to accomplish this. It would be hard on George for a while, but that could not be helped, and in the long run George would come out far better than he could if he continued to drift with Boone Helm.

The nearest Boone came to letting the boy know that he understood was just before he walked out of the bunkhouse. He said: "Listen to me, partner. Every man deserves one honest chance in his life, and most men get that one chance. This is *your* chance. For both our sakes, take your time, grow up slow and thoughtful, don't lie and don't steal. Otherwise, you'll get vices, as we all do sooner or later, but be honest with the colonel and the men you work and ride with, and you'll never feel like you feel right now, ever again."

Boone reached roughly to rumple the lad's hair, then he turned on his heel, walked out of the bunkhouse, and went down to the horse barn where he went to work saddling his black horse.

The night was well along by this time. Just before Boone mounted up, a lean, fine-boned silhouette appeared in the barn opening. The colonel studied Boone, studied the way he had rigged out—for the road—and ambled into the faint light of the log barn as he spoke quietly.

"Odd thing, how people have presentiments about other people."

Boone guessed what lay behind that statement and replied to it casually. "Nothing very strange about it this time, Colonel. You'd know damned well no range rider ever saves up four thousand dollars."

Old Bonner brushed that aside. "I felt it before I knew you had four thousand dollars, Boone. I felt it that first day you rode in. You'd leave directly. Well, have you told the lad?"

163

"Yeah. A few minutes ago."

"How did he take it?"

Boone finished saddling and turned toward the front opening. "About like you or I would have, Colonel, at his age, if you'd just been cut loose for the second time in your life." Boone paused in the doorway. "I hope to hell it'll be the last time for him. Nothing's very easy about being a youngster in New Mexico Territory, not these days."

"Don't worry about him," murmured the colonel, extending a hand. "Good luck, Boone. I'm right obliged to you. Whatever the reason for you having to ride on tonight . . . good luck. If you ever get back this way . . ."

They shook, Boone smiled, said—"Sure, Colonel."—and stepped up across his saddle. "You aim to tell the boy someday how all this worked out?"

"Yes, indeed. When he's eighteen or twenty. By then he ought to be about as good a cowman as they have out here. I'll explain the whole story to him . . . well, as much of it as I know."

Boone said: "You know as much as either one of you have to know. Good bye, Colonel." He lifted his rein hand, and the black horse obediently stepped forth into the cool, delightful night.

Boone did not intend to ride far; he was weary to the bone. He intended to go just far enough to be well out of the country of Red Rock Ranch, then bed down and sleep away whatever remained of this night, and maybe tomorrow morning, too, if he got a chance.

Afterward, he thought he might just as well ride on down to Zuñi and see the old couple he'd originally struck out southward to visit, when he'd had George along. He was in the country, and the way he felt tonight, what he particularly wanted and needed, was another few weeks of loafing, like the weeks he'd spent back up there by Gunnison Butte.

There were a million milky stars in the pitchblende setting above him, while all around, down below where he allowed the black horse to pick his gait and his route, the land was hushed and slumbering. It was a good time for crossing this Southwestern desert country in summertime. Even if it hadn't been hot during the day, crossing the countryside below Gallup and west of the mountains where snake-eyed raiders kept a deadly watch could be done most safely at night, any time of the year.

Boone told the black horse they were on their own again, and, although he would miss George, he was, still and all, glad to be unencumbered once more, and this time, he told the black horse, he was *really* unencumbered; he didn't have but two silver dollars in his pockets.

THE DRIFTER

I

Under the pale green sky of early dawn, a tawny
prairie ran on, misty and flat and silent, until it
met the sharp edge of a rising sun, and the world
burst alive. That racing, golden brightness struck
down hard upon rusty tin roofs in the middle
distance, making some little no-account cow town
look like El Dorado—a place of gold. Closer at
hand, where the rider sat his leggy chestnut horse,
were some creek willows in a shallow draw, dim
and silvery, still shrouded by vagrant dregs of the
gone-away night. In that direction he heard the
musical lift and fall of water, and rode over that
way to wash and perhaps shave, for while he did
not always use his razor, when there was a town
to be passed through he usually did.

He was in some ways a nondescript-looking
man; he was neither particularly tall nor short; his
attire was that of any range man—wide-brimmed
hat, low-slung, hip-holstered gun, scuffed black
boots, and faded blue shirt and slightly darker,
shinier blue pants.

It was when he kneeled at creekside, tossed
aside his hat, and sunshine struck his face that
the difference showed. He was not as young as
most drifters; there was a thin, light brush stroke
of silver at his temples. His eyes were quiet

blue and rock-steady. His face was not boyishly handsome; it was maturely strong and solid, the face of a man who'd looked into his share of sunsets, who'd survived his share of trouble, sorrow, and whatever else life had thrown his way. In build he was sinewy, square of shoulder, and lean of thigh. He was angularly heavy of bone and lithe of movement. He could have been many things, from the looks of him—a gunfighter perhaps, a good hand with rope and hot iron, or nothing more than just an ordinary cowboy on the loose with perhaps not too much silver in his jeans.

About his kind one never knew until the key of circumstance or the sting of violence released some inner spring. But one thing was fairly obvious; he was a drifter, one of that fraternity of quiet men who eternally sought the end of some private rainbow. Sometimes, when they got along in years, this kind of man, though, lost direction, lost perspective, and drifted just to be drifting. Every spring brought them out by the score to seek work in the cow camps, along the cattle trails, and sometimes—although not too often— in the cow towns. They were the easy-going ones, usually, the quiet-eyed ones who didn't have a lot to say, who fitted in almost anywhere and never stayed too long.

This one's name was Jared Carson. He had come north out of the south country where winters were warmer and sunshine brightened nearly every lifelong day. Now, when he finished cleaning up, he rode on downcountry toward that cow town as easy in the saddle as a man can be who has nothing on his mind and nothing on his conscience.

In the middle distance a clutch of ranch buildings firmed up in that new-day soft brightness. He considered them, considered particularly the look of prosperity over there because it never paid off working for some starved-out ranch; sometimes a man got his pay, but more often than not he didn't.

But this place looked good. There was a big old windmill, a sturdy log barn, and a much smaller house that looked as though it might belong to a bachelor, which suited Jared Carson fine because, although he did not dislike women, he had no use for them in his world of men and cattle and horses. He looked ahead at that town, flipped a metal coin, and decided to head for the cow outfit first. If there was no work, then he'd light out for the town.

Coming in at an angle toward the small house he sighted two men, standing face to face, out in the dusty yard there. One of them had obviously just come up because he was holding one rein of a big, ugly bay horse that was saddled and bridled. It seemed to Carson a trifle early in the day for callers to be out; still in a new country a wise man kept still, looked and listened. Every land had its different customs.

Closer, he saw that the man holding that ugly bay horse was big and broad with a high-bridged, hooked nose. Closer still, with the sound of his coming making its quiet little sound pattern in the pleasant morning, he saw that big man twist half around to gaze out at him, and that man had hard blue eyes that fastened themselves inhospitably upon Carson. The other man also looked over. As Carson halted twenty feet out, he thought he saw immense relief in this one's face.

That second man was gray and grizzled. He had a tough-set mouth and a weathered look. He was easily fifteen years older than the larger, hook-nosed man. Also, in Carson's view, he looked fearful of something, as though he and the blue-eyed big man had been fiercely arguing about something before Carson rode up. It was sometimes a wait for Carson when he rode in; sometimes he was civilly invited to dismount, to come up to the house. Here, though, those two stood there, gazing steadily up at him, saying nothing, assessing Carson, his horse, his attire, even the expression on his face, all the while saying nothing at all.

Finally the grizzled man inclined his head the slightest bit, saying: "Morning, stranger. Get down and rest your legs."

Carson swung off, stepped to his horse's head, stopped there, and turned hip-shot in his stance and speculative in his expression. The grizzled man was relieved that Carson had ridden up, but the hard-eyed bigger man was not. Now that one said: "Who are you and what do you want here?"

There was an arrogance in those words that rushed at Carson full of unfriendliness, full of challenge. He said back to the hook-nosed man: "Your outfit, mister?"

"What difference does that make?"

"I'm looking for the owner."

The big man made a disdaining smile. "Drifter," he said. "The springtime brings you fellers out like prairie dogs." That disdaining smile turned indifferent, scorning. "You'll want work and a place to bed down. That's what life is to your kind . . . someone's barn to sleep in, someone's table to push your feet under." The big man broke off, swung back toward his companion in front of the house, and said: "Go ahead and hire him, but he won't do you any good, Clem."

The big man turned, stepped over beside his horse, and reached up. Carson's quiet voice halted him.

"Mister," Carson said, "you talk too much."

The big man eased away from his saddle animal and gave Carson a long, careful study, his expression smooth and unreadable, his sharp blue eyes looking for something in Carson he

173

may have overlooked before. Carson, not accustomed to being weighed and probed like this, kept close watch on the big man's face for a sign of change. None came for a long time, then the big man made a wintry little smile.

"It's always the same," he said, speaking as much to the grizzled man as to Carson. "They ride in with their down-at-the-heel look, their too-long hair and their battered old saddles . . . and their pride." He looked straight out at Carson. "That's it, isn't it?" he asked. "Your pride makes you talk big. You ride in here with maybe five dollars in your pocket, lookin' for work, but you're full of pride."

The big man wagged his head, swung up, and shortened his split reins. "Hire him," he said to the grizzled man he'd called Clem. "Go ahead, the pair of you'd make a matched team."

The big man spun his horse and loped on out of the yard southbound for that town Carson had seen earlier. Both Carson and the grizzled man stood silently, looking after him, their thoughts perhaps not too entirely different.

Carson fished around for his makings, dropped his head, and began working up a cigarette. He felt embarrassed for the grizzled man. He also wondered if his hair was indeed too long. He lit up, lifted his head, and found the other man carefully looking him over.

"The name," he said softly, "is Jared Carson,

and I reckon one thing Hook Nose said was true enough . . . I'm looking for work."

The grizzled older man kept his thoughtful gaze on Carson. "I'm Clem Forsythe," he said. "And that man you called Hook Nose is Harry Brogan."

"I'll remember," murmured Carson, meaning he would not forget either Brogan's face or his name. "Now, about that work?"

Forsythe had already come to a decision on that; he'd had plenty of time to do it in. "Forty a month and found. There's a cot in the harness room at the barn. You cook one week. I cook the next week. That sound tolerable to you, Jared?"

"Yes. You run this place alone, Mister Forsythe?"

"I do. Let's start off right, Jared. I'm not Mister Forsythe, I'm Clem." The grizzled cowman made a lop-sided small grin. "No man's 'Mister' in this country unless he's got a thousand cows. I only got four hundred."

"How many's Brogan got?"

"He's not in the cow business. Brogan owns a big slice of Cinnebar, that town you saw south of here when you rode up." Forsythe loosened at the shoulders. For the first time since Carson had come up, Forsythe turned loose and easy where he stood. Carson thought that this was the real Clem Forsythe, this near-to-smiling, relaxed man. The other stance, stiffly unnatural and apprehensive, had been occasioned by Brogan's presence and whatever Brogan had been saying when Carson had ridden in.

"Put up your horse at the barn, if you wish, or in one of the corrals. Dump your bedroll in the harness room, then come on up to the house. I'll have breakfast cooking."

Carson nodded, watched Forsythe turn toward the house, dropped his smoke, trod upon it as he turned, and went along toward the log barn. Ordinarily this would be exactly the type of cow outfit Carson liked to work for; only one or two other men, no women, plenty of open country and some backdrop mountains far out sort of to catch a man's glance now and then, sort of to hold his soaring thoughts down to this one place.

He offsaddled at the barn, turned his horse into a little round corral that fronted on a network of other, larger corrals, dragged his rig into the harness room, and dropped it. But this might not be the pension he was looking for; that Brogan, if he was as big a man in the area as Forsythe had implied, had not come riding out this early in the morning and this far from his town just because he liked riding. There was something brewing between those two.

Carson untied his bedroll from aft of the cantle, tossed it carelessly upon the iron cot, shucked his rider's short-waisted coat, and strolled back out to the barn's big doorless front opening. There, he swung to gaze northward where the strong early rays of morning sunlight struck burnishingly against those rough hills and peaks, breaking them into crags and buttresses. Well, hell, wherever a man went, there was always something. He lifted a dark hand, ran it along his neck at the back, let it fall down, and told himself that Hook Nose had been pretty observant at that; he *did* need a haircut.

In a far corral some horses nickered at Carson's chestnut in the little round corral. Carson went back into the barn, took down a fork, pitched up a large flake of loose hay, and walked down where those other animals were. He fed them, looked them over with an experienced eye, found them good, serviceable animals, returned to the barn, and fed his own animal. These were simple things to do but they gave a rider his initial proprietary feelings about the outfit he worked for.

He walked on across the brightening yard toward the house. Someday, he told himself, this was precisely the size outfit he wanted to own himself. Not so big he'd need a bunkhouse full of cowboys, but no smaller, either, because with fewer than four, five hundred cows, a man didn't make a worthwhile living; he only survived. He even liked the simplicity, the functional austerity, of Forsythe's ranch. No unnecessary buildings, no flowerbeds around the house, just a big log barn, a good, livable house, a windmill to keep the troughs full, and a stout network of working corrals.

Sometimes a man ran across something that fitted him as perfectly, as comfortably, as an old woolen coat, and usually, when this happened, it was such a gradual, easy thing, that the man did not immediately appreciate it. But Carson did. He was by nature a thoughtful and observant man, a person who arrived at conclusions without any considerable difficulty or without a lot of hampering reservations. He was not a complicated man.

Forsythe met him at the kitchen door around back, beckoned him on inside where that good, tangy aroma of boiling coffee and frying meat rushed at Carson, bringing into sharp relief his forgotten early-morning hunger.

"Have a chair," said Forsythe, motioning toward an oil-cloth–covered table in the kitchen's center. "Be ready in a minute. Did you bait your horse?"

"Yes. I also tossed some feed to those other animals."

"Thanks. That's what I was going to do when Brogan rode up."

Carson watched Forsythe at the wood stove. Brogan again. He waited for Forsythe to enlarge on Brogan, but Forsythe never did. Carson mentally shrugged; he was a patient man, he could wait. Sometime Forsythe would bring up the topic of Harry Brogan again. Folks didn't have trouble in the forefront of their thoughts without someday mentioning it.

II

The first two days Forsythe rode with Jared Carson, showing him the cattle, the limits of their range, the water holes and salting grounds. They would not fetch in the critters for another few weeks, Clem said. A lot of the cows hadn't been to the bull until late, so they wouldn't calve for a while yet.

"No sense in working one bunch, then having to bring 'em all in three, four weeks later, and work the balance of them. We'll let things drift until all the calves are on the ground."

That made sense to Jared. He didn't say so, but he nonetheless agreed.

They found a dead heifer near a tree fringe upon the northward foothills. Wolves had pretty well worried the carcass; there was no way to tell what the critter had died of, at least not from the saddle.

"Well," philosophized Clem, "those things happen. If she's the only one I lose this year, I'll count myself plumb lucky."

Jared got down from his saddle, went up, and

bent over the carcass. What Clem had said was true enough except for something a man standing close could see and a man lounging off a little distance in his saddle could not see. There were two bluish punctures in the heifer's head from right to left.

"Come on!" called Clem casually. "We've still got to get you acquainted with the rest of the range an' time's running out for today."

Jared walked thoughtfully back, stepped up over leather, and without saying anything reined on out beside his employer. That, back there, had been a bullet hole through the heifer's head. She hadn't died naturally; she'd been shot.

After a couple of miles of quiet riding, Jared said: "Who shares this range with you?"

"Two adjoining ranches," answered Forsythe. "Keith Winston of Pothook and Casey Hedrich of Circle Dot." Clem made a roundabout gesture with one arm and hand. "There's more'n enough feed for the three of us." He let the arm drop. "Sometimes in the late fall a drive or two passes through from down below Cinnebar. Those cowmen down there often put their herds together and trail north over the mountains to rail's end. From there, they ship their cattle to Kansas City or Chicago, wherever the market's the best at the time."

"You get a lot of hunters up here?"

Clem looked around. "Hunters? Now and then,

I suppose. In the fall when snow gets deep in the high country, game drifts down here. Otherwise, there's not much to hunt."

They rode in a large westerly circle, crossed some lava-rock country where breaks and low spires stood, then headed back for the ranch. They had covered nearly eight miles of good cattle country; except for the lava rock and the forested northward foothills, every foot of it was deep-soiled grassland, the kind of country that put tallow under a critter's dark hide.

As they were coming down into the yard again, with shadows marching down from those far-away hills, Forsythe said: "I thought I might go into town this evening. Care to come along?"

Jared smiled. "It wouldn't hurt none," he said. "I could use a drink, but more'n that I could use a haircut."

They ate supper, snaked out fresh mounts, and rode out for Cinnebar twenty minutes ahead of a rising moon's soft brightness. It wasn't a long ride at the gait they chose, but Cinnebar was still a good five miles southward from Forsythe's Five Pointed Star outfit. It appeared over the murky horizon as a clutch of bright, yellow lights in an otherwise gloomy, blue-velvet world of great distances and great silence.

Where they slowed to a loose walk a half mile out, Clem blew out a big sigh and said:

"Something I got to tell you, Jared. Something I should've told you and kept putting off."

It doesn't take long for two men living as close as these two were living for each to come close to surmising what lies in the other's thoughts. Jared fixed his gaze dead ahead upon the clustering lights and waited; the thing about Harry Brogan, whatever it was, would now come out. They were nearing Brogan's town; they would probably meet Brogan. All the little facets were coming together. Only one was missing, so Jared slouched along, waiting for Forsythe to supply it, and he did.

He said: "That first day you rode in. That morning Harry Brogan was out at the ranch. We were having a disagreement." Clem was picking his words carefully, and he, too, was staring straight ahead. "You see, I came into this country fifteen years back, put up my buildings, brought in my seed stock, and ever since then I've had my beak worn smooth keeping it against the grindstone."

"Be damned," muttered Jared. "A woman."

"What? What's that you said?"

"Never mind, just get on with it," grumbled Jared, sounding quietly disgusted.

"Yeah. Well, last year I was at Circle Dot's roundup, repping for my Five Pointed Star iron, and met Casey Hedrich's aunt."

Jared looked around, astonished. "Aunt!"

"Sure. She's Casey's mother's youngest sister. She's about six, seven years younger'n I am. Prettiest thing you ever saw, I swear it."

"Get on with it."

"I took her to a couple of socials."

Jared reached up, removed his hat, scratched his head, and crushed the hat back on. "Clem, one time I worked for a man over in Idaho who couldn't say he went to the corral and roped himself a horse. He had to say he went first to his saddle in the barn, took down his hard-twist, seven-sixteenths scant Manila lariat, walked on through out back to the corrals, built himself a little bear-cat loop, and went on through the gate and roped his horse."

Forsythe understood this lengthy innuendo and, without taking offence, nodded his head up and down. "All right, I took her to a couple of dances, then Brogan saw her."

"And moved in."

"Yes. He moved in. But she still went with me now and then."

"So he rode out the other morning to tell you to run your brand on something else, this heifer belonged to him."

"Correct." Forsythe turned his grizzled head. "You understand why a feller might be reluctant to tell a stranger?"

"I understand. But why now . . . why tonight?"

"Like I already explained, Jared, Brogan owns

a big piece of Cinnebar. He's got men working for him in the saloon and the livery barn, not to mention the dry-goods store and the Land Office."

"And you figure I'm entitled to know he just might send some of these employees of his to part my mane with a singletree, right?"

"You were pretty short with him the other morning."

Jared cleared his throat, spat aside, swung to view the buildings that were now less than five hundred feet onward, and grunted: "I was, wasn't I?"

Cinnebar, that one earlier glimpse of it Jared'd had, didn't look a lot different at night than it did in early morning. It lay flat out upon the plain, its solitary main thoroughfare astraddle the north-south stage road. A number of other roadways came in toward it from far out and it seemed, for no larger than it was, a bustling, up-and-coming village. But it was functionally ugly. There were no trees, the buildings were constructed of unsurfaced pine, tin roofs predominated, the roadway was needlessly wide, and those opposite ranks of buildings were nearly all of the bat-and-slat type of architecture. In fact, Cinnebar reminded Jared Carson of something thrown up in a hurry to catch some transient trade before that trade headed for some other town with its money and its goods.

"Used to be mines back in the northward mountains hereabouts," explained Forsythe, seeing Jared's critical assessment of the town. "When they petered out and the cowmen came in, Cinnebar turned from a miner's town to a cowman's town."

They reined over to step down and tie up before the Cinnebar Palace Saloon. There was considerable roadway traffic, mostly horsemen, cowboys from outlying cattle outfits. There was the distinct noise of a piano, too, but coming up from southward where another saloon was blazing with yellow lamplight.

"The Palace belongs to Brogan," said Forsythe, finished with his tying and waiting for Jared to complete his slow, thoughtful study of the town.

"And the livery barn," mused Carson, letting his gaze take in that aromatic building across the way.

"Yes. So does the Land Office and the dry-goods store."

Jared went on around their tied animals, stepped up onto the rough boards of the plank walk beside Clem, and hooked both thumbs in his gun belt.

"Tell me something," he said softly. "How long's Brogan been around here?"

"Four, five years. Came from Kansas or Missouri, so the story goes."

"And in four, five years he accumulated himself a town."

"He had money when he arrived here, but he's made more, too, since those days."

"Another question, Clem. He's never married?"

Forsythe wagged his head. "Like me, I expect. Too busy up to now just trying to carve something out for himself."

Jared spied the barbershop. It was lit from inside and outside both. "You go on in," he said. "I've got to get shorn first. I'll look you up later."

Forsythe studied Carson's dark profile. He said dryly—"Yeah."—and turned away.

Men passed on behind Carson, some with the ring of their spurred boots identifying them as cattlemen, others, wearing bowlers and similar narrow-brimmed hats, showing themselves to be townsmen, merchants of one kind or another.

Three riders came loping abreast out of the sooty east, swung southward, and slowed as they came even with the Palace. They called casually back and forth, ignoring the dark shadow of Jared Carson there on the plank walk. A shiny-wheeled top buggy went spinning past. One of those riders raised up and turned.

"Hey, Casey!" this man called to the driver of that top buggy. "I'll buy you a drink!"

The rig slowed but did not stop. A quite youthful-looking man leaned far out to call back: "That you, Keith? I'll be back in a minute."

Carson swiveled to let his gaze drop fully upon the man called Keith. Forsythe had mentioned a Keith Winston as sharing the range with him. Carson studied that rider there at the hitch rack with kindling interest. Keith Winston was a raw-boned, lank, lean man with a careless grace and long stride to him. His face was open, bronzed from wind and sun, and about as uncomplicated-looking as the average range man's face usually was. He did not, in Jared's view, look at all like a man who would deliberately shoot a heifer through the head and leave her to rot.

Then the man called Keith, along with his two rough companions, stamped on up to the plank walk, shouldered past Carson, and entered the Palace Saloon.

It was a pleasant night for early springtime. The customary chill of a stubbornly unrelenting winter was not in the air. This seemed to bring more people out. Jared watched them ebb and flow, young lovers strolling hand-in-hand, older people taking a constitutional to settle their supper and get them in the mood for a good night's sleep. Even a few range men strolling, or standing here and there softly talking, quietly enjoying this slack time when no chores or obligations or responsibilities nagged at them.

Jared stepped down into the roadway's floury dust, crossed over to the barbershop, and entered. He'd been waiting for the cowboy in the barber chair to get shorn, had watched this operation through the barbershop's front window, and had timed his own entrance to coincide with the rider's departure.

The barber beamed upon him, flicked a big white sheet, and said good-naturedly: "I'm sure gettin' my share of long-maned ones tonight. Step right up, mister."

Jared stepped right up.

III

In a strange town there were usually three excellent places for a man to pick up worthwhile gossip, traveling directions, and sly tales concerning local natives. One was the livery barn, another was a saddle shop, and the third was, traditionally, the barbershop.

"You're a stranger in town, aren't you?" asked the barber of Jared Carson as he smiled, studied Jared's mop of thick brown hair, and edged up with poised shears to attack it.

"Yup. Been hereabouts exactly three days."

"Working for Winston?"

"Nope."

"Hedrich?"

"Nope."

The shears clicked a little viciously, a little impatiently. "Who, then?"

Jared considered. He did not like personal questions, did not ordinarily answer them, and disliked the people who asked them. Still, in order to get information sometimes, you had to give information. "Clem Forsythe," he said.

"Oh."

The barber had nothing to add to that one-syllable word for a long time. He cut out chunks of hair, clicked his scissors, and moved from left to right and back again.

"Seems like a pretty good man," prompted Jared. "Not the best cook in the world but decent enough otherwise."

"Clem? He's a hard worker," said the barber as he stepped back to survey his work thus far. "Got good stock and takes care of it."

"Must be lonely, though," suggested Jared, "living alone out there all the time."

The barber stepped around, met Jared's gaze with a sly look, and smiled. "Hear tell he's trying to remedy that. Hear tell he's sweet on Casey Hedrich's aunt."

Jared said disinterestedly: "I've heard that, too. Better late than never I reckon. You know her? Sounds awful old to me, being an aunt and all."

The barber stepped back in and stood poised with his shears again. He chuckled. "It's clear to see you're sure enough a stranger in these parts." The shears swooped. "Mister, that woman's just about the handsomest thing that ever came down the pike."

"But . . . somebody's aunt . . . ?"

"Hah! Let me tell you, cowboy, she's not a day over twenty-five. They say she was Casey Hedrich's mother's youngest sister." The barber thought of something, lifted his head, and laughed. "I wish I'd had an aunt like her, so help me Hannah, I surely do." The laugh faded. "But Clem's got competition. You've heard of Harry Brogan, haven't you?"

"Yeah."

"Well, sir, Harry's after her, too."

"Is that a fact?"

"Yessirree, and what Harry Brogan goes after he gets. Let me tell you that. Besides, he's a younger and handsomer man than Clem Forsythe."

"Maybe," murmured Jared dryly, "the lady likes character instead of just a flashy front and a big hooked nose."

"Money!" exclaimed the barber, with a cunning wink at Carson. "Women like money and Brogan's got it. He owns most of this here town."

"Well," said Jared pointedly and dourly, "if auntie wants Brogan for his money, I sure hope she gets him. Because then she'll have a sidewinder, and maybe that'll teach her a lesson about men . . . and about money."

The barber looked long at Carson's profile and afterward changed the subject. It suddenly struck him that this down-at-the-heel cowboy Clem Forsythe had hired not only did not like Harry Brogan, but also he looked like a good man not to cross.

"They tell me," he said getting back on safe ground again, "the beef price out of Kansas is strong this spring."

Jared lifted his level gaze to the barber's face, saw the fresh non-committal look there, and understood perfectly what had happened between them. It didn't bother him; he'd verified everything he'd been curious about anyway. Almost everything anyway. He was still puzzled over that shot heifer, but a town barber wouldn't know anything about things like that.

An abrupt, muffled six-gun blast shattered the lesser noises of the roadway outside and the quiet of the barbershop. It startled both Jared and the barber. No second shot sounded so Jared eased back down again in the chair. The barber, though, stepped to his roadside window peering out interestedly.

"Came from over at the Palace," he said, and swung around. Jared was pushing up out of his chair. He stood up, yanked off the sheet, balled it, and tossed it backward.

"Wait," said the barber. "I haven't finished with the edges yet."

Jared stepped outside, watched shadowy silhouettes across the way running northward toward the Palace, and swiftly crossed over to join them.

It was a bad premonition that led Jared to twist his way roughly through the thronged doorway into the saloon. Men turned frowningly to see who this was, punishing them that way. Jared did not heed them. He crossed over where a stocky man with a star upon his shirt front was standing, wide-legged, looking downward, elbowed his way up beside this lawman, and halted stockstill.

Clem Forsythe was lying there in the churned sawdust looking dumbfounded, looking breathless. There was a glistening stain of spreading crimson upon his white shirt. Near Clem's twitching right fingers lay a cocked six-gun.

Jared dropped to one knee, shoved his hat under Forsythe's head as a pillow, and said: "I'll get a doc. Rest easy, Clem."

"Jared?"

"Yeah, I'm here, Clem. Just lie easy a minute. I'll fetch a sawbones."

"Jared, listen. Like I told you on the way in . . . fifteen years I worked to . . . build up my Five Pointed Star . . ." Forsythe's clouding gaze passed above Carson's hunched figure. "Al? Sheriff Al?"

That burly man with a badge kneeled down. "Yes, Clem?"

"Al, witness this for me. Jared Carson here . . . he's my heir. He gets my Five Pointed Star outfit . . . all of it. You hear, Al?"

"I hear, Clem. Sure I hear. I'll witness this for you, but now you just lie easy. We'll send for the doctor."

"No," murmured Forsythe. "No time for that, Al. We been friends . . . ?"

"Sure, Clem. Good friends for a long time."

"You'd do me a favor . . . Al?"

"Just name it, Clem."

"Don't let anyone take the ranch away from Carson here. Promise me that, Al."

The sheriff solemnly nodded, his voice going soft, very soft. "I promise, Clem. Jared Carson here gets the place."

Forsythe's head weakly rolled, his lips parted forming words. "Jared, I'm sorry. I should've kept you out of it. I'm . . . sorry . . ."

Jared heard the lawman make a little rattling sigh and looked around. "He's dead," the sheriff said, and for the first time lifted his gaze to put it fully upon Jared.

"Who did it, Sheriff?"

But the lawman did not reply to this question, he said instead: "He had no kin, mister, so I reckon you just inherited yourself a pretty good little cow ranch."

"I asked who shot him, Sheriff."

The lawman pushed heavily upright, turned, and spoke to some of the silently standing men. "How about a couple of you boys taking Clem over to Doc's place?"

A number of men stepped in and leaned far down. Jared was coming back upright again when someone pushed Forsythe's cocked, unfired pistol into his hand. Jared looked at the thing, eased the hammer off, and turned as the sheriff rapped his arm.

"Come and have a drink with me," said the law officer, sounding routine about this, sounding glum and tired.

Jared did not at once move. He instead looked at all those quiet, carefully locked faces, recognized none until his gaze went farther out and met the pushing, unwavering gaze of Harry Brogan. A shock passed back and forth between those two, something antagonistic and uncompromising. It made Jared's stomach tighten; it ran out to the raw ends of his nerves. Brogan had no gun showing but something told Jared as emphatically as it could that Brogan had been in some way responsible for Forsythe's killing.

A wispy, dead-eyed–looking man standing with Brogan abruptly turned and sauntered toward the door. From behind Jared along the bar that stocky lawman sang out, halting this individual: "Pete, stick around. I'll want to talk to you in a little while."

Jared threw his glance farther out, where that man called Pete had turned to look back. Maybe Brogan, Jared told himself, had engineered

Clem's killing, but he was right now looking at the man who'd done the actual firing.

"Carson?"

Jared did not turn. He still held Forsythe's gun in his right hand. He and the wispy man called Pete steadily watched one another. Eventually Harry Brogan gave his shoulders a little careless shrug and turned to pass on through the quiet, watchful crowd, and this movement seemed to bring things almost back to normal. The talk did not immediately become noisy again, but it started, became a murmur almost like a sigh throughout the saloon, and people moved, went back to the gambling tables or the bar or on over where a chuck-a-luck cage resumed working. Even that dead-eyed man called Pete ambled off, putting his back to Jared.

"Carson, come on and have that drink."

Jared went over, put Clem's gun on the bar top, and looked across into the carefully non-committal face of a bartender. "Whiskey," he said.

The sheriff nodded twice at the barman, twisted from the waist, and looked Jared up and down. "How long have you known Clem?" he asked.

"Four days tomorrow."

"Well, Clem was a good man. I knew him since the day he first came riding into Cinnebar fifteen years back. If Clem judged you a good man,

Carson, I'll abide by that. He knew men and horses and cattle."

"But not women," said Jared, accepting his drink from the barman, throwing his head back, and downing it.

"What do you mean by that, Carson?"

Jared pushed the shot glass from him, turned, and looked sardonically at the lawman. "If you don't know, Sheriff, I couldn't explain it to you."

For a moment those two stared steadily into one another's eyes. "All right," said the lawman gently, "I know. I just didn't think, in four days, you'd know. By the way, my name's Al Putnam. Sheriff Al Putnam."

"I'll remember that," said Jared. "A question, Sheriff. Who was that smoky-eyed, skinny feller standing over beside Brogan . . . the one with the tied-down gun?"

"Pete Aleo. Listen to me now, Carson. Don't get some ridiculous idea about Pete."

"Why did he kill Clem?"

"I didn't hear the argument, too much noise in here. I just heard some fool woman squeal, turned quick, and saw both of them drawing."

"Fair fight, Putnam?"

"It was fair. Whatever the argument was doesn't matter. What matters is that Clem had an even go for his money."

"How long'd you say you'd known Clem?"

"Fifteen years. Why?"

"He said you were a friend, Sheriff."

"What're you driving at, Carson?"

"You standing here drinking and calling that a fair fight. The murder of your old friend, Forsythe."

Sheriff Putnam's gaze drew out narrowly. His mouth went thin in a sucked-back way. "You," he said very softly, very clearly, "better be satisfied you just inherited a damned good ranch, Carson, and keep your thoughts to yourself."

"Yeah," drawled Jared, matching Putnam's bleak glare. "Just one more comment and I'll go on over and make arrangements for Clem's burial."

"Say it."

"Pete Aleo's a gunman. He stinks of it. You've seen a dozen just like him and so have I. Now, Sheriff, where I come from we never call it a fair fight when a hired killer sets up a working cowman and shoots him."

Putnam hadn't lifted his shot glass. It lay in the curve of his brawny fist with Putnam's knuckles showing white around it. "All right, Carson, you've had your say. Now maybe you'd better do like you said . . . go on over and make arrangements for Clem's burial."

Jared pushed off the bar, half turned to leave, and Putnam spoke again, halting him, bringing him back around.

"I'll be out to see you tomorrow or the next

day, Carson. There'll be papers for you to sign."

The solid disapproval between these two crystallized then and there. Jared felt it; he knew Al Putnam also felt it.

"Sure," he said, "any time, Sheriff." He brushed past big Harry Brogan on his way out of the saloon.

Night was fully down with its leavening quietude and its eternal mystery. Jared paced slowly through it on his way over to the doctor's lit doorway with its black-on-white little sign.

IV

It was early morning of the day following the killing of Clem Forsythe that two riders walked their mounts down into the Forsythe ranch yard. Jared saw them coming while he was out feeding the corralled livestock. He didn't know either of them, but probably wouldn't have anyway because the only people he thus far knew in the Cinnebar country were in town, and these riders were approaching from the west. A prudent stranger in a land where trouble had erupted did not go out to meet strangers unarmed, so Jared went back to the house, buckled on his gun belt, lashed the holster to his leg, and stepped outside upon Clem Forsythe's little front porch, waiting.

While those two were still a hundred yards off, Jared recognized one of them; it was the same Keith Winston he'd seen in town the night before. He thought he also recognized the slighter, much younger man riding with Winston, but the light had been poor and this man had been driving past at a good clip in a top buggy. Still, he thought this one would be Casey Hedrich. He was correct in both instances. When his visitors halted before the house to sit a moment gazing gravely down at Jared, they introduced themselves. After that, though, they seemed to have difficulty thinking of what next to say.

Jared could have helped them but he didn't; he had no good feelings toward anyone he'd met thus far in the Cinnebar country. Furthermore, he'd done some deep thinking the night before, when, unable to sleep, he'd come to a solid conclusion. Whoever Clem Forsythe's enemies were, he'd probably inherited them along with Forsythe's ranch. That was the only reason he could imagine for Clem to tell him, in his last moments, that he was sorry for dragging Jared into his personal affairs.

Rusty-headed, powerfully put together Keith Winston eventually said somberly: "That was a bad thing, last night. I don't know how close you were to Clem, stranger, but everyone who knew him as well as Casey and I did liked him real well."

"Were you in the Palace when it happened?" Jared asked with deceptive mildness.

"Sure was," said Winston. "It was a bad thing."

"You already said that, mister. As for liking Clem so much . . . if you were there last night, how come you to sit back and let a professional gunman kill him?"

Winston, caught unprepared for a remark like this one, sat his saddle looking down and across at Jared, saying nothing. But gradually his face got very pink and his eyes turned sharp, turned antagonistic. "You too, sonny?" Jared said to youthful Casey Hedrich. "Did you see it happen, too?"

"No. I didn't walk in until after it was all over."

"Then," said Jared looking straight out at Hedrich, "I'd like to invite you to his funeral. It'll be tomorrow morning at ten o'clock in Cinnebar."

Those two horsemen stared. That Keith Winston had not been included in that invitation was painfully clear.

"Listen, mister," said Winston finally, his voice roughening. "Whatever you believe, I was as good a friend as Clem Forsythe had in these parts, and whether you like it or not I'll be at his funeral."

Jared put a saturnine gaze at the powerfully built older man across from him. "Suit yourself," he replied. "It'll be a public funeral. Now, you fellers didn't ride over here just to shed a tear for Clem Forsythe. What else is on your minds?"

Casey Hedrich was slim and boyish. He didn't look to Jared Carson to be over perhaps twenty-three or -four years of age. His face was smooth and unlined; his hands, lying upon the saddle horn, were unscarred and uncallused. Whatever young Hedrich did for a living, he didn't do it with his hands. Also, there was a look of affluence to the younger cowman that Jared had never before encountered in working ranchers. His boots were expensive-looking, as were the rest of his accoutrements; even the horse under Casey Hedrich was better by far than the usual working cow horse.

It was this somewhat miscast younger man who answered Carson's last question by saying: "We thought you'd want to know about our mutual range. You see, Al Putnam told us last night after you'd gone on, that Clem left you his outfit."

"Go on," said Jared, conscious of the dis-approving stare he was getting from silent Keith Winston.

"Well," continued Casey Hedrich, "we keep other cattle than our three brands off this range. We take turns in salting. We work together at keeping the water holes clean in summertime and sometimes, when things coincide, we get together for our roundups." Hedrich made a little deprecating smile. "It's about the same as anywhere, Mister Carson, where three outfits share the same range."

"I'll remember," said Jared. "Anything else?"

"Yeah," growled big Keith Winston. "One thing. You better get rid of that chip on your shoulder, mister, or someone might get rid of it for you."

Winston was lifting his rein hand preparatory to turning away when Jared said: "You, Winston?"

That moving rein hand grew suddenly still as Winston faced back toward Carson again. "Maybe," he said, biting the word off.

Jared's expression turned sardonic. His gaze up at the larger man was pushing. "Naw," he quietly commented. "Not you, Winston. But if someone else wanted to try it, you'd stand back and watch."

This innuendo did not escape either of Jared's visitors. Casey Hedrich shot a quick, alarmed look over at his companion.

Winston sat still a moment considering Carson. He measured and appraised him with that long, long glance, then he said: "You got a burr under your saddle blanket, Carson. I can understand that. But you're making the wrong kind of impression hereabouts. I'm not going to fight you this morning, but you keep pushing and someone'll take you up one of these times. You think what you want about last night. I don't have to alibi my actions to you or anyone else, but I'm going to make one last stab at being your neighbor. I'm going to tell you exactly what I saw last night. Nothing. Nothing at all until I heard a woman squeal. I turned then, but it was all over before I'd even completed my turn. That's the truth, Carson. Think what you like."

Winston spun his horse, hooked it, and went loping out of the yard. Casey Hedrich hesitated a moment as though he meant to say something to Jared, but in the end he didn't speak, only turned, and went hurrying after his friend.

Jared waited until those two were small in the westerly distance, then he slumped, reached up to ease back his hat, and gently wag his head. He hadn't handled that at all well. Sure, he felt that Forsythe's friends should have interceded—if he'd been in the Palace when Pete Aleo challenged Clem he'd have jumped in—but you couldn't always expect others to think as fast or move as quickly when trouble came because people were everlastingly different.

He went back into the house, finished eating a cold breakfast, cleaned up his mess, and returned to the yard just in time to meet Sheriff Putnam riding in over by the log barn. Putnam nodded, his expression wooden, and his gaze unfriendly. As he swung down, he said: "I brought out those deeds and transfers for you to sign, Carson. I've been authorized to witness your signature, too."

Jared swallowed his bitterness and said: "Care for some coffee, Sheriff?"

Putnam finished tying his horse, slowly turned, and slowly put his dead-level gray gaze upon Jared. For the space of a long moment he did not reply, but eventually he said: "All right. If you've got it made." There was no overture of friendship in that assent, though, and Putnam's gaze was wary and suspicious.

They went over to the house, passed on around back, and entered the kitchen from the rear door. Putnam removed his hat, put it upon the table, and eased down beside it, watching Carson go to the stove. While Jared's back was still to him, Putnam shrugged, his wariness dropped away, and he brought forth several crinkly papers, spread them upon the oil-cloth table cover, and puckered his brow over them.

"One of these," he said without looking up as Jared brought two mugs of black coffee over and sat down, "is the transfer of Clem's brand . . . the Five Pointed Star . . . from his name to your name. When you've signed it and I've witnessed it, the thing gets sent to the capital for recording. Then the Five Pointed Star becomes officially and legally your registered brand."

Jared sipped coffee and nodded. He understood this but it didn't seem real to him. He'd never owned a registered brand in his life.

"This here paper is the deed to the Forsythe Ranch, lock, stock, and chattels."

"Chattels?"

"Yeah. That means all Clem's livestock and such like."

Putnam brought forth a pen, put a thick finger where Carson was to sign both papers, and handed over the pen. Jared signed, pushed the papers away, and returned the pen. That easily he had become a landed cowman.

Putnam signed as Carson's witness, carefully, very deliberately folded the papers, and returned them to his pocket. Not until then did he lift his eyes, pick up the coffee cup, look over the rim of it, and quietly say: "Clem knew he didn't have more'n a minute or two left, last night. He had a fast decision to make and he made it."

Jared ran that remark through his mind a moment before replying to it. "Are you implying he did the wrong thing, Sheriff?"

Putnam put his cup down. "No," he said slowly, thoughtfully. "What I am saying, Carson, is that he knew you three, four days, and he knew just about anyone you could mention hereabouts from five to fifteen years."

"Including you, Sheriff."

"Yeah, including me. But it doesn't matter, Carson. Not really. It's just a thing that pops into a person's head, is all." Putnam finished the coffee, looked straight at Jared, and said in a brisker, less pensive tone of voice: "I hope old Clem did the right thing."

"But you don't think he did."

"I don't know, Carson," said the lawman quietly, persisting with that dead-level look. "Last night you made some pretty hard remarks. I didn't repeat 'em to anyone because there's no point in helping you make folks dislike you. But they didn't sit too well with me."

Jared's resentment was rising; he checked it with an effort, held his voice low, and said: "Tell me something, Sheriff. After I left, did you have your talk with Brogan's hired gun, Pete Aleo?"

"I had it, yes," Putnam replied as he leaned back in his chair. "I ordered Aleo out of the county."

"You got that authority, Sheriff?"

"No," said Putnam candidly. "Only a court of law has that kind of authority. But you see, Carson, there's more'n one way to skin a cat. I told Pete how popular Clem was. I suggested to him that no matter how good with a gun he is, no man can buck an entire countryside, and before Clem's molding in the ground some of his friends just very well might lay for Aleo and kill him."

"And?"

Putnam picked up his hat, examined the inside sweatband, dumped the hat atop his head, and stood up. "He told me he'd pull out when he damned well felt like it, or when Harry Brogan told him to . . . paid him off. Not until then."

Jared accompanied the sheriff back outside and

onward across the yard where Putnam had left his tied horse. They walked along slowly, each busy with his private thoughts.

When Putnam bent to untie his horse, Jared said: "Sheriff, was it over the woman?"

Putnam turned, considered the reins in his hands, and nodded. "There's never been much love lost between Brogan and Clem, but there's never been anything but the woman to make 'em fight each other, either. Yes, I'd say it was the woman, Carson." Putnam lifted his head. "Want some advice?" he asked.

"Shoot."

"Don't take it up for Clem."

"Look around you, Sheriff, that barn behind you, that range land out there. Even those corrals and the horses in 'em, not to mention four hundred cows out where we can't see 'em from here. All that adds up to fifteen years of hard work and sweat out of a man's life. Now, Putnam, if that man had given you all this . . . and he'd died like Clem Forsythe died last night . . . would you be content to just take and not give a little in return?"

Al Putnam ran a grave look out over the sunlit, golden countryside behind and beyond Jared Carson as he answered. "When a man gets to our age," he quietly said, "he does a heap of thinking about things sometimes. Carson, last night when Clem lay there dying, he said he was sorry to drag you into his affairs. What d'you suppose he meant by that?"

Jared searched for his reply to this and had it formed on his lips. But he didn't get to say it because the sheriff spoke out again.

"I'll tell you what I figured out about that. Like I told you, Clem was a right good judge of horses, cattle . . . and men. He'd sized you up as a rough, straight-shooting feller. Clem knew he was dying, Carson. He knew it as sure as the devil, but he didn't mean to go out without making sure of something. That's why he gave you his ranch, his cattle . . . and his problems. He knew damned well you'd never rest at just inheriting from him, unless you also inherited his fight with Harry Brogan."

Putnam stopped speaking. Silence settled in the yard. Jared Carson stood there, gazing at the lawman for a long, long time. It had never once occurred to him that things might be as Putnam had just said.

V

Clem Forsythe's funeral was large, for the Cinnebar country. All the local cowmen and their riders were there. So also were the townsmen, the merchants, gamblers, saloon men, and freighters who had known and liked Forsythe. Carson had gone in early, not only to attend to the last-minute details but also to purchase a black suit. He was grim-faced when, at graveside, he looked up and caught the cold, sardonic gaze of Harry Brogan fully upon him in the crowd. He half expected to see Aleo beside Brogan but there was no sign of Forsythe's killer at all.

Brogan was well-dressed. In fact he seemed to be the only man in a suit at the funeral who looked as though he might be entirely at home in a suit. Mostly the cattlemen looked, and were, uncomfortable in their creased black pants and Prince Albert coats with little shoe-string black neckties. Keith Winston was there. He and Carson exchanged only one long look. After that neither of them sought out the other man again.

Casey Hedrich was also there, in his handsome top buggy. He looked more boyish than ever but Carson passed him over with only one glance, for by then he'd noticed how the others were gazing askance at him, how only burly Al Putnam came over to stand with him when the first handful of crumbly soil was dropped in upon Clem's coffin, and afterward said quietly: "You bought him a fine send-off, Carson. Folks'll remember that."

"Be better," muttered Carson, "if they'd just remember *him*."

When the crowd was breaking up, some wandering back to town from the cemetery, others mounting up for long rides back to their ranches, Al Putnam strode along beside Carson.

"I heard about the run-in you had with Winston," he said casually. "Too bad. You two fellers've got to be neighbors now unless . . ."

"Unless what, Sheriff?"

"You decide to sell out and drift."

Jared halted and turned. "You don't have too high an opinion of me, do you, Sheriff?"

"Well now, have you given me reason to have, Carson?"

Jared stood, considering Putnam's open, weathered face. "No," he ultimately said, "I guess I haven't."

Putnam smiled. It was the first time Jared had seen him look any other way than grim and forbidding. Putnam said: "You know, I've got a theory about men, Carson. When one admits he isn't likely to be right always, there's hope for him."

Putnam walked off without looking back, bound onward into town. Carson watched his thick, powerful body swing along.

A hesitant voice came on from behind, bringing Jared around to face Casey Hedrich. But it wasn't the youthful cowman that caught and solidly held Carson's attention; it was Hedrich's companion, a beautiful girl in black whose smoky eyes met Jared's stare and gave back all the dull fire without wavering. This then, Jared knew at once, would be *the woman*. She wasn't tall but she was willowy. Her face wasn't pretty, as he'd been told, it was beautiful. If she were an "aunt," then it was one of those idiosyncrasies of Nature that had made her one, for if Jared had ever seen a girl-turned-woman without losing any of the wholesomeness, the vibrant sweetness of girlhood, he was staring at her now. Her eyes were the autumnal color of a slate hillside on a wintry day. Her mouth was long with a heaviness that sang over the little separating distance to Carson, and her ebony hair with its heavy curl and luster struck down into him, bringing on a shallowness to his breathing. He had never in his life seen a woman such as this before. He would never in his lifetime see another like her, either. He was definite in his thoughts about that, too.

Young Hedrich was introducing them. Jared heard the words and acknowledged them, but he could never afterward remember them at all. He stiffly nodded and stiffly stood there, knowing very well his face mirrored every thought, yet without the will to change that, or even the wish to change it.

She said: "He was a fine man. I liked him very much."

There was something in the depths of her gaze, something cautious and considering, as though she'd heard things and was trying now to fit them to the man in front of her. Jared drew in a big breath and silently let it out. How did you say to a beautiful woman that except for her a man would not now be in his grave? You didn't. You thought things like that, but you didn't say them.

Casey Hedrich spoke up, hesitantly again, tentatively, as though he wasn't quite sure how to handle that bronzed, tough man in front of him. "You did right by him. It was a fine send-off."

Jared's eyes moved a fraction to young Hedrich. For an interval of quiet he said nothing. Then he struck his legs with his hat and murmured: "He had it coming. He's got a lot more coming, too."

Casey read into this something that made his face pale. He said, rather hurriedly—"Well, see you again, Carson."—and took the beautiful woman's arm. As those two went across to Hedrich's rig, Jared thought of something. He hadn't heard Casey say what her name was.

He was the last to walk away from Forsythe's grave. Back there, where laborers were shoveling in dirt, the grisly rattle of sod upon the wooden box sounded infinitely sad and final. Jared put on his hat, went along to town through back byways, and got his horse at the livery barn. Ordinarily he'd have had a drink or two. Today he wanted only to get back to the ranch. He was a man whose outer armor only seemed to be of iron. Pain could reach him. It often had in his lifetime. Pain and sadness. You didn't have to be a lifelong acquaintance of someone to feel grief over their passing. It didn't entirely have to do with the dead person, either. It had to do with the removal of a good man's shadow from this earth, with the ending echoes of a strong man's laughter, his roaring anger, his tender moments. For some men, it was not an easy thing to shake off all this. For Jared Carson, the drifter, it was not easy at all.

Back at the ranch he wasted the balance of that day puttering. He cared for the corralled horses, racked up firewood outside the kitchen door, cleaned two stone troughs beneath the windmill, and along toward evening he saddled his chestnut horse and rode out where a lowering sun was turning the world a dull, coppery color. He had no particular destination in mind, but, while it was yet light, he found himself in the vicinity of that shot heifer. He rode out and around to approach the carcass upwind, dismounted, and stood back a little distance, worrying at this small riddle that had never ceased nagging from some dark inner place of his mind. Why? What possible reason could anyone have to shoot deliberately one Five Pointed Star animal? It hadn't been a hunter; he was positive of that, because none of the meat had been taken. It certainly wasn't because the heifer had been on the prod; she had no calf to make her belligerent. It wasn't some vendetta, otherwise a vengeful killer wouldn't have stopped with just one Five Pointed Star animal.

His gaze wandered in and around that acid-scoured patch of earth. It touched briefly upon the nearly whole hide where wolves had scuffled with it. It swung away, then slowly back. There was a neat, large hole in that red hide. A hole larger than a man's fist. It was far too round and neatly made to have been gnawed out by scavengers.

Jared went forward, picked up a little stick, and kneeled. He probed that hole, which was only slightly smaller than the crown of a man's hat. He tossed aside the stick, grabbed the hide, and dragged it out flat. The hole was beginning to assume important dimensions to him. It was when the hide had been yanked flat, precisely over the rib cage where Forsythe always branded his critters.

Jared stood up. He walked around the hide. He bent over and, afterward, straightened up again. Someone with a very sharp knife had deliberately cut the brand out of that hide. He walked back a little way, caught his horse, and stepped up over leather to sit for a long time, staring downward. It was reasonably clear now what happened here. Someone had first shot the heifer, then carved out her brand. But why? He turned his horse, let the reins hang slackly, and permitted the beast to strike out in a long-legged walk for home.

There would be a reason for whatever that unknown cow killer had done back there, but it wasn't a very pleasant reason. Someone had tried working over Forsythe's Five Pointed Star into some other brand, had either failed or glaringly botched the job, and had then been obliged to destroy the evidence by shooting the heifer and cutting off the worked-over brand.

Jared rode all the way home unmindful of everything else. He didn't even become aware that a saddled horse was standing drowsily at the hitch rail in front of his barn until his own animal suddenly sighted that strange beast and drew up sharply to peer ahead through the dusk.

"You ride like a man in a trance," said the recognizably drawling voice of Sheriff Al Putnam. "I figured, it being suppertime and all, I'd wait a spell before heading back."

Jared rode on up, stepped down, and began offsaddling. Over the seat of his saddle he studied Putnam's shadowy face. "Glad you did," he said. "Tonight I need company for supper."

Putnam was leaning upon the barn's log front. In the same non-committal tone he'd used when he'd accepted Jared's offer of coffee two days earlier, he now said: "All right, I won't say I'm not hungry. But first off, I brought you out Clem's passbook."

"Passbook?"

"From the bank in town. As soon as the inheritance papers were probated and filed, they sent for me to come over to the bank. They gave me

Clem's passbook and another paper for you to sign."

"You'll have to make it plainer than that," said Jared, walking forward toward the round corral where he turned loose his chestnut gelding.

"Clem had seven thousand dollars in the bank, Carson. It's yours, too, along with everything else. This here is the passbook from the bank, showing when he deposited and withdrew money."

Putnam pushed the little book out. Jared took it, turned it over, turned it back, and lifted his eyes to Putnam's face. "I don't like this," he murmured. "It's sort of stealing. This isn't my money, Sheriff. I didn't earn a cent of it. In fact I never dreamed it existed."

"Well, it exists all right. Seven thousand dollars' worth." Putnam pushed off the barn front. "Now, about that supper . . ."

They hiked on over to the house, entered, and Jared lit a lamp. There, he paused to frown at the passbook once more. He put it down upon a little scuffed table in the parlor, jerked his head at Putnam, and passed on over into the kitchen. "You plumb certain Forsythe had no kin?" he asked from over at the cook stove.

"Plumb certain," affirmed Putnam, watching Carson go to work. "Want me to make the java?"

"That'd help," assented Carson. As Putnam walked over, he looked at him, saying: "Listen,

Sheriff, I don't want that money. I don't feel right about it."

Putnam turned, his expression ironic. "How about the rest of it, the land and cattle and all?"

Jared's brows rolled inward and downward. "I'm getting used to that. Those are things I understand and can make out with, like tools. But the money . . . no. It just doesn't sit right with me, taking that, too."

Putnam resumed his work. He used the stirrup pump at the wooden sink to fill the coffee pot. He meticulously measured out the coffee and with all the delicate care of an old-time alchemist ladled it into the pot. He said nothing until he'd placed the pot over a burner. "Like I told you once before, Carson, men our age sometimes get to thinking."

"Well, go on."

"On the way out here, and even after I was waiting around out there in the dusk for you, I sort of wondered exactly what your reaction would be to taking Clem's money."

Jared whipped around, his gaze hardening toward the sheriff. But Putnam knew his man now; he didn't brace into that swift anger; he simply put up a hand without changing expression at all. "Now wait a minute before you blow off steam. Hear me out. I got to wondering what to do if you wouldn't take this money. I thought of a heap of things that could be done with it, until I remembered that under the law when a feller dies intestate . . . that means without leaving a will . . . his estate reverts to the people, which is to say, it reverts to the state, of course with a slice of it going to the federal government."

Jared was listening closely. "You mean to tell me that if I don't take that . . . ?"

"Exactly. If you don't take it, Carson, it goes into the general fund for this state, and that's the end of it."

"Well, hell, Putnam . . ."

"I said hear me out. Shut up for a minute." Putnam rummaged his pockets for the makings and went to work manufacturing a cigarette. "Suppose you were to take it, Carson. Suppose you were to use it to build a first-class school in Cinnebar and name it the Clem Forsythe Public School of Cinnebar." Putnam lit up, exhaled, and peered through blue smoke at Jared Carson. "Well," he said. "What about it?"

"How much of a school would seven thousand dollars build?" asked Jared, after Putnam's idea had lost its surprise for him. "I don't know much about schools."

Putnam gravely smiled. "I don't, either, but I know for a fact that seven thousand dollars would build just about the finest school in the whole danged state. The one we got now in town cost two thousand . . . and that was with all the fellers around town pitching in to put it up, and charging nothing for labor." Putnam suddenly gave a start. "Hey, that damned meat's burning!"

Jared spun around; the skillet behind him was beginning to send up ominous puffs of oily dark smoke. He removed it, plugged the fire hole, and turned back to catch and hold Al Putnam's gaze. "Done," he said. "You just talked up a school for your lousy town, Sheriff."

"Lousy town, Carson?"

"That's what I said . . . lousy town."

"If you feel that way, maybe you'd better just forget . . ."

"Why penalize the little kids, Putnam? They didn't fix it so's Brogan can call the shots down there."

"Whoa," said the lawman softly. "Brogan doesn't call the shots. Him nor anyone else, as long as I'm sheriff."

"Putnam, go tell that to the slab they put up over Clem today."

For a moment Sheriff Putnam's face turned yeasty, turned dangerous. Then he spat out a rough word and crossed to the table, dropped down, and wagged his head back and forth. "You've got a bad habit," he declared. "Someday you're going to needle the wrong man and I'll wind up buying you a hole in the ground beside Clem. As for Brogan . . ."

"Yeah?"

"Forget it, Carson."

219

"Afraid I'm not built like that, Sheriff."

"No, and Clem knew you weren't, too, dog-gone him. All the same, keep your nose out of Brogan's way. He belongs to me. Someday he'll slip up. They all do sooner or later. When that day arrives, Carson, I'll nail his hide to the door so tight no one'll ever be able to pry it loose again."

"You just might have to stand in line and await your turn for that, Sheriff," replied Jared, taking two loaded plates and the coffee pot to the table, putting them down there, and returning for the cups. "But there's someone else who comes first."

As Jared seated himself, the lawman said: "If you're thinking of Pete Aleo . . . don't be a fool, Carson. He eats cowboys for breakfast."

"I wasn't thinking of Aleo. I'll get around to him one of these days, but right now I'm thinking of someone who was a threat to Clem, and is now a threat to me."

Sheriff Putnam sat with a fork poised half-way to his mouth, staring across the table where yellow-orange lamplight made Jared Carson's strong features look like dull bronze. "What the devil are you talking about?"

"Can't say just yet, Sheriff, but within a day or two I'll be able to say." Jared looked up, meeting Putnam's perplexed gaze. "One of the bad things about people is that a feller sometimes reads them wrong. The most inoffensive-looking ones occasionally turn out to be the snakiest."

"You're talking in riddles, Carson."

"Can't help that. Eat your supper and let's discuss the Clem Forsythe Memorial Public School for Cinnebar." Jared didn't smile, but he looked close to it; his near humor was inspired by Al Putnam's disgruntled, tart phrase and his annoyed expression as he resumed eating.

After a while Putnam's curiosity prompted him to say: "Now what's coming? I thought the Aleo-Brogan outfit was your only worry."

"No, Sheriff. It's one of my worries. The other one . . . the one I figure to do something about right away is rustlers."

Putnam's head snapped up. His eyes grew large. "Rustlers? In my bailiwick? Since when?"

"I don't know since when. I only know they're around and they're active."

"How do you know that? What proof have you got?"

Jared met Putnam's stare and gently shook his head. "In a day or two, maybe," he answered. "But not now. Not tonight."

"You figure to take on Brogan first? Carson, I'm beginning to think you're a fool."

Jared finished the last of his meal, drank his coffee, and stood up. Sheriff Putnam was also finished, so he came up, too. They stood a moment, looking straight at one another.

"Think what you like," said Jared. "I never like accusing folks of things until the proof is solidly against them." Jared picked up Putnam's hat and held it out. "Good night, Sheriff. See you in a few days . . . when I have something for you to sink your teeth into. Meanwhile, go ahead and get your town council, or whatever you've got in Cinnebar, to work up the plans for our school."

Al Putnam would have persevered, but he was coming to know and understand Jared Carson, so he said no more, only put on his hat, left the house, and hiked over to his horse by the moonlit big old barn. Jared went with him. When Putnam was astride, he made a wry face downward.

"I want to give you a little warning," he said to Carson. "Amateur detectives have a way of getting killed. Don't increase the odds that already are piling up against you."

Jared made a little farewell gesture with an upraised hand. "Good night, Sheriff. Thanks for coming out . . . and thanks for the advice."

VI

When Putnam rode on southward out of the yard, Jared did not return to the house. He instead waited until those diminishing hoof falls completely faded out before going over to his corralled horse, bringing the beast over to the hitch rail, and rigging it out. When he left the yard, he rode in the opposite direction Al Putnam had taken, going north and east.

There was a crooked old moon above and the good, soft scent of a velvety night all around. The corralled horses left behind nickered long after Jared had left the Five Pointed Star yard. This sound carried well. He heard it, liked it, and kept on going out over the range in the direction he felt sure would bring him to either Keith Winston's ranch or Casey Hedrich's Circle Dot outfit. Eventually it was the scent of a white-oak fire that led Jared's horse out upon a low hill overlooking some dark-hushed buildings lower down and farther out.

There were lights coming from one of those buildings. Jared went slowly onward, got close enough to make out the corrals, the barn, some rickety old outbuildings, and decided this had to be the Winston place. Keith Winston had looked like the kind of cowman who did not labor over non-productive things around the ranch. He would care solicitously for his cattle, but not for his buildings.

It was a good guess. By the time Jared came down athwart the wagon road leading into that yonder yard, he came upon a rough, carved sign giving Winston's name and brand—the Pothook. A long parallel bar that was burned across an animal's ribs, with both ends hooked upward as though to hold pots, was exactly in the shape of a true pothook.

Jared halted near some willows where the scent of cattle was strong. On ahead up at the buildings a dog began to bark furiously. Jared neither heeded the dog nor the buildings; instead, he eased out along that creek, seeking cattle. He found them when, the sounds of his coming carrying on ahead, a number of wicked-horned heads were suddenly thrust out of the thicket. He did not ride in among the cattle but gently eased them on out where the moonlight would strike them. There, he saw that big, long rib brand. There, too, he made a cigarette, lit it behind his hat, and quietly smoked it.

He had not thought the rustler would be Keith Winston but he had wished to see some of Winston's branded animals. Having done this, he went along southward until Winston's ranch lights were lost in the gloom, then cut westerly a little, seeking another road or trail.

He found the road. It was broad and much used. Dust churned into puffs around his horse's legs. Once, where this road passed through a particularly light patch of some alkali like pale earth, Jared got down, walked ahead, leading his horse, saw what he was seeking—buggy tire tracks—remounted, and booted his animal over into a long lope.

He did not spy Casey Hedrich's buildings as

readily as he had Winston's for the elemental reason that the Hedrich Ranch lay upon a long plateau above the rolling, westward plain, and it was hidden by huge old trees. It was the high whistle of a stallion on ahead, among those shielded buildings, that caused Jared to stop, to keen the night a moment, then pass on again, but much slower now.

He was almost within sighting distance of the Hedrich buildings when he spooked a little bunch of drowsing cattle beside a stone trough that was fed by a rusted old pipe coming directly out of the near hillside. As before, over at the Winston place, these animals sprang up and peered, but did not bolt, although it was clear that they would do so the second Jared came too close. He dismounted, glided ahead, saw the big Circle Dot branded on the right rib of those Hedrich critters, returned to his horse, and stood for a long time, gazing on over toward the buildings.

Here, there were two lighted buildings. One appeared to be a rather large house while the other building, easier seen from the distance, less obscured by trees because it was near the barn and working corral where no trees had been permitted to grow, was clearly a bunkhouse. This fitted in with what Jared had deduced about young Casey Hedrich. Unlike Clem Forsythe and Keith Winston—and now Jared Carson—the Hedrich Circle Dot outfit was not a one-man operation. Casey Hedrich had hired hands. But there was something here that did not jibe with Jared's thoughts. That big ranch yonder was obviously prosperous; the buildings were well cared for, the corrals were strong and large and in good repair, and obviously those cowboys in that lighted bunkhouse were paid regularly, otherwise they would not be there. Then why, Jared wondered, was Casey Hedrich a cattle thief?

Perhaps it wasn't young Casey. Possibly it was some man working for Circle Dot. It was not unusual for overly ambitious riders, wishing to get their own stake, to rustle on the side while in the employ of perfectly honest cowmen. As Jared mounted and swung away, he considered the most profitable thing for him to do now was to ask questions, find out all he could about Casey Hedrich and his riders. This posed a problem, though. Aside from Al Putnam there was no one he could interrogate about Hedrich, and, after the remarks he'd made at supper this very night, he could not now even ask Putnam, otherwise the sheriff would guess who Jared suspected. But there was one other way. He could catch Casey Hedrich by himself and do his questioning where the answers would have to be first-hand.

All the way back to Five Pointed Star he turned this over in his mind. Hedrich, he knew, was wary of him. He'd seen it in the younger man's face when he'd choused Keith Winston in his own ranch yard. He'd also seen it at Clem Forsythe's funeral down at Cinnebar. Still, he needed some answers, and, lacking an alternative, he would seek out young Hedrich alone and ask them. If, afterward, trouble came as a result of those questions, he would be sure of his ground. No man fights hard in his own defense unless he believes himself in danger; this was just as true of rustlers as of honest men. Anyway, there would be trouble regardless, over this rustling, so, he told himself as he came down out of the quiet night into his own yard again, it might as well be now as later.

He offsaddled in front of the barn, heaved his rig over the hitch rail, put up his animal, and went on across to the house. That big old lop-sided moon was almost directly overhead by this time, its soft-silver light turning the roundabout world into a place of gentled harshness and melancholy quiet. Over by the barn his chestnut gelding nickered at the other corralled animals. The others nickered back. It was a good sound, a sound of homing animals content and drowsy. A long way off a cow bawled, and nearer a bull made his incongruous, broken wail, which was altogether different from the sound he'd have made if there were danger.

Jared hooked both arms around a porch upright and leaned there, looking far out where northward hills lay softly crumpled. He thought of many things, his mind slipping its normal shackles to touch here and there upon little figments, mostly out of context, until after a while it settled down upon the image of that beautiful woman he'd seen some ten hours earlier at the graveside of the man who had given Jared all this.

Then his thoughts turned inward, turned alternately bleak and warm. It was not the least bit difficult to understand why Brogan had killed Clem Forsythe now, but it made Clem's death all the more bitter to think about. If anyone had a reason to hurt Clem, it hadn't been Brogan—it had been the beautiful girl. Jared pulled upright off the post, struck it lightly, and scowled. Just what, he wondered, did Clem mean to her, or for that matter, what did Harry Brogan mean?

VII

He was in the saddle again before dawn, but this time astride one of the Forsythe horses, a solid big black beast with a light rein and a knowledgeable way of traveling. He crossed the range roughly in the same manner as the night before, passed far out and around the Winston place, and struck ahead for that dusty roadway with the buggy tracks. There, he did not hurry. It was still too dark to be seen, which was why he'd come out this early, and being in the general vicinity of Hedrich's place in the dark, which was what he wished for, he had no need for haste. Killing time until sunup, he rode out and around the Circle Dot buildings, assessed the range there, found it good, then went back easterly until he came upon a little wooded barranca overlooking a ragged erosion gulch. Here, he dismounted, put his animal back out of sight, left it tied, and strolled on out to the barranca's lip to squat down and make a smoke for breakfast.

It was by this time beginning to brighten somewhat off in the watery east. A gradual steely softness settled upon the world, making it possible to see around and ahead. He hunkered there, watching those yonder buildings across his gulch firm up, take shape and substance and dimension. A rooster crowed over there. Some impatient horses nickered in a corral. Southward somewhere a cow bawled, other cattle answered, and Jared could imagine them lumbering up out of their beds, hungry and impatient for first light.

He could, from this slightly northward position, get a good look across onto Hedrich's plateau. He could even see the main house now, which he hadn't been able to see the night before. It sat deep among cottonwood trees, appearing old and comfortable and low-roofed. A man emerged from the bunkhouse, stood a second in the dusty yard, looking right, looking left, and pleasurably scratching his middle. All Jared could make out about this man was that he was not young; being hatless—shirtless, too, for that matter—his balding head shone palely in morning's milky light. The man cleared his throat, lustily spat, turned, and stumped along toward the barn, evidently with the intention of forking feed to those impatient horses.

Time passed, the eastern horizon brightened, a delicate shade of blue firmed up, brightened, became diluted by pink, and somewhat later the sun itself came popping up over a far-away pinnacle. Light rushed down across the land, striking dazzlingly against glass windows over on Hedrich's plateau, striking with a fierce flash upon bits of metal here and there. The range jumped forth out of night's murkiness. It became an unburdened, empty-looking world all its own. Men left Hedrich's bunkhouse. Jared counted three of them. Including the older cowboy who'd emerged earlier, Circle Dot apparently had four full-time riders. With no knowledge of just how many cattle Casey Hedrich ran, Jared calculated, from the number of his riders, it would have to be between four and five thousand head.

He made another smoke. Not because he felt any particular inclination to smoke, but because he was bored with his grim resolve to catch young Hedrich riding out and stalk him. But the thing didn't taste good, so he punched it out after just one inhalation. The riders ate at Circle

Dot's cook shack, went along to the barn, rigged out, and loped away from the ranch in pairs. For security's sake Jared watched those men very carefully. He did not mean to be caught squatting up there like a bronco Indian horse thief, and because he so intently kept track of the cowboys he neglected to see another person go from the main house to the barn, also saddle up, and also ride out. He didn't sight that fifth rider until, where the trees thinned out southward, he sighted swift movement. He became instantly alert and annoyed with himself. Obviously this solitary rider bearing southward had come from Circle Dot. Just as obviously, it very well could be Casey Hedrich.

Jared went to his own animal, swung up, and eased away eastward until he was reasonably certain no one could identify him from the ranch, assuming someone might be watching, before he shook out the reins and went loping southerly at a wide angle so as to intercept that other rider. By this time there was a good warmth settling upon the range. The northward hills stood out starkly clear and seemingly close enough to touch. Cattle, grazing as was their custom in small bunches, looked up warily as Jared went past. Once he came up onto a pair of yearling coyotes worrying an ancient pile of bones, and caused those two fleet animals to explode into fleeing puffs of gray-tan hair, one heading rapidly west, his companion racing off in the opposite direction.

Jared caught sight of that other rider where the land dipped in a long swale. Horse and rider came up over the easterly rim of that swale, picked up speed, and loped along for nearly a mile before slowing to an easy walk again. Jared ran on behind his prey, slowed when only a mile separated them, and closed the distance carefully. It was apparent the other rider had no inkling that Jared was behind, stalking him. Not until he was well within hailing distance, a matter of a hundred yards or so, and he called out sharply, commandingly, did that forward horse get hauled up short and reined around.

At less than three hundred feet Jared saw his mistake. That rider over there wasn't Casey Hedrich at all; it was his aunt. Jared, never once in his recent pursuit, had dreamed that other person would be anyone but young Hedrich, so he was surprised now, and later disgruntled with himself, too. But he had those intervening yards to think of something, so when he came up and halted, he leaned both hands upon the saddle horn and said: "Good morning, ma'am. It's kind of unusual to find folks riding out before breakfast."

Those gunmetal, liquid, large eyes coolly studied Jared. That full white blouse rose and fell. "Not on Circle Dot range, Mister Carson, and if you mean me . . . I do this every morning

232

when the weather is good. I love the beginning of day and its shadowed ending."

"I thought you were someone else, ma'am."

"Casey? He'll be along after he's finished some work at the office. I was going on over to one of the troughs to see if it needs repairing. One of the men reported yesterday that it was broken." Those interested, gray eyes considered Jared a moment. "Would you like to ride along? That way you'll see him when he gets over here."

Jared turned and went along slowly beside her. A dozen questions ran riot in his head but he asked none of them, not right away at any rate. They cut around a large herd of fat cows with calves, spied two shaggy bulls with those cows, and eventually came to a solitary old windmill standing in the middle of nowhere with a stone trough at its base. She lifted an arm, pointing toward that trough.

"One of our riders said two bulls started fighting there. One of them struck the trough and broke it."

Jared looked ahead. He saw no break but he did notice a dark stain around the trough's base where water had settled into the earth.

"It happens," he philosophized. "Tell me, Miss Hedrich, how many cattle does Circle Dot run?"

She turned, gazed steadily at him for a long moment, then looked straight ahead, over at the nearing trough. "Four thousand cows, Mister

Carson . . . and you don't have a very good memory, do you?"

Jared turned, considered the handsome profile, rummaged his memory for any reason she might have to make such a remark, and said doubtingly: "Ma'am . . . ?"

"My name is Lisa Crandall, not Hedrich. We were introduced at the funeral, remember?"

Jared's eyes whipped away, also went ahead to that trough. He muttered a fumbling apology, thankful for the weathered darkness of his skin so she could not see him redden. But if Lisa Crandall had meant for her rebuff to be as pointed as he took it, she gave no sign of this at all when they hauled back near the trough and she swung down, went ahead, and peered into the trough.

"It's broken all right!" she called back where he was holding their horses. "And here's some dark hair. The cowboy was right, it looks like there was a bull fight here." She straightened up, half turned, saw Jared's solemn gaze upon her, and sank down upon an edge of the stone trough, put her head slightly to one side, and returned his look. "Mister Carson, I'm curious about you."

He had his ready answer for this. "And I'm curious about you."

She nearly smiled over at him. She said softly: "I know. I saw it in your face when you rode up. I think I saw it in your face at the funeral, too." She got comfortable upon the trough's rough edge, settled herself, and said: "All right, ask what you like."

"Clem Forsythe," he murmured, and she nodded at him.

"It would have gotten around to him sooner or later, wouldn't it have, Mister Carson? He was a kind man. I was fond of him."

"Just fond, ma'am?"

"Just fond, Mister Carson. If he told you anything else, then it was one-sided."

"He had you in his mind. He wanted to marry you."

A shadow passed across her face and was gone. "I'm sorry," she said very quietly. "But if I'd wanted to get married, he'd have been the kind of man I'd have looked for."

"Instead of Harry Brogan?"

Now her expression altered, the buttermilk richness of her cheeks and throat faintly colored. Those gunmetal eyes that put Jared Carson in mind of a wintry day got hard, steely. "Harry Brogan," she declared, enunciating with a sharpness, "is nothing to me and never has been. I don't like him. I don't trust him, and I've told him so."

Jared shifted weight over where he stood, still with the reins of their horses in his hands. He was uncomfortable now, under that cold stare, and muttered: "Well, that's all my questions I guess."

"Then," spoke up Lisa Crandall, her tone becoming less cool, less formal, "it's my turn, Mister Carson. Why did you practically throw my nephew and Keith Winston off Five Pointed Star the day they rode over to introduce themselves to you?"

"Yeah," he growled low in his throat. "I figured that'd be first. Well, ma'am, as I told those two . . . where I come from we don't stand back and see a good man shot down without a chance. That was sticking in my craw the day they showed up." Jared glanced away from her, and then at her again. "All right, I was hasty. I was wrong, doing that. I know that now."

Lisa Crandall looked solemn. "I thought it had to be something like that. In fact, on the way home from Clem's funeral, that's what I told Casey. You see I'd met you then, and I knew that was the kind of a man you are."

"What kind, ma'am?"

"Quick-tempered. Fiery, Mister Carson. Intensely loyal. Probably good with weapons, too, because you're not a boy any more and yet you're still alive, in spite of that hot temper."

He studied her beautiful features and the easy, supple length of her. She was everything any man could ever hope for in a woman, but it annoyed him that she could read him like this, so he said a trifle tartly: "If you had a man, ma'am, you'd know how it is with all men, all men that grow up with the same values in life."

She hung fire just a second, then said: "I had a man, Mister Carson. We were to be married, but he was killed during the war."

She added nothing to this, nothing that would alleviate his sudden feeling of wishing to bite off his tongue. She let him stand there with his awkwardness and his embarrassment until he knew he was being deliberately whittled down.

But after a while she got up off the trough, crossed over slowly, and halted in front of him. She was a head shorter than he was; she had to tilt her face to look into his eyes. "I didn't say I blamed you for being as you are, Mister Carson. As a matter of fact I told Casey that the Cinnebar country has needed a man like you for a long, long time. But I also told him he shouldn't become too involved with you because you brought trouble with you, when you came here, and there is a very good chance you'll die here."

"Brogan again," said Jared. "No, ma'am, I may die here but it won't be Brogan who does that job." He could catch the fragrance of her hair; it was in him powerfully to reach out and touch her. Instead, though, he half twisted from the waist, ran a narrowed look far out, and said: "Rider coming."

"That will be Casey."

"I want to see him alone. Maybe it'd be better if you went on back now, Miss Lisa."

"Why? Why do you want to see Casey alone?"

"I'd rather not say."

She touched his arm very lightly, bringing his face back around. Her gaze up at him was cool and challenging. "In that case," she murmured to him, "I'll stay."

He stood very close to her, their similar steely eyes dueling. "Then stay," he said, his tone roughening. He pulled in a shallow breath and spoke again, this time saying something that was overpoweringly in his mind but that had little bearing on anything either of them had said to the other up to now. "I don't blame Brogan. You're worth killing for. Only Brogan did it the coward's way. I aim to settle with him for that."

VIII

When Casey loped up, looking curious about the man with his aunt, a peculiar kind of tension existed there around the stone trough. Lisa was over by the windmill seemingly engrossed in a re-examination of the broken trough, while Jared Carson was standing by their two horses, a cigarette drooping from his lips, his hat thumbed far back, and his expression, which was turned toward Casey, carefully speculative and deceptively blank.

Casey got down, nodded at Jared, looked

over at Lisa, and said: "Got here quicker than I figured. Is the thing busted like Frank said?"

Lisa kept her eyes carefully upon Casey when she replied: "It's cracked badly enough not to hold water. I think if you sent a man over tomorrow with one of the wagons and some cement, he could repair it."

Casey nodded, swung back, and confronted Jared. "You're a long way from home. Must've left before sunup to get over this far so soon."

Jared removed his cigarette, considered its little red tip, knowing very well that over by the trough Lisa Crandall was watching him, waiting for his answer. He dropped the smoke, ground it out, and raised his head. Lisa's dead-level gaze pushed up against him across that little distance. While still regarding her, Jared growled—"Yeah."—to Casey, turned on his heel, swung up, and reined around. As he hooked his black horse over into a loose lope, he heard Casey say something but he did not look back.

He rode a goodly distance before he slowed, spat, and told his horse that, if that woman had belonged to him, he'd have bent her over one knee and whaled her good for interfering in the business of men. But what he really thought was that he just was not mean enough to accuse Casey Hedrich of being a rustler, woman or no woman.

By the time he got back to the ranch most of that sour resentment had been winnowed out of him by the lovely day, the good warmth, and the fact that he'd encountered several handsome bunches of Five Pointed Star cattle, all of them in good shape, all of them contentedly grazing.

He offsaddled and turned the black horse loose. There would be other times, he told himself, and other places; he'd get Casey Hedrich off by himself one of these days. He left the barn area for the house, was midway between those two buildings when out of the eastward distance a Winchester's flat, sharp bark broke the hush. Something struck fiercely into the ground five feet onward, blowing up a stinging geyser of sharp-sided little gritty stones. Jared flinched but did not drop; instead, he broke away in a hard run, got to the porch, and, six-gun fisted, flattened back in cool shadows against the house.

The silence returned. Everything was as serenely bright and golden as before. It was as though he'd imagined that gunshot, that near miss. But he hadn't; where that bullet had struck there was a gouged-out place. There was no one in sight, though; the land was seemingly quite empty, quite benign. Over by the barn his saddle hung where he'd tossed it, over the hitch rail. Farther along, those corralled horses were snuffling, ambling aimlessly in their confinement with good sunlight upon them.

He swiped sweat off his forehead without otherwise moving, and intently scanned that easterly run of land. There was nothing moving out there. There was no sound. If that bush-whacker had not sped away as Jared rushed for cover, when he wouldn't have noticed it, then whoever the man was, he was still out there. But except for one spindly little stand of creek willows, there was no cover for a killer—or his horse. At least not that he could see.

For a long while he was content for things to remain as they were, but after an hour had dragged by without another shot, without a man becoming visible anywhere around, Jared put up his gun, and sidled along toward the edge of the house. There, beginning to loosen in the shoulders, he stepped on around. This time the Winchester's blast was much closer. This time the slug did not entirely miss. Jared felt the tug at his shirt side at exactly the same instant he heard the muzzle blast. He jumped back around the corner upon the little porch, his breath coming short. Whoever that ambusher was hadn't gone away; he'd simply belly-crawled southward where he could see under the porch overhang and along the east side of the house. And he'd come down much closer, too; that gunshot had been much louder, the bullet much closer.

Jared backtracked to his front door, reached behind, lifted the latch, kicked the panel inward, and jumped inside. He closed the door very carefully, put up his six-gun for the second time, passed into the bedroom where his saddle gun stood propped upon the wall in its boot, yanked the carbine out, and stealthily made his way out to the kitchen. A man didn't have to survive two near misses to be incensed against an assassin, but it certainly augmented his resentment if he did survive.

From a kitchen window he made a minute examination of that quiet land east of the house. There was no movement out there and he had not actually expected to see any. Whoever that assassin was, he was no novice at this stalking game.

An hour passed, an hour and a half. The overhead sky was mottling with brassy clouds from where the sun was slipping off westward, its color changing subtly from yellow to orange. Jared put aside his Winchester, made a meal, and ate it. Still nothing changed anywhere in his sight beyond the house. He cleaned up his dishes, taking a lot of time at this. He even shaved, being prudent enough to place his six-gun beside the basin ready at hand while he did this, but afterward, believing the assassin had finally given up and departed, he took up his saddle gun, glided silently out of the house by the rear door, moved along to where a gunman could partially see him, see movement anyway, and held his breath.

No shot came. The roundabout hush was as

serene, as deep and solid as ever. He stepped out into full view. Still no shot came. He grasped the Winchester in both hands across his body and started walking straight out eastward.

He found a shiny spent bullet casing, with the aid of a co-operating sun, where this brass object had been ejected. He also found grass pressed flat and boot-toe marks where a fairly tall man had been lying. The elbow indentations were also there, as well as the faint impression of a big belt buckle.

He tracked that man back nearly half a mile until he found where the assassin had left his horse just beyond the curve of eastward land. He paused here to study those shod-horse marks. He kneeled for a long time, then went along to where more tracks led him directly to the more distant spot from the house where the ambusher had initially fired down into the yard. Here he picked up another spent casing and pocketed it. But what puzzled Jared now was that those ridden horse imprints came out of the west, the same direction Jared himself had also come not much later than the assassin's tracks indicated he had ridden, somewhat earlier.

He went back down to his barn, put aside the Winchester, and fed the horses. Afterward, with daylight fast fading, he returned to the house, eased down there upon the porch, and furrowed his forehead in puzzled thought. Initially he'd thought it might have been a Circle Dot rider who'd drygulched him. But this didn't hold water unless Hedrich had sent a man out before he knew Jared was over on Circle Dot range, which wasn't likely, for as yet Hedrich had no reason to want him assassinated. At least no reason Jared could imagine. He also thought of Keith Winston. Those two were the only people he knew west of Five Pointed Star. He'd been a little disagreeable with both Winston and Hedrich, but not nearly unpleasant enough to warrant an attempt on his life.

Ultimately, though, he discarded the notion that either Winston or Hedrich had anything to do with his near killing. Casey wasn't a killer; Jared couldn't controvert what he knew of young Hedrich into a gunman no matter how he tried. And Keith Winston, well, while there was a bird of a different color, he couldn't make a killer out of Winston. If Winston wanted a man, he'd go after him in a stand-up, face-to-face fight. Still, whoever that man had been, he'd just about matched Winston in build, and he'd come riding out of the west. It was a genuine riddle. Perhaps some hired killer, some envious cowboy from Circle Dot maybe, or just some local gun hand who fiercely resented Clem Forsythe's giving his ranch to a total stranger.

Jared made a smoke, lit it prudently behind his cupped hands, and instantly blew out the light. A coyote made its sad cry far out and an owl swooped low in front of the porch. He heard these things, and then saw them, but paid them no attention. Somewhere, coming softly down the dark, settling night, was a ridden horse; he made out its even-cadenced walking easily in the quiet night, took up his Winchester, gauged the distance, and ran lightly, swiftly over to the barn. There, he paused to listen, to assess the correct direction, then ran on northward until the last protective corral was reached, where he dropped deliberately to one knee, cocked the Winchester, half raised it, and waited.

That oncoming horse neither slackened its gait nor increased it. Neither did it deviate from its onward course. Jared lowered his Winchester. Instinct told him that it was no enemy, or, if it was, it wasn't a very astute enemy, riding on in without making an attempt to conceal his approach. It was that in-between time when the sun was quite gone and the moon had not yet risen. There was no worthwhile light to see by, only a diaphanous vagueness that heralded day's end and night's beginning.

That rider out there abruptly halted. The silence became greater than ever for a quiet moment. Jared strained to sight a silhouette and failed. The horse started moving again, came right on down into the yard, and at the last moment Jared made out both animal and rider. He got up, struck at dust on his knee, cradled the Winchester, and stepped out almost directly into the horse's path. At once the animal snorted and set back, stiff-legged. A ripped-out hard curse came from up above where the rider was abruptly pitched forward against his saddle swells.

"Good evening, Sheriff," said Jared. "You know, if you're going to slip up on folks in the dark, it might not be a bad idea for you to carry a lantern."

"What the hell's the matter with you!" snapped Sheriff Putnam, steadying himself to dismount, his voice rushing angrily at Carson. "What'd you think you're doing . . . sneaking around like this?"

Jared grounded his carbine, fished for the two brass Winchester casings, and, when Putnam stamped angrily up, he held them out in his open right palm. Putnam bent, made a face, reared back, took the two cartridge cases, and held them up close to his eyes.

"Someone left those behind this afternoon, Sheriff," Jared explained, "when he tried to bush-whack me."

Putnam's eyes swept up and slowly widened. "Bushwhack you?" he said in a rising way. "Are you plumb sure?"

Jared smiled at this question. His strong teeth shone white. "I'm sure all right. When he missed me the first time, he lay out there eastward of the house, crawled down closer, and tried a second time. If it wasn't so danged dark, I'd show you right where he left his horse and right where he lay belly-down both times he tried to wing me."

Putnam, his earlier annoyance entirely forgotten, caught up the reins of his animal and walked along beside Jared toward the barn. He kept jingling those two cartridge cases inside one big fist. As he was tying up, he said: "You got any ideas, Carson?"

"All I can tell you for certain, Putnam, is that he came from the west."

"The west? Hell, man, there's nothing out there but miles and miles of range."

"Correction, Sheriff. Keith Winston is out there. So is Casey Hedrich's Circle Dot with a bunkhouse full of cowboys."

Putnam yanked upright. "Don't be foolish," he expostulated. "Neither Winston nor Hedrich would try a bushwhack."

"How about Casey's riders? Can you say as much for them?"

The lawman looked down into his hand again. He jiggled the casings and muttered: "Let's take these things up to the house and light a lamp."

"They won't tell you anything except that someone who owns a Winchester carbine fired 'em, but come along. I need a cup of coffee anyway."

Jared led off, still with his Winchester cradled across one arm. He told Putnam what had happened as they crossed the yard, and once inside, where he lit a lamp and took it prudently away from any windows, he said: "I'll make some coffee. You had supper?"

Putnam nodded without speaking. He was intently examining those two casings, his face screwed up and his eyes narrowed into slits. He turned them over and over, studied the firing-pin indentations a long time, and finally drifted on over into the kitchen where Jared was working at the stove.

"Nothing," he said. "Unless I could match them with other casings fired from the same carbine, they tell me nothing."

When the coffee was ready, Jared brought the pot and two cups over to the table, sat down, and exchanged a wry look with Al Putnam.

IX

"It doesn't make much sense, though," said Putnam. "Maybe you've been a little short with folks and maybe a few might resent you riding in and inheriting Five Pointed Star as easy as falling off a log. But, hell, Carson, those aren't reasons enough for someone to want to shoot you."

"Then why, Sheriff . . . and who?"

Putnam carefully placed those two brass casings upon the table in front of his half emptied coffee cup and morosely wagged his head back and forth. "I don't know. I can't imagine. Outside of Winston and Circle Dot, there's no one west of here." Putnam's face brightened. "Maybe he didn't really come from the west. Did you think of that? Maybe he just rode up from that direction to throw you off."

"Well," murmured Jared dryly, "he sure succeeded. But that's not the point. What I want to know more than why he tried it, is who is he? The trouble with living alone is that, if someone's out to assassinate you, he's got all the advantage. All you've got, Sheriff, is the carcass for him to aim at."

Putnam seemed to be silently agreeing with this as he took up his cup and drank off the dregs of his coffee. As he put the cup aside, he said: "You could move into Cinnebar."

"Sure. I could saddle up and slope, too, but I don't figure to do either. Tell me, Sheriff, how come you to ride out here tonight?"

Putnam made a rueful face. "You think I did it? Let me tell you, Carson, if I had, I'd have finished it."

Jared reached far over, refilling the lawman's cup, and leaned back again. He was smiling with his eyes only. "He was taller and thinner than you are, Sheriff. He wore a big belt buckle and had feet a yard long. No, it wasn't you. What brought you out tonight?"

"Well, I did like you said. I talked to the town councilmen. They were bowled over with surprise and about as tickled as a kitten in an asparagus patch over your offer to give 'em a seven-thousand-dollar brand spanking new school. I think, if I'd pushed it, they'd have voted you in as honorary mayor."

"But I'm not giving the school . . . Clem is."

"All right, have it your own way. Clem's name'll be on it. That's all settled. The council wants to know when you can ride into town and talk about this with its members."

"Tomorrow," said Jared. "That satisfy you?"

"Yup," said Putnam, and, although there was nothing further to say, he sat on. After a while he said: "One other thing."

Jared's eyes gleamed again. "Yeah, I had you pegged for a stubborn cuss, Sheriff."

"What do you mean?"

"The school was only half the reason for you to ride this far tonight."

"All right, what's the other half?"

"What I said about rustlers."

Putnam bobbed his head up and down, saying: "Correct. You said you'd have something to tell me in a day or so. Carson, I'm a calendar watcher."

Jared left the table, got a pencil and some paper, re-seated himself, and drew his brand, the Five Pointed Star. He looked up. "You following this, Putnam?"

"Like a fish after a bucket full of green worms. Go on with it. That's your brand . . . Clem's old Five Pointed Star."

"And this," said Jared, drawing a large circle with a dot in the center, "is Casey Hedrich's brand. Right?"

"Right as rain."

"Now," said Jared, drawing an altogether new brand beside the other two upon the same sheet of paper, "this is a combination of my brand and Hedrich's mark. You take my Five Pointed Star like this . . . you watching?"

"Of course I'm watching."

"Next, you draw a circle plumb around my Five Pointed Star, like this."

"All right, now you've drawn a wagon wheel. What about it?"

Jared leaned back and tossed aside the pencil. He told Putnam of the shot heifer, how her rib brand had been cut out of the hide in a circle, and sat there, waiting for Putnam to grasp the significance.

Putnam did, almost at once, but he said nothing; he, instead, reached over, caught up that marked piece of paper, and studied it for a long while in total silence. After he carefully put the paper back down, he glanced over at Jared, his eyes kindling with a slow anger.

"Hedrich?" he asked. "But it doesn't make sense, Carson. Let me tell you something about that boy. His pa built the Circle Dot from scratch in the early days when a man branded his critters with one hand and kept a cocked pistol ready in his other hand. After twenty years the old man had as good a ranch as there is in this state. He wasn't rich but he was damned well off."

"That was a long time ago, Sheriff."

"Sure it was. But the Hedrichs've been making money ever since. Besides, I've known Casey since he was a little kid. He'd no more steal cattle than he'd fly."

"And his riders . . . how about them?"

"Hell, no," insisted Putnam. "They're old Circle Dot hands to a man. Why, old Frank Silvius, the range boss, has been with the Hedrichs since I first hit this country."

Jared threw up his hands. "Then who shot that heifer, Sheriff, and who designed a new brand?"

"You don't know for a fact that anyone did, Carson. All you know is that someone shot a heifer and cut out her brand."

"Sheriff," said Jared quietly, "that's enough for me. As for Circle Dot . . . that's the only outfit around here that could work my brand over into something also using the Circle Dot brand. Winston couldn't. He's got a pothook. None of the other branded critters I've seen since lighting in this Cinnebar country could, either."

Al Putnam removed his hat, placed it carefully upon the supper table, and stared hard at it.

"Something's beginning to bother me," he mused aloud. "Let's just assume you're right, Carson. Let's just assume someone *is* rustling. You know what it looks like to me? Not that anyone from Circle Dot is moving in on your herd, but more like some third party is moving in on *both* you and Circle Dot. Listen a minute. An ambitious rustler who'd want to build up a big herd fast couldn't do it just off your four hundred or so cows. But if he rustled from *both* the Five Pointed Star *and* the Circle Dot, reworked both those brands over into his wagon wheel . . . hell, man, within a year he'd have more cattle than you've got right now."

Jared turned this over thoughtfully in his mind. It made sense. In fact it made very good sense, and he felt like kicking himself for not having thought of it himself. "I came awfully close to making a bad mistake today," he murmured, thinking back to Lisa Crandall and Casey Hedrich over at the broken stone trough on Circle Dot range. "Putnam, I came within an ace of calling Hedrich a cow thief this morning . . . and with Miss Lisa standing right there, too."

Putnam made a rumbling sound deep in his throat. His gaze turned punishing. "Carson, when are you going to quit acting like a buck Indian on the warpath around here? I told you before you weren't making it easy for folks to like you. When are you going to learn?"

"I'm learning, Sheriff, I'm learning. I said I *almost* called him a cow thief. I didn't say I'd actually called him one."

"Yeah, but sometimes it's as bad to think evil of a man as to accuse him of evil. Did you talk to Casey at all about this?"

"No," said Jared, and winced at the recollection of his rudeness back at the Circle Dot water trough. "I didn't say anything in fact, just got on my horse and came home."

"Well, at least you did one right thing anyway." Putnam leaned back in a teetering way upon his chair. He studied the ceiling for a while before bringing his gaze back down and fastening it upon Jared Carson. "Who would be doing it?" he asked.

"I've been in your lousy country one week, Sheriff, and you've been here probably fifteen years. Why ask me a question like that?"

"Thinking out loud is all," muttered Putnam. "Say, do you know if any of your critters are missing? I mean, have you made a tally yet or held a roundup?"

"No. When Clem was alive, he said we'd hold off on rounding up because some of the cows'd be late calving."

"How about Casey? You reckon he's started gathering yet?"

Jared shrugged. "Got no idea," he said. "Although, when I was over there today, there was no sign of a chuck wagon being rigged up for the range, or anything."

Putnam brought his chair back down with a crash. "You know something?" he exclaimed. "If this isn't just a myth, we're up against a damned smart rustler. I'll tell you why. If neither of you fellers even knows yet whether you're being stolen blind, it's because that damned rustler realizes neither of you've begun rounding up yet. If he's been working, say, for two or three months and working hard, I'll make you and Casey a little bet. I'll wager he's cleaned the pair of you out of better'n a hundred head already."

This, too, made sense to Jared. He felt around for his makings, dropped his head, and scowlingly began twisting up a smoke. He lit up, exhaled, and stared flintily over at Sheriff Putnam. "I'll ride out and take a look tomorrow," he said quietly. "Clem told me he had something like four hundred cows."

"Go one better than that," said Putnam. "Ride over Circle Dot range, too. They're supposed to have close to four thousand cows."

"That's what Miss Lisa told me today. That's right. All right, Sheriff, this is going to take more than one day, but I'll do it."

Putnam's face began to cloud a little. "Miss Lisa told you?" he said. "That's the second time tonight you've mentioned Lisa Crandall. You're not figuring to move in on Brogan's territory like Clem did, are you, Carson?"

"For the record, Sheriff, she told me she liked Clem but did not love him, and that she had no use whatever for Harry Brogan."

"That personal, was she?" said Putnam, his voice turning thoughtful, his expression becoming speculative.

Jared felt his face reddening, turning hot. He said a little sharply: "It was an accident. I thought she was Casey when I rode up behind her. As for it being personal . . . forget it, Putnam."

"Sure, Carson. Sure. I'll forget it. But what about Brogan? If he hears . . ."

"Well?" demanded Jared, seeing Putnam's expression undergo a complete change.

"Maybe he *did* hear, Carson. Did that occur to you? Maybe he heard about you and Miss Lisa already."

Jared stood up. He was angry now and it showed. "What nonsense are you figuring out now?" he demanded.

"Carson, you said you doubted that the feller who tried to bushwhack you was Winston or Casey Hedrich. You said you had no idea who it might have been or why he tried it. Well, let me remind you of something. Clem Forsythe took Miss Lisa out a few times."

"I didn't take her . . ."

"But you were alone with her out on the Circle

Dot range. You could've been seen with her. I've already told you Brogan's got quite a bunch of men working for him. Any one of those men could've been riding over there and seen you with her, Carson, and, if that's so, don't you ever think they wouldn't be willing to plug you and earn an extra five hundred dollars from Brogan for doing him such a big favor."

Jared reached for his chair, sank down again, and stared at Putnam. "But . . . hell, Sheriff, I wasn't alone with her more'n maybe twenty minutes." Suddenly Jared remembered how close they had stood. During that time an army could have ridden up, seen them, and ridden off again, and he wouldn't have seen it.

"Sheriff, whoever he was, he *did* come riding down here from that direction."

"He was here ahead of you, wasn't he?"

"Yes."

Putnam got up, put on his hat, and said: "Listen, do us both a favor. Don't go near her again while I'm out of the country. Wait until I get back. Promise me that, will you, Carson?"

Jared looked at him, then got up. "Out of the country . . . ?"

"Sure, what'd you expect? Look, if someone's going into the cow business on a big scale in this state, he's got to have a registered brand. I could wire the capital for information about whoever's got a wagon wheel brand registered down here, but telegraph clerks sometimes get awful loose tongues, so I'll take the stage out in the morning, check the records myself, and come fanning it right back. The trip, going and coming, will take maybe four days. For a lousy four days promise me you'll stay plumb away from Lisa Crandall."

Jared nodded. "I'll promise, only I can't answer for her."

Putnam squinted, snorted derisively, and hiked out to the front door. There, as he passed over into the outside starry night, he heaved a big sigh. "Every damned time I come out here, it's something. Well, good night."

"Good night. Make a fast trip and look me up when you get back."

"That I will," mumbled Putnam. "That I will."

X

Jared had two things to do the following day. He was supposed to ride into Cinnebar and see the town council, and he'd promised Al Putnam he'd go look over two large herds of cattle. There was only one way to keep his word in both cases so he arose before sunup again, rigged out, and left the yard with the world drowsily quiet and gloomy around him.

He began meeting his Five Pointed Star cattle a mile out. He angled back and forth over the range for two hours, even after sunup, estimating numbers of critters in the bunches he encountered. In this manner he arrived at a rough tally of his cattle—three hundred head!

He paused for a while up in the shade of some foothill oaks, juggled the figures in his head, and came up with the same number again. He made one more big sashay down across his own range, then swung west and rode slowly while he totaled up the figures again. This time he came up with slightly under three hundred head, and this time he'd been closer with his counting. It was beginning to appear that Sheriff Putnam had been right, that whoever the rustler was, he'd been active for a long time before this. Perhaps for a long time before Clem Forsythe had been killed.

Over where Circle Dot's critters grazed, with good springtime sun across his shoulders, Jared began another tally. This one would take much longer and encompass a lot more countryside, but he was confident he could make it before sundown if he hurried. He had not forgotten Hedrich's riders, though, and in order to see them before he himself was seen, Jared made a point of staying to either the high ground or the sunken places where a man on horseback would be hidden from casual view.

Hedrich's cattle were in top shape. His cows appeared to be nearly through calving, which appeared to Jared to be the result of timed breeding; no stockman worth his salt wanted cows calving while snow was still upon the ground, but every stockman wanted his calves dropped as soon as the final snow melted off and springtime grass began pushing through, for then cows made good rich milk and lots of it, which, consequentially, raised big, stout, greasy-fat calves. That's the way it looked over on Hedrich's range. The cows were dark red and blooming, the calves were loose hided and sassy with health. But because Jared was not entirely familiar with the range over here he had to waste a lot of time feeling his way. Still, by midday it began to appear to him that Hedrich did not have very many replacement heifers, the young she stock open-range cowmen usually raised and relied upon to replace older cows when the older critters began to loose their teeth so that they could not winter well.

The more he rode, the more this lack became apparent. He encountered some replacement heifers, perhaps three or four hundred, but this was a very low figure—no more than ten percent or under—of the number of cows Circle Dot ran on the range. He was interested in this. So interested that he passed up over a little land swell, halted upon its wind-scourged top-out, and thoughtfully rolled a smoke without paying the slightest attention to the trees around him or the total absence of birds in those trees. He lit up, exhaled, pushed back his hat, and gazed out where perhaps two thousand cattle grazed onward and downward from this spot.

"You cover a lot of ground," said a quiet voice out of the rearward trees.

Jared stiffened without appearing to. He slowly lowered his cigarette and slowly twisted to look back.

Lisa Crandall strolled out of tree shadows on foot, leading a big raw-boned sorrel horse along after her. She was not smiling. She seemed to be appraising Jared, to be viewing him with curiosity, with a skeptical attention devoid of fear but wary.

He kicked loose one booted foot, slid down, and dropped his smoke, stamped on it, and watched her cross over. "You do pretty good yourself," he said.

This time, though, her wintry gaze was not amused, not the least bit light or casual. "Why are you over here again?" she pointedly asked. "You'd need a good reason to leave Five Pointed Star two days straight running, hours before sunup, and ride this far, Mister Carson. You'd need a very good reason."

"It could be you." He remembered Putnam's admonition and scorning it.

She shook her head very gently at him. "You're not the Brogan type or the Clem Forsythe type.

You don't casually do things or have gentle inclinations."

"Ma'am," he said, "I don't like this habit of yours of digging for the worst in men."

"Worst?" She looked faintly rueful. "What I told you I saw in you yesterday didn't mean it was all bad."

"Then what did it mean?"

"Mister Carson, it meant that you're an intense, intelligent, strong person, that you have no shades of gray to your thinking, things to you are either black or white, either right or wrong . . . never gray . . . never in between."

"You don't make it sound exactly complimentary, ma'am."

"You wouldn't want me to compliment you."

He stood there, studying her. She was disconcerting. Not only her uncommon beauty, her fullness and her promise, but her honesty and quiet wisdom reached out to him, leaving its impression, its mark. The way her gaze lay upon him without wavering or dropping away, as though challenging him to break the composure of her beautiful face. The way her heavy mouth lay closed but without pressure, richly compelling, full at the centers. He felt like making another reckless statement, something like he'd said to her the day before just before Casey had come up.

They were like this with perhaps twenty feet

between them for a long time, neither speaking to the other, neither conscious of anything else around them. He saw a gradual heaviness come to her eyes, a veiled look of want. Then it broke, showing a hunger and a tenderness. Jared dropped his reins, stepped over close to her, reached out, caught her at the waist, and swayed her to him. He kissed her, full and heavy, on the lips, and stepped back.

She said: "It was easy wasn't it, Mister Carson?" Something close to pure wrath burned against him from her. She made an unpleasant little laugh but did not turn away as another woman might have done. Her bitter gaze shamed him.

"I apologize, Miss Lisa, but you've got a power to draw a man against his will."

"Is that an excuse, Mister Carson?"

"No," he answered a little sharply. "It's not an excuse. It's a fact."

She lowered her head slightly, gazed steadily out over the immense run of land southward. For a while she had no more to say. He watched her, then turned also to look southerly.

"It is a strange thing about this country," she finally said to him without looking back. "It seems always to bring out what's basic in men. Take Clem for instance. He was a frugal man, honest and hard-working and unimaginative. His word was his bond."

"Is that bad?" he asked.

Now she looked up at him again, put her head slightly to one side, and said: "Don't always be on the defensive with me, Mister Carson. I'm not trying to hurt anyone. I only say the things I see. No, it's not bad, it's good."

He did not look at her; far out two horsemen were jogging along side-by-side. They would be Hedrich riders, he knew.

"And Brogan," Lisa murmured, continuing to think aloud. "He was never any of the things Clem was. He's always been ruthless and grasping and scheming. I suppose in his own way he's strong, but it's not a good way."

Still watching those two far-off horsemen, he said: "What exactly are you telling me, Miss Lisa?"

"I'm telling you that this is not an easy country, that it brings out the best and the worst in people. I'm telling you, Mister Carson, that a hundred men have come and gone and not one of them was the right man."

Now Jared turned to face her. "And I?" he said. "I make one hundred and one, is that it?"

She met his gaze steadily, her eyes blacker than he'd seen them before, her lips lifted at their outer corners with a quiet, soft bitterness. "No, Mister Carson . . . you make *the* hundred and first."

Now she turned away from him, dropped her eyes, and moved back where her raw-boned big sorrel horse stood. He thought she was perhaps annoyed with herself for having said that, and yet he wasn't sure. He didn't really know women very well. One kind he knew, but not *this* kind. He went over to lay a light hand upon her reins and looked up where she sat easily in her saddle.

"Tell me something," he said quietly. "How is it that you're Casey Hedrich's aunt?"

She considered his face for a moment, then smiled downward. "It's a very natural thing, Mister Carson," she replied, her tone turning crisp again, and normal, the way it had always been with him up until he'd kissed her. "My sister was twenty years older than I was. She married Casey's father and I came West to live at Circle Dot with them. You see, my sister and I were orphans and my sister raised me as though I were her daughter."

"I see," he murmured. "That was none of my business, of course, but it's been sticking in my head. When someone told me you were the aunt of the feller who owned Circle Dot, I had visions of a nice little old lady."

"In long black dresses," she said, her slate-gray eyes laughing at him, "and with a shawl around her shoulders. Sitting by the fire of an evening with a cat in her lap."

Jared listened, found that this fitted perfectly the idea he'd had, but which he'd never thought through this far, and laughed. It was a rich, good sound. "I reckon that's about it."

Her gaze became gentle, softly approving of his smile and his laugh. "You should do that more often," she told him. "It erases the tension in you."

He looked up but did not say anything.

"I'd like you to answer a question for me now," she said. "And like your question, it's really none of my business. What, exactly, has brought you over here these last two days?"

"I could say it was you, ma'am."

"You could say so but you won't, Mister Carson, because that wouldn't be true and you're not a liar."

"Well," he said, "I'm afraid I can't tell you."

"I see." Her gaze did not harden against him; it simply lingered upon his face for a while before she said: "It has something to do with Casey, with the Circle Dot, with our range or our cattle, hasn't it?"

"Something like that," he admitted. "Listen, Miss Lisa, for now let's just leave it like that. I don't want to appear bull-headed and make you mad. All right?"

"All right. Just tell me this . . . will you tell me when you can?"

"Yes'm."

"And when might that be, Mister Carson?"

He got a sly little twinkle in his eye. "Maybe,"

he drawled up at her, "the day you quit calling me Mister Carson, and call me just plain Jared."

She met his twinkle with a matching look. She shortened the reins. "Tomorrow, perhaps, *Mister* Carson?"

He had entirely forgotten Sheriff Putnam's entreaty for him not to see this woman under any circumstances. He said: "Tomorrow, Miss Lisa."

"Over at the stone trough where we met yesterday. It's not such a long ride from Five Pointed Star. It's almost midway between both ranches."

He released her horse, nodded, and stepped back to watch her ride off into the little fringe of trees. For a long time afterward he remained as he was, but eventually he went back to where his patient horse stood, carelessly caught up the reins, and stood for a while, gazing out over Circle Dot's range southward, westward, and eastward. Those two jogging cowboys were no longer in view. In fact even the bunches of cattle had broken up, re-formed, and were grazing in a different pattern now. He did not until then realize how much time had gone by since he'd come up onto this little promontory.

He stepped up, dropped down, and turned his horse, heading eastward off the little hill. Behind him in the flaming west the sun was fast falling toward its meeting with the earth, far out. The sky, the land, even the grass and underbrush were softening into a dying-day pattern of sweeping copper. Reddish tints showed here and there. Shadows, anemic now but strengthening gradually into dark substances, came out underfoot as he paced along homeward.

He did not think any more of Circle Dot's cattle. He did not even think of his own animals. He instead thought of Lisa Crandall, of the soft firmness of her mouth, of the fullness and promise of her, of the heaviness that he had sighted in the depth of her gaze, and all of these things went down deep into him bringing on a sensation of pain and powerful longing. Not once did he recall Al Putnam's warning.

When he got back home, dusk was thickening on all sides. He changed horses, went to the house, cleaned up, changed his shirt, his pants, ate no supper, went back out, and got astride. He rode southward this time, in the direction of Cinnebar, still with the same compelling thoughts, rode slowly and easily, going over everything that had happened up there on that little hill, until, after five miles, the light patterns of Cinnebar brought him unpleasantly back to the present.

XI

Cinnebar, in its nighttime attire, was not the languid village it appeared to be in broad daylight. It seemed to Jared a threatening place, a town of deviousness and silent peril to him. Somewhere down there, he thought, was a tall man with big feet and a large belt buckle who had tried to assassinate him. Down there, too, would be the man he felt was behind that assassination attempt—hook-nosed Harry Brogan. Remembering things he'd been told, he did not now ride on into the livery barn as he'd normally have done. He instead circled around town, entered from the west, passed up through crooked byways, and left his horse tied behind a dark store where it would not likely be noticed. After that, he passed down between two buildings to emerge upon Main Street, and stood there a long time, gauging Cinnebar.

Across the road and northward was the Palace Saloon, its hitch rack full, its windows pouring square patterns of orange lamplight out into the roadway. Noise came over the batwing doors, laughter, catcalls, loud voices raised in reckless exuberance. He hadn't been in the place since the night Clem Forsythe had died there on the Palace's sawdusted floor; he did not mean to go there now, either, at least not right away. He made a smoke, popped it unlit between his lips, and ambled along as far as the first store he came across that still showed lights. This was a bakery. He entered it, considered the paunchy, elderly man who looked up from behind a counter at him out of pale eyes, and asked where he might locate some of the town's councilmen.

The baker's eyebrows ran up. "So late at night?" he said. "Young man . . ." The words trailed off, those high brows abruptly dropped, the baker's face screwed up, and in a quite different tone he said: "You're the feller who inherited the Forsythe place." He made a statement of this, not a question.

Jared said: "Yeah. I'm the feller."

"Well now, young man, I heard about your offer of a new school. I think that's a fine thing you're doing. I think . . ."

"Listen," said Jared sharply. "Just tell me where I can find a councilman if you don't mind." That bubbling praise discomfited and embarrassed him.

"Did you try the Palace? There's usually one or two of the councilmen over there in the evenings. Or try the livery barn. Sometimes Brogan is there. He owns the livery barn, you know."

"Brogan? Is Harry Brogan a councilman?"

"Sure. Why shouldn't he be? Brogan owns a lot of property in town, mister. He's a very influential man. They say he's even branching out, going into the cattle business, too."

Jared walked out of the bakery, stood a moment wondering why Putnam had not told him this, then headed up toward the livery barn. He was still three doors south of the barn when a tall man swung out up there, astride a big seal-brown horse. Jared looked up at this rider and in return caught the man's casual southward look upon himself. Something immediately jangled in Jared's mind about this man. He was not close enough to make out the rider's face clearly, but he saw enough of it to know it if he encountered it again. What he did see, though, as the rider reined southward was faint, reflected light off a big belt buckle.

This brought Jared slowly around, watching that horseman until he was an indistinct blur down the roadway. For a moment he considered that man, fitting him, in build and general appearance, into the pattern he carried in his mind of the ambusher who had almost shot him at the ranch. The stranger fitted perfectly.

Jared went on to the livery barn, saw a hostler with a rake returning from deeper down the wide, dirt alleyway separating two banks of horse stalls, and went down to meet this man. He passed a lit room where two other men were idly seated, talking back and forth. That room looked to be a combination office and harness room.

The hostler, spying Jared, slowed, halted, leaned upon his rake, and waited for the younger man to come up. He said: " 'Evening. What can I do for you?"

"Tell me the name of that tall feller who just rode out of here."

"Sure," agreed the hostler, expectorating a dark stream and shifting his cud of tobacco. "That was Will Amber."

"Where does he work?"

"Right here. He's the day man." The hostler expectorated again, puckered his eyes, and studied Jared. He seemed curious but not curious enough, because whatever lay in his mind he did not put into words. "He'll be back directly, if you want to wait around. Just rode out to Brogan's place to fetch in a horse that needs shoeing."

Jared nodded. "I just might do that," he murmured. "Tell me something. Was yesterday Amber's day off?"

"Yup. Sure was."

"Did he take a horse and ride out?"

"He sure did. Went over to the Circle Dot to fetch back a pair of shoeing nippers he'd borrowed from Frank Silvius out there a month or so ago."

Jared dug out a silver dollar, dropped it into the night man's hand, and said: "Thanks. Have you been working here long?"

"Couple months is all."

"You like the boss?"

The hostler slowly reversed his cud, chomped down on it for a moment, then said: "Mister, you're sure full of questions."

Jared dredged up a $5 bill. "Are you full of answers?" he asked.

The hostler's squinted eyes widened. "Five dollars' worth of answers," he said, plucking away the money and plunging it deep into a trouser pocket. "Let's see now. You asked was I fond of the boss. Well now, that'd be Mister Brogan, wouldn't it?"

"It would."

The night man spat aside again, stepped one step forward, and said in a hoarse whisper: "Mister, I think he's a first-class skunk."

"And Will Amber . . . what about him?"

"A second-class skunk."

Jared faintly smiled. "Then do us both a favor. Don't tell Amber I was around asking about him."

"That's all I got to do?"

"That's all."

"Mister, you just bought yourself the closed-mouthedest feller this side of the Missouri River, yes sirree."

Jared left the livery barn, hadn't progressed back southward a hundred feet before a man hailed him from on across the road. He whipped around, did not recognize either the man or his voice, and stood easy, waiting for that hurrying, dumpy figure to approach.

This man was elderly, fat, white-haired, and rosy-cheeked. Jared thought he'd make an ideal Santa Claus. Even his voice had a depth to it that was resonant and cheerful. "I'm Elisha Evans, Mister Carson," this cherubic individual said, shoving out a pudgy hand. "I own the bakery shop where you stopped in a while back and asked my brother where you could find a councilman."

Jared shook and dropped that soft hand.

"Well, sir, the council waited around most of this afternoon, waiting for you, Mister Carson. You see, Sheriff Putnam told us . . ."

"I know what he told you," interrupted Jared. "That I'd be in town sometime today. I didn't say when I'd be in, only that I'd be in."

"Of course. Certainly, Mister Carson. Now, about the school . . . we've had donor's papers drawn up for your signature. They're over at our council rooms, and, if you'd like, we could go over right now and sign them."

"Not tonight," said Jared. "Not until Putnam gets back. I want him to explain something to me first."

"Explain something?" said the baker, his voice trailing off.

"Yeah. Explain to me why he didn't tell me Harry Brogan was a councilman."

Evans's expression lost some of its cherubic

look. His eyes, fully upon Jared, dimmed out a little. "I see," he muttered. "I see, Mister Carson. It's about Clem Forsythe's killing, isn't it? I mean . . . you feel that Brogan was . . ."

"That's exactly how I feel, Mister Evans."

"But you see, Mister Brogan was only appointed to the town council three days ago, Mister Carson. He was appointed to fill out the unexpired term of a man who was previously on the council and who moved over to Healdsville."

"Then why didn't Putnam tell me that three days ago?"

"Probably, Mister Carson, because he didn't know it. The council meets only once a month, unless, of course, something real urgent comes up, and Al Putnam's not a member. In fact, you see, it's the council that pays our sheriff. He wouldn't know anything about changes on the council right away. In fact, I don't expect many of the folks in town would know . . . not right off, at any rate."

Jared thought on this for a while, found it plausible, but his mood was not affable or co-operative, so he said: "Putnam'll be back in a few days. I'll come in when he returns and sign over the money."

Southward, a solitary horseman came ambling along, leading a haltered animal behind him. Jared sighted this shadowy rider, remembered at once what the livery hostler had told him, and stood there, straining for a good look at this approaching horseman. Elisha Evans also stood there, but he was ignoring the rider and studying Jared's face with a worried expression. Obviously Town Councilman Evans had been shaken badly by Jared's curtness and his hard look.

That lanky man came up, dropped a casual look downward where Jared and Evans stood in formless shadows, then paced along northward toward the livery barn. Jared turned, stepped around Elisha Evans, and followed the rider up to where he dismounted, called down into the livery barn for the night man to come take the horses he was holding, and there Jared went up to this taller, looser-built man, looked down at his belt buckle, then stepped back again. The tall man put a scowling look around. Almost at once his face cleared with sudden recognition. He stood rooted, staring at Jared.

The night man walked up, glanced at these two, took the horses, and without a word or a second look proceeded into the barn with them. He didn't turn to look back even when Jared spoke, his voice bell-clear and cold. "How much does Brogan pay for near misses?"

The lanky man turned very slowly and deliberately. He was standing in a big patch of light from within the barn, was framed in this light. He dropped both arms, the left one hanging easy, the right one just the slightest bit crooked at the elbow with the fingers within inches of the man's holstered handgun. "What you talkin' about?" he asked Jared, but his tone was hollow. "Who d'you figure you're talkin' to . . . stranger?"

"The next time," said Jared, "don't wear a buckle that leaves such clear imprints on the ground."

"I don't know what you're talkin' about, mister."

"You're a liar," rapped out Jared. "A liar and a bushwhacker, Amber, and before I kill you, you're going to tell me whether Brogan sent you, or whether you tried that on your own."

Amber stood there like stone. For a long moment he said nothing, only carefully appraised Jared. Then he said: "No one calls me a liar, mister. No one at all. You made a mistake. You've mistook me for someone else, an' I'm goin' to give you five seconds to realize that."

"In five seconds you'll be dead, Amber. Only one thing's going to keep you alive. Did Brogan send you out to Five Pointed Star to drygulch me, or did you try it on your own?"

Amber let his breath out very slowly. His lips drew out thinly. He moved his right hand. Opposite him no more than fifteen feet away, Jared's right hand also moved. It was more a blur than a movement. Amber's breath choked off. His hand was firmly around the six-gun butt without having had time to draw the weapon; he was staring into the tilted black muzzle of Carson's gun. Jared distinctly cocked the weapon.

"Go ahead and complete it," he said very gently. "You've started . . . go ahead and finish it. I can kill you whether you do or don't."

Amber's shoulders gently slumped. His eyes lifted. He looked strickened. "Brogan didn't send me. He only said that, if any of us boys as work for him, got a good bead on you, he'd pay us two hundred dollars."

"Why?"

"Well, I ain't sure, Mister Carson. But I saw you 'n' Miss Lisa yesterday over by Circle Dot's windmill. I was comin' back from . . ."

"So you had a reason . . . two hundred dollars and your filthy thoughts." Jared dropped his gun back into its holster. He straightened up again, his face ugly with cold anger. "Now draw it," he challenged. "Go ahead, you've still got your hand on it."

But Amber declined to do this. He very slowly brought his hand forward and let it hang down, well clear of his holstered gun.

"Did you tell Brogan you tried to drygulch me?"

"Yes, I figured if you went to Putnam there'd be talk, so I went to Mister Brogan as soon as I got back to town."

"And you told him why. You told him you'd seen me with Miss Lisa."

"Yes, I had to tell him why I tried to bushwhack you, Mister Carson. Otherwise . . ."

"What did he say, after you told him you'd seen me with Miss Lisa?"

Amber shifted his weight; he ran a furtive, helpless look over toward the Palace Saloon. He licked his lips and looked apprehensively back across to Jared Carson. "He said he'd pay a thousand in gold to the man who killed you."

"Was Aleo around when he said that?"

Amber nodded forlornly.

Jared eased off, made a motion with his left hand, and said in a voice full of scorn: "Get your horse, Amber, and be out of Cinnebar within fifteen minutes. Don't come back, and, if you try to go over to the Palace and tell Aleo or Brogan we've talked, I'll drop you on sight. You understand?"

Amber nodded again, jerking his head up and down with enormous relief. "Now?" he whispered.

"Right damned now!"

Without another word Will Amber turned, walked stiffly down into the barn behind him, and bawled out for his horse. Jared pressed back into black shadows and waited. In less than ten minutes Will Amber came out of the livery barn in a swooping run. He rode north and didn't even look back.

XII

Jared rode home, put up his horse, and went to bed. He didn't go to sleep right away; he'd had his faith in Al Putnam badly shaken and it took a little while for this to ease off its nagging. He also had the knowledge that he was worth $1,000 dead to keep him wakeful. But perhaps more than anything else, the image of Lisa Crandall kept breaking in upon his other thoughts. One man had already died because of her. Now another man's life was on the line—$1,000 for simply being in her vicinity, for simply briefly talking with her.

Finally he thought of Harry Brogan. These were bitter, vengeful thoughts. He thought of Brogan's killer, too, Pete Aleo, but he could understand a man like Aleo; he had seen others like him, knew how they thought and acted. Aleo was a simple man, a hired killer with no vast intelligence, only the instincts of a lion or a weasel, the instincts and the perfect physical co-ordination to kill. Aleo would be dealt with in the only way a man could deal with his kind, but it was Harry Brogan that occupied Jared's wakeful thoughts until after midnight.

Brogan was not a simple man, but he was as ruthless as Aleo. More ruthless perhaps because he didn't kill for money, he didn't kill at all, not directly. He simply made up his mind someone annoyed him, reached into a cash drawer, and counted out in dollars and cents what that annoyance was worth to him. The Pete Aleos of this world were, in Jared's thoughts, understandable. The Harry Brogans were not. He surely knew Lisa Crandall disliked him. Even if she hadn't told him, he would have sensed it by now. Then why did he persist in keeping all men away from her?

Probably, Jared reasoned, to force her into a loneliness that might eventually drive her to him. If this were so, he thought, then Brogan had a blind spot; anyone who'd ever studied people, good or bad, could see that Lisa Crandall might break, but she would never bend. But there was another possible reason, too, for Brogan's intense possessiveness. He perhaps wanted Lisa to see herself as responsible for Clem Forsythe's death and, if possible, for the death of Jared Carson, too. He wanted her to realize the power he had to make her despised throughout the country-side, which she certainly would be if any more deaths resulted from her knowing other men. But sometime and somewhere, Lisa Crandall, as overpoweringly desirable as she was, would attract a man Harry Brogan could neither kill nor intimidate.

Jared fell asleep with this thought uppermost in his mind. When he awakened, it was still there to remind him that he was to meet her over on Circle Dot range. He shaved again, ate a big breakfast, did his outside chores, then saddled his chestnut gelding, and rode out of the yard with his Winchester under the saddle fender, his Colt .44 thonged to his right leg, and his eyes up and moving, for he'd been warned by what Amber had told him that he was a marked man.

Still, riding now with good morning freshness and warmth upon him, the wild anger that had kept him awake last night could not now sustain itself, so it became instead a cold fury, a fixed and patient purpose. The kind of fixed and patient purpose that was infinitely more deadly than wild wrath ever was.

He crossed the golden countryside without seeing a soul. He passed bunches of Five Pointed Star cattle and later on bunches of Circle Dot animals. As before, he made rough mental tallies as he went along, found things as he'd already observed them to be, and wondered which of his problems would explode in his face first, the rustled livestock dilemma or the attempted murder Harry Brogan was planning, with him as the victim. The third problem, he saw, was down there at the stone trough, while he came out over a land swell and began a slow descent. She had her raven-black, heavy head of hair caught up severely at the base of her skull with a small green ribbon, and her white blouse stood out proudly against the darker shades of that old trough, the overhead windmill, and the miles of empty countryside behind her.

She saw him coming, stood up, and walked out a little distance. Her horse, the same raw-boned big sorrel gelding, was tied at the windmill's base, standing loose and easy, looking drowsy. He made up his mind as he rode closer to tell her of the rustling. He knew Al Putnam wouldn't approve, but he didn't care. He needed some answers. The only way to get them was to push this unpleasant thing out where others would see it, would have to comment upon it. But even more than that, he had a strong feeling about Lisa. If he couldn't trust her, who could he trust?

She smiled when he swung off and, trailing his reins in one hand, walked over to her. She smiled but he did not.

She said: "What is it . . . what's bothering you?"

"I'm worth a thousand dollars dead," he answered. "That's a big pile of money, don't you think?"

Her smile winked out. "Brogan?"

"Brogan."

"How do you know?"

"Someone tried to drygulch me at the ranch. Last night I caught up with the man who tried it. He told me. Lisa, that bushwhacker saw us together. Up until then I was only worth a couple of hundred dead. Afterward . . . one thousand."

She swung away from him, facing west, facing the old stone trough with its glaring, fresh patch down one side. "He told me he'd do it, Jared. He said he'd make me famous for being the cause of Clem Forsythe's death, and any other man who came near me." She swung back with her face gray-white, with her eyes huge and very dark. "He told me that the day of Clem's funeral."

Jared made a wry face, took her arm with his free hand, and guided her over toward the trough. "He's got a streak in him I never found in another man. There'd be a name for it, but I wouldn't know it." At the trough he turned her toward him, eased her down into a sitting position, and stood gazing down at her. "Forget Brogan. For now let's just forget all about him. You wanted to know what I've been doing out on the range. I'll tell you."

He did. He told her everything he and Sheriff Putnam had come up with regarding the cattle thefts. He then asked her about Circle Dot's replacement heifers. She didn't answer right away. She seemed shocked, momentarily speechless. Her mouth hung slightly open, her eyes round and inquiringly large.

Finally she said: "Last week Frank Silvius, our foreman, told Casey it looked as though most of the young she stock had drifted off, perhaps up into the northward foothills."

"Did Casey go look?"

She shook her head. "He said that would be all right, that we wouldn't have to bother with them until late in the fall anyway." She got up off the trough. "Now, Jared, now Casey should be told what you suspect."

"Not for another couple of days, Lisa. Not until Al Putnam gets back."

"But if it's a big band of thieves . . . ?"

"Two more days won't make a lot of difference. What I want from you is a solemn promise you won't mention this to Casey or anyone else. Not even to your sister, Casey's mother. Do I have it?"

She nodded, beginning faintly to frown at him. "You have something in mind."

"Yeah," he murmured. "I've got something in mind all right . . . forty feet of hard-twist lass rope over the stoutest limb of an oak tree up some nice, secluded cañon."

She searched his face a moment, saw that this was no jest, and turned slightly away from him. It was while she was standing like this that she sighted the horsemen and said quietly: "I think Frank and Casey are coming."

He whipped around, staring ahead, a warning flashing down through him. There were two riders, loping toward them, but they were not coming from the direction of Circle Dot at all. They were coming directly onward from the east, from the direction of his own home place.

He said quietly, forcing his voice low to make it sound unconcerned: "Lisa, go get on your horse and ride on home."

She turned, perplexed by this order, saw his flinty look, and gradually stiffened. Without obeying, she swung back around to stare out where those two riders were beginning to angle inward and downward, toward where she and Jared stood beside the old stone trough.

"Jared, who are they?"

"The only answer I have to that," he replied, keeping up an intent watch, "is that I don't know either of them."

She moved over until they touched at shoulder and hip. "Come with me," she murmured swiftly. "We can still get to Circle Dot before they can catch us. Frank and Casey and the others are there. Come with me, Jared."

"No," he said sharply, and moved off from her, moved ahead toward those oncoming riders. "You go. Get on your horse and get out of here. They won't bother you."

"Jared . . . !"

He kept on walking until she was a hundred yards behind. She called his name twice more, but he neither heeded her call nor allowed his attention to be diverted. Out where he halted the distance was too great for a handgun, but within moments those two oncoming men rode into carbine range.

They slowed to a walk, said something back and forth, turned to studying Jared standing alone out there, well away from the windmill and the trough, and finally halted. One of them dismounted, lazily dropped to one knee, brought up his Winchester, then failed to snug it back.

Jared had not heard her coming up behind him until she touched him with something hard and cold. "Take it," she said, pushing his saddle gun at him. As he reached back, the man out there who had not dismounted called out.

"Lady, get away from him. Go on back where you were!"

Lisa started to answer that shout but Jared turned, broke across what she'd meant to say repeating the same order: "Go back, Lisa. They're Brogan's men. I saw them in the livery barn office last night. Go back or you might get hurt."

She heard him out with her eyes darkening, turning defiant and resourceful. She stepped out beyond Jared. "If I leave," she called to those two assassins, "and you kill him, I can identify you both!"

The man on the ground swung his head to say something to the other man. For a moment those two consulted, then the mounted man called back lazily: "Lady, he's going to fight us! That's not murder!" The man paused. "It wasn't murder when Forsythe went for his gun, either!"

During that little interval when those two out there had been conversing before this, Jared moved up. Now he said—"Go back."—and this time it was an order. He put a hand upon her arm. She flung away from him.

"Brogan will pay you one thousand dollars for him dead!" she cried out. "*I* will pay *two* thousand for him *alive!*"

Now the kneeling man grunted up to his feet, grounded his carbine, and said something sharply to his companion. The pair of them gazed steadily ahead, obviously prompted by Lisa's offer and their own personal greed.

"You got it with you?" the mounted man asked.

"No, of course not. Who rides around with that much money?" retorted Lisa. "But you have my word. Ride off now, tell me where to leave it, and I promise you that you'll get it!"

The mounted man stared a moment longer, barked at his friend, who mounted up, shoved his Winchester back into its boot, and gathered his reins.

"All right, lady!" called the mounted man. "You get that two thousand, an' you keep it on you! We'll see you again!" The two of them swung around and loped back the way they had come.

Jared grounded his Winchester, swore quietly as he watched those hireling killers grow small, and eventually turned to put a cynical glance upon Lisa.

"You didn't have to do that," he said. "They were well in range."

She swung on him. "Two to one? They with horses for shields, you with nothing?" She shook her head, brushed fingers over his arm, and started back toward their horses. "Jared, how many killers can he hire? How many will try it?"

Pacing along at her side, he remained silent. There was no point in answering a question with such obvious answers. Back at the stone trough he eased down, hooked both arms around his carbine, and leaned upon it, considering her.

"They'll come for that money, Lisa. One day they'll just appear out of nowhere. That's why they didn't tell you to put it somewhere. That kind is wily as an old coyote."

"I'll have the money." She swung around, sat down next to him, and exhaled a big breath. "Something like that takes the starch out of a person." She smiled ruefully. "Do you know what I thought of doing first?" she asked, and drew forth a little nickel-plated revolver from a skirt pocket.

He looked at that little gun, looked up into her face, and dryly said: "It's a good thing you didn't. That thing's no match for two Winchesters and two Colts." He stood up, swung his head for a long look roundabout, went over, got her horse, and led it back. "Go home now," he said, taking her arm, drawing her up off the trough, holding the stirrup for her. "Go home and don't leave there until I come see you in a day or two."

XIII

Sometimes a man's anger draws him inward, turns him away from everything with its force and its power, makes him abandon everything else to concentrate wholly upon its own self-feeding flames. That's how it was with Jared Carson after that near assassination over at Circle Dot. He rode all the way home thinking of nothing else, thinking of the casual, almost contemptuous way those two killers had come out, workman-like, to finish him off for Harry Brogan's $1,000.

He did his chores early, while the sun was still visible off in the reddening west. He cooked himself a meager supper, then sat for half an hour cleaning and caring for his guns. After that, when it was turning gloomy outside, he selected a bay horse he hadn't ridden before, rigged it out, and started southward toward Cinnebar. He rode slowly, working out some details as he passed down the lengthening dusk. Putnam wouldn't approve at all of what he had in mind. Neither, for that matter, would anyone else, least of all Lisa Crandall, but neither Lisa nor Al Putnam was in his boots or felt as he felt. Every man has a limit; some come to it sooner than others, but all have it. One nearly successful attempt on his life was Jared Carson's limit. Two such attempts, although the second one had only brushed him with its peril, was more than he could stomach, particularly when the man responsible in both cases had been involved in neither attempt, really, but had remained comfortably at his saloon in town. This was in itself a kind of direct insult. Brogan didn't consider Jared Carson worthy of any direct action; he remained at his bar, casually drinking, joking with his customers, living his pleasant life undisturbed by dust or sweat or danger.

It was dark when Jared came into town from the west, left his horse tied in the same spot again, and walked along to the back alley entrance to the livery barn. Back here the light from up front was poor, the shadows were solid, and there was no one to see him glide through and fade out southward where tie stalls effectively hid him. He waited for that night hostler to appear. He had included this man in his plan, but after a long enough time and the night man did not show himself, Jared stepped forth and began an onward march toward the livery barn office. He knew only that he'd recognized those two as being the same pair he'd glimpsed the night before sitting in there idly talking. He did not know that they were there now, but he did know that, after agreeing to spare him for Lisa's $2,000, they wouldn't say anything of this to Harry Brogan. To best greedy men you must take advantage of their greed. It was an old axiom, and a true one.

When he was near the office, Jared eased over where two padded nail kegs stood, improvised chairs for daytime idling, got right up next to the door, and considered the lamplight coming out of that smelly little room with its pegged harness and its racked saddlery. Not a sound came from the office. He twisted forward in a half turn to peer in. There was only one man in there, the same hostler he'd spoken to the night before. He stepped out into full view, opened the door, and watched that man's head come around, watched his faded eyes lift and brighten faintly with recognition. The hostler had been making entries in a fly-specked ledger. Without speaking he now matter-of-factly closed the ledger, put aside his stub of a pencil, scooped up his hat, and indifferently dropped it atop his head, all without a greeting, a question, a sound of any kind.

"Come outside," ordered Jared.

The hostler dutifully rose up and walked on out of the office, turned, and moved over into shadows where Jared also moved. There, he halted, kept that faded unwavering gaze upon Carson, and finally spoke. "Mister, if you came here alone, you're in bad trouble."

"I'm alone," said Jared. "Or am I?"

The hostler's eyes flickered. He understood but made no commitment, only stood there waiting.

"How much does Brogan pay you a month?"

"Twelve dollars and a cot in the office."

"For twenty-four dollars a month would you consider changing employers?"

"If that's an offer, Mister Carson," said the liveryman quietly, "you just hired yourself a cowboy who's sick to death of working in a livery barn."

Jared relaxed. He studied that battered, whiskery face with its dead-level eyes and its square, tough jaw. "What's your name and how come you to know mine?"

"Hank Phelps, and I expect everyone knows who you are. It's not every day a drifter falls into a barrel of horseshoes like you did with Forsythe."

Jared nodded. Hank Phelps was a forthright, soft-talking man who said what he meant in few words. This was Jared's kind of man; he was himself of this same breed.

"Those two men who were in the office here last night, who are they and where are they now?"

Phelps shifted his stance, plunged both fisted hands into his trouser pockets, and said: "Mister Carson, let me tell you something before I answer that. I heard what you told Will Amber last night. I didn't see you outdraw him but I was watching

Amber from down here in the barn, so I know that's what happened. Now, Brogan and Aleo and those two fellers who were in here last night in the office have been going all over town today looking for Amber. They can't figure out what happened to him."

"What of it?"

"Mister Carson, I'm a little older'n you are. I know that when you got folks worried you got 'em half whipped. Now, I'll tell you where those two men are, but, if you're smart, you won't gunfight 'em here in town at all. You'll just take 'em out of town where no one'll hear a thing, then do whatever you want with 'em. Three disappearances in twenty-four hours'll just about bring Brogan and Aleo down to earth."

Jared speculated on Hank Phelps and what he had said. There was an iota of good logic here; certainly Brogan might suspect Carson was behind the disappearances, but a man like Brogan would have other enemies, too. He and Jared hadn't openly clashed yet, so there existed a possibility Brogan might think someone else, or perhaps even a number of other men, might be involved. "And you," he said to Phelps. "What about you?"

Phelps shrugged. "I'm just a down-at-the-heel rider who drifted in, down and out and hungry. There are lots of drifters, Mister Carson. Whoever pays attention to us?"

Jared smiled slowly and pleasantly. "Should've run across you before, Hank, damned if I shouldn't. All right, where are those two?"

"Over at the Palace having a few." Phelps turned, looked out into the roadway, looked back, and said: "Stick around, they'll be back. One of 'em said something about taking a ride out west of town tonight."

"Yeah, over to Circle Dot maybe."

Phelps shrugged, waited for Jared to elaborate, and, when he didn't, Phelps said: "If I was you and wanted those two bad enough, I'd ride west a half mile or so and wait 'em out. They sure won't be expecting anything and you will be."

That, Jared decided, then and there, was what he'd do. He brought out some money from a pants pocket, counted out $24, and handed it to Phelps. "Your first month's wages," he said, "in advance. Stay here, keep right on working for Brogan. If something goes wrong and I don't make it all in one piece, no one'll ever know about you and me, Hank. If things work out, I'll be back in a few days for you."

"Sure," murmured the old cowboy. "Good luck." He turned and re-entered the livery barn office. Jared heard him ease down again upon a squeaky chair in there, and walked back on out of the barn the same way he'd entered it.

Jared rode west of Cinnebar and within the first thirty minutes had two false alarms when whooping bands of cowboys returning homeward went rushing past in the soft-lit night.

An hour later when impatience was inspiring all sorts of dire thoughts in him, Jared heard two riders approaching slowly, casually speaking back and forth, riding easy and slouched, when they came into view. He remained far northward of those two, standing at his animal's head to prevent the horse from making any sounds. He could not see the horsemen any better than they could have seen him, had they been looking for him, which they were not, but he recognized one of their voices as belonging to the man who had not dismounted over by Circle Dot's stone trough, and that was all he waited for.

The riders drifted slowly on past, still desultorily speaking to one another. Jared let them get several hundred feet onward before he swung up, eased out, and cut in behind them. He trailed them within hearing distance, heard them speak of hitting out for Wyoming after they got that $2,000, was satisfied with this, and dropped off until they were well ahead, then swung southward, out and around them in a long lope, and made his final halt a mile ahead.

This time, although the wait was seemingly endless, he was there on foot when those careless voices came on ahead of the men owning them, and afterward in the gloomy light the men came into view, too. He let them get up very close before rising up off his belly and confronting them with a cocked gun in his right fist. One of those men saw him; Jared heard that one's breath suck back in a strong gulp. The other one was turning perplexedly toward his companion when Jared spoke.

"Hold it. Keep your hands in plain sight. Sit still and don't make a sound."

Both those men hauled back, staring ahead where Jared's silhouette blended with the sooty earth. They looked dumbfounded at first, then they looked fiercely angry.

"Get down. Watch it now . . . don't try an offside dismount. One wrong move and hell busts loose. Easy now."

The men dismounted. They did not seem cowed exactly but they did seem unsure and worried about exactly what course to pursue, and because this is precisely how they did feel, they did nothing at all.

"Shuck your six-guns."

They obeyed this order, too, their faintly discernible features wrathful but shaken.

"Now, about that two thousand dollars," said Jared, holstering his own weapon. "I'm going to gamble with you for it, one at a time." He pointed with his left hand at the larger, heavier of those two. "You there, pick up your gun."

"Huh?" said the bigger man. "Why?"

"I'm going to gamble that I can outdraw and

outshoot you, mister. If you win, go on out to Circle Dot and collect the two thousand. If I win . . ." Jared lifted his shoulders and let them fall, the answer to his second statement obvious without being stated. "Pick it up!"

"Wait a minute," protested the large man. "How do I know you won't drop me when I bend down?"

"You don't, mister. That's part of the gamble."

"The hell with you," growled the big man, standing very straight and looking very defiant. "I should've let my pardner drill you, woman or no woman."

"Why didn't you? He wanted to do it."

"Sure he did. He's stupid sometimes. That there lady belongs to Harry Brogan. If a stray slug'd hit her, Harry'd have skinned us both alive."

"The gun," said Jared. "Pick it up."

"No, by God, I won't do any such danged thing!"

"Amber did. He wasn't a coward."

"What? You . . . you shot Will Amber?"

Jared solemnly nodded. He didn't verbally reply because he doubted that his voice would sound convincing. As Lisa Crandall had once said, and as Jared knew, he was not a very convincing liar.

"Will was pretty good with a gun, Carson."

Jared smiled. "Pick it up, bushwhacker, and find out if I'm any better."

Now the shorter, thicker of those two spoke up. His voice was nasal and he dragged out each word slowly and ponderously as though the process of thinking was more difficult for him than the process of physical activity. "What's wrong with just lettin' us go get that two thousand? You ain't hurt none, Carson."

Jared looked at this man's low forehead, deep-set, dull eyes, and over-balanced big massive jaw. "I've got a better idea," he said. "You pick up your gun."

"Don't do it," said the other one quickly. "Don't let him bait you into nothin'."

Jared was briefly silent, then he jerked his head at the shorter man. "Get away from him," he ordered. "Move off fifty feet."

The short, thick man moved off obediently. His partner suddenly looked worried. "Not in cold blood," he said huskily.

Jared walked closer. "Turn around," he snapped. "Move!"

The big man turned, his shoulders drawn up, his body ramrod stiff. Jared picked up this one's gun, dropped it into the man's holster, stepped away, and said: "Face me, mister."

"No! Damned if I will!"

"You yellow, mister? Both our guns are leathered. You've got a lot better chance than you deserve."

"Yeah," muttered the shorter man from out

where he was watching all this intently. "Turn around, Cliff. You got an even break with him."

The big man loosened a little. Moonlight fell, gray and watery, across his troubled countenance. He had to turn, to take his chances. He lived by that code. He drew in a breath, slowly let it out— and whipped around, lunging for his gun.

As before, Jared's enemy froze with his six-gun half clear, his unbelieving eyes wide and bulging. He had been outdrawn by a full second. Jared cocked his weapon and tilted it to bear steadily upon the big man's chest. "Draw it or drop it."

Out where the burly man stood came an unsteady loud sigh. "God a'mighty, Cliff, did you see that draw?"

The man called Cliff brought his gun hand forward away from his weapon. He slowly raised his eyes, looking strickened. "Don't," he said hoarsely to Jared. "You win, Carson. Don't pull the trigger."

"Toss it down," Jared ordered. "Now, the pair of you, listen to me. You've got five minutes to get back on those horses and light out. Leave the Cinnebar country and don't ever show your faces here again. That . . . or fight. Which'll it be?"

The man called Cliff looked over at his partner. He said: "That lousy Brogan . . . he done that on purpose. He said Carson was a pilgrim." He swung back toward Jared. "We're goin', Mister Carson, we're goin'."

Jared put up his gun, watched those two get back astride, and said: "Don't worry about Brogan. I'll settle with him for you. Now move out and keep on moving."

The pair of renegades hooked their horses hard and went flapping off into the night, northward.

XIV

For a while after he was back astride and alone in the night, Jared considered returning to Cinnebar. He still wanted a showdown with Harry Brogan. In the end, though, he thought of something else. It was not entirely improbable that those two renegades he'd just vanquished without firing a shot might not be as fearful as they'd seemed, or as Will Amber evidently had been. They might, with the powerful incentive of $2,000 to encourage them, try a quick swoop westward toward the Circle Dot. He reined off in that direction, riding easily, not convinced what he was doing would prove worthwhile, but unwilling to risk Lisa in case those two did weaken and make a swift strike at the Hedrich place.

It was a long ride and a tiring one all the way from Cinnebar out to the Circle Dot. Long before he came within sight of Hedrich's tree-studded plateau he had to make a cigarette and smoke it to keep awake and alert. He did not see or hear another rider, but he hadn't really expected to, for by the time he got close to the Circle Dot it was well past midnight. He came across a shaggy old uplands wolf, probably a gummer, stalking a pregnant Circle Dot cow near to birthing and therefore unable to shake the wolf or turn on him, either. He could not risk a shot so he took down his lariat, shook out the knotted end, and went careening after the old wolf.

For a mile he ran that shaggy old animal back and forth, popping him every once in a while with the lariat. He could have roped the wolf but any range man with a lick of sense knew better than to do that. Anyway, the old gummer wouldn't ordinarily bother cattle; he was gaunt and considerably slowed by age, the only reasons for his being down where he was upon the plain.

Jared turned off, letting the old lobo keep to his beeline for the foothills, when he spied a tiny square of lamplight on ahead, showing through big cottonwood trees. Someone was still awake over at Hedrich's house, but the bunkhouse, in fact every other building at the ranch, was sunk in total blackness.

He sat a while, watching that light, imagining that Lisa might be sitting in the house over there, perhaps reading. He decided to ride on in, and he did, following the Circle Dot road almost into the yard, then swinging off southward into the cottonwood grove that surrounded Hedrich's house for several acres. There he swung down, took his carbine, and began a cautious trip of exploration.

Circle Dot had been laid out by an experienced, shrewd cowman. The working corrals were out behind the barn. The bunkhouse and shoeing shed were nearer the barn than the house, and all of it was arranged so that nothing impeded the northward mountain view from the house, or the westerly view, either, except where those carefully cared-for big old cottonwoods stood in deep shadows in the moonlight. There was something to this ranch that lingered in a man's heart. Jared thought that this would be what he should work toward, a home made comfortable and warmly inviting by good management down the years, a place of quiet serenity, so quiet that when a horse blew its nose over by the shoeing shed that sound carried, bell-clear, all the way to where he stood in the formless dark beneath a huge old tree.

He yanked upright suddenly. There was no corral by the shoeing shed. The nearest place where horses should be, unless they were tied over there, was a good three hundred feet from that shed. Unless they were tied over there. . . . He pushed off the cottonwood, rummaged the shadowy yard for movement, saw none, and began a very cautious approach through the shadows and big trees, on toward the shed. He saw the horse finally. It was saddled, bridled, and tied. No cowman would have forgotten his animal like this. He edged closer, straining to see that animal better. It occurred to him that, if this beast belonged to one of those renegades, the pair of them had made very good time getting out here from where Jared had last seen them. It also occurred to him that there must be a second horse somewhere close by. He concentrated on locating this other beast, and never did find it.

He was retracing his steps away from that tethered horse when he heard men's voices, two of them, coming softly through the night around in front of the house. He sank from sight in formless gloom, waited until there was discernible movement to see along the house, then took two long steps forward to intercept that lank-moving shadow. At the very last moment he recognized Keith Winston and halted stockstill, his breathing running out in a slow, relieved sigh.

It had not occurred to him that Casey Hedrich might have had a visitor tonight. But now that he saw this was so, he was divided between being angry with himself, and being curious about Winston being at the Circle Dot so late at night. It crossed his mind to step forth and ask Winston about this, but he didn't, and meanwhile Keith crossed over to his horse, untied the animal, stepped up, and kneed the horse out in a loose walk, heading due east in the direction of his own home place.

Jared watched him, turning loose all over, letting that earlier tightness dwindle, curious about what Winston and Casey could have to discuss that wouldn't wait until daylight, or at least which had to be pursued into the small hours of this night. He was so intent upon these things that he did not at once hear the softly abrasive sound of a shod hoof passing over stone, northward, until the sound was repeated. He turned, looking now on over toward the cattle corrals, toward that big old ghostly-looking Circle Dot barn.

The sound was not repeated. He thought it perhaps had been made by corralled horses— except that there were no corralled horses. He'd verified that earlier when he'd made a thorough reconnaissance of the Circle Dot's yard and buildings. There were five stalled horses in the barn, but none outside of the barn. He stood a long time totally silent and motionless, considering that once-heard and faintly abrasive sound, trying to place its location, and never quite succeeding.

There came into the night's great hush now, a kind of sinister breathlessness. It was something felt; something that touched along a tense man's nerves, bringing him up to full alertness, full wariness. Keith Winston could not have made that sound; he was riding due east. The sound had come from northwest, somewhere in the vicinity of the barn or corrals. It might have been made by a loose horse or even by a cow wandering sleeplessly out of the westerly night. Also, it could have been made by two stealthy renegades unable to resist the considerable temptation of $2,000 that Lisa had told them she'd have handy.

He started back toward the shoeing shed again, this time moving with the swiftness provided by knowledge of the route. From the shed he went northward with the Hedrich house directly behind him, low and totally dark now, in the cottonwood grove. He did this deliberately, knowing he could not be skylined.

Something man-high flitted across open ground between barn and corrals. Something this phantom was carrying milkily glistened. Jared dropped like a stone, lay flat, and drew his handgun. He had been right; those renegades had been unable to resist the temptation. A second phantom whipped across into the protective shadows of the big barn. This one, though, had no bared gun in hand. Jared, prepared this time, followed that shadow with his eyes from its place of origin on across to where it faded out. He recognized that one by his big old floppy hat, by his bulk and heft and bear-like movements. That one was the larger of the renegades, the big one who had refused to fight him.

He very carefully pushed his six-gun out ahead, trained it upon the gloom where he knew those two would be stalking along, and waited. He was directly in their path. Nothing happened, though, for so long he wondered if the renegades hadn't gone on through the barn from back to front for a frontal approach to Hedrich's house. Such a course was not prudent because the bunkhouse had to be passed and the yonder yard was moon-lighted and barren of any cover at all. He lay on, speculating about the thoughts of those two, waiting and wondering and shallowly breathing, until, fifty feet ahead, something eased over into paler shadows near the barn's southward corner, halted, and stood motionlessly until a second, larger silhouette also eased forward. The range was good; he was positive of the identity and purpose of those men, so he deliberately canted his gun and fired.

That thunderous explosion blew the night apart with a crimson flash of flame. Inside the barn a horse, evidently asleep when Jared fired, made a shrill squeal of terror and fought its tether rope, making hammering sounds. From the barn's southward corner a gun flamed back at Jared's muzzle blast. Its slug was close but not close enough. Jared thumbed off two fast shots, rolled clear, thumbed off another shot, and sprang up running. He was a goodly distance off when two six-guns flashed and roared, the smell of their dirty smoke turning the night air acridly unpleasant. From within the bunkhouse came a man's high shout and the sound of other men striking the floor from topside bunk beds.

Jared angled out to the nearest corral, kneeled there to reload, sighted upon a flitting shadow, and fired. That shadow, in the midst of a retreating dash, sprang high into the air and lit down in a threshing heap. Very gradually those wild convulsions lessened until the man lay utterly still in the moonlight, a bundle of disheveled clothing and nothing more, flat and sprawled and very, very still.

The surviving renegade had evidently reloaded his handgun because he now dumped four furious shots toward Jared's corral corner, at the same time letting out a great, savage roar. That one, Jared knew, would be the big renegade, the one who hadn't wished to fight. Jared counted each shot that man fired, then waited, hoping the renegade would be taking advantage of this intervening lull frantically to punch in fresh bullets. He called over to that man.

"I told you to get out of the country! Now you're going to stay here permanently."

"Carson," that hidden man gasped. "Carson!"

Jared sighted on that sound and fired. He missed. He knew that when the renegade frantically fired back. But he hadn't really expected to hit the man; he'd only wanted to upset the renegade badly enough for the man to fire back, which he'd done, and now Jared fired three times, fast, giving the renegade no time to get away before three carefully placed slugs slashed toward him. The renegade gradually stood up, stiffened his shoulders against an inclination to sag, turned, and dazedly started walking northward. Jared could see him plainly after the barn had been passed and the renegade no longer had any protective cover. But he did not fire. That renegade was hit; Jared knew it as certainly as he knew anything.

He lowered his gun, watched the man go almost a hundred feet northward from the barn, then halt, wilt, and buckle over to slide down face first into the dust. Moonlight etched a soft, sad light pattern over that man. He did not move.

Jared stood up, reloaded, holstered his gun, and turned. Twenty feet behind him stood a shock-headed big cowboy with a sawed-off shotgun in both his hands. This man, like the shorter, paunchier, and nearly bald man standing beside him, was attired in underwear and pants, but that was all.

"Drop it," said the balding, older man. Jared dropped the six-gun. "Now turn around, mister, and hike straight ahead out into the yard. You make a run for it an' it'll take two coffins to bury you."

XV

A light had come on over at the main house. Jared saw that as he was driven out into the faintly lighted yard by his captors. There, two more cowboys came padding up, also barefoot and only partially dressed, but armed and ready.

The balding, shorter man stepped around. "Who are you?" he demanded.

"Jared Carson from over at Forsythe's place."

This registered; Jared's captors looked at one another and at him, their expressions turning speculative. "Who are those two you downed?" asked the same balding man. "And just what the hell's going on?"

Before Jared could reply another man came quickly forward, this time from the direction of the house. Jared recognized this one at once, and said: "Hullo, Hedrich."

Casey had his gun belt strapped around him. He was fully dressed and his face was full of urgent inquiry. The balding man, who evidently was Circle Dot's range boss, said: "Damnedest thing . . . there's a couple of dead men around behind the barn, an' we come onto this one after he shot it out with 'em. I was just tryin' to find out what it's all about, Casey."

Young Hedrich looked down at Jared's empty

holster and up again. With not as much suspicion in his voice as the range boss's voice had held, Casey said: "What happened, Carson?"

Jared looked over toward the main house and back again. He said, after a thoughtfully quiet moment: "Maybe we'd better go up to the house, Hedrich."

Casey faintly frowned, looking still more puzzled, but he jerked his head. "Lead out," he said to Jared, and to his riders: "Go on back to bed, boys. I'll handle it from here."

The riders looked lamely at their employer, their faces full of suspicion and interest. The balding man growled something as Jared and Casey Hedrich started off, then the cowboys put up their weapons and went shuffling toward the bunkhouse, tossing little speculative sentences back and forth.

Jared turned when he and Casey were a hundred feet onward. "Hey," he softly called to those riders. "When you're through looking over the bodies, one of you bring my gun up to the house."

He and Casey paused upon the verandah, twisting to listen. Eastward, a hard-running horse was sweeping overland toward the Circle Dot.

"Who's that?" asked Casey sharply. "Another one?"

Jared listened a moment, shook his head, and

said: "Winston coming back, I expect. Those gunshots made a lot of noise."

Casey seemed placated. He led Jared into a spacious, soft-lit big parlor where cherry embers of a burned-out fire sullenly glowed upon the field-stone hearth. Two women were in there, both wrapped around with robes, both looked big-eyed and apprehensive. One was Lisa. At sight of Jared her lips faintly parted in astonishment. Casey, seeing the questioning looks of these two, introduced Jared to his mother and his aunt. Young Hedrich's mother was a stately copy of Lisa; she was in her late forties or early fifties, a strikingly beautiful woman.

Casey neglected to see the look that passed between his aunt and Jared Carson; he was impatient to hear what Jared had to say. The women said nothing at all. They remained over in the shadows, waiting and watching.

Jared turned, ignored Casey's mumbled invitation to be seated, and said: "Those two were Brogan's men. They came out here to get two thousand dollars."

Behind Jared, Lisa faintly gasped. Casey stepped sideways, gazed over at his aunt, but said nothing because Jared went on speaking.

"I met them earlier, ordered them out of the country. They agreed to go and left. But I thought that two thousand dollars might be too much temptation, and it was. I rode out here to make

312

sure they wouldn't shoot anyone, saw them, traded a few slugs with them, and they're lying out back of your barn."

Young Hedrich's forehead furrowed. He looked steadily at Jared, puzzled and bewildered. "What two thousand dollars?" he asked. "And how come you to be ordering Brogan's men around?"

Jared twisted to gaze over at Lisa. She gazed back, her face pale, her hands clasped tightly across her stomach. "Casey," she said, "two men tried to assassinate Jared this morning over by the broken trough. I offered them two thousand dollars not to shoot him."

Both Casey and his mother stared.

"You see," continued Lisa, "Harry Brogan has a bounty of one thousand dollars on Jared's head."

Casey ran bent fingers slowly through his hair. He looked from Lisa to Jared and back again. He said: "Lisa, I don't understand anything of this."

"All you have to know right now," said Jared, breaking in upon these two, "is that those two were Brogan's men. They came here to get that two thousand dollars, and now they're dead."

A big fist rapped hard upon the front parlor door. Everyone in that room whipped around. The door opened and big Keith Winston entered, blinked at the light, and stood framed in the opening, looking from face to face. He had a six-gun in his right hand. Without a word he passed over beside Casey and held that gun out to

313

Hedrich, his eyes fixed hard upon Jared Carson.

"It's his gun," explained Winston. He was breathing hard. "I heard the shots and came dusting back, Casey. Frank Silvius showed me the bodies and gave me Carson's gun."

Hedrich took the pistol, scowled at it, slowly pushed it out to Jared, and said: "Those two came out here to rob us, Keith. Carson trailed them, or something like that, and the three of 'em shot it out."

"Yeah," muttered Winston, still staring in the same unfriendly way at Jared. "You mention that other thing to him, Casey, what we talked about tonight?"

"No. I'm still trying to make sense out of this gunfight. Carson and Lisa . . ." Casey shrugged, dropped his hand back to his side when Jared took back his gun, looked over to his aunt, and said: "Lisa?"

"Yes."

"You and Carson are friends, is that it?"

"Yes."

"I see. Well, I sure had no idea you two even knew each other." Casey looked around at Keith Winston. He murmured dryly: "I've got to get out of the office more often."

Jared heard that and didn't like it. "You have some objection?" he demanded.

Casey's mother now spoke up for the first time. "Of course he hasn't, Mister Carson. None of us have. But you see, well, none of us know you, and all this is quite a surprise. I, for instance, have never before laid eyes on you, and I'm sure you'll agree that this first meeting of ours is . . . to say the very least . . . very dramatic. It's after three in the morning, there are two renegades dead out behind the barn, and here you are."

Jared turned to look over at Casey's mother. She had a tart little smile upon her lips, and, like Lisa, she looked a man straight in the eye. He reached up, pulled off his hat, and smiled over at her.

"Excuse me, ma'am. It's been a long night and a long day. I'm a little edgy. I apologize."

Mrs. Hedrich's smile brightened. "Please sit down," she said. "Lisa and I'll make some coffee."

The two women departed, Jared sat down, lifted his gaze skeptically, watched Winston and Casey. "We know each other," he said quietly, speaking of Lisa. "And we know about Brogan's notion of keeping Lisa unattached by having men like Clem Forsythe killed. Did you boys know about that, too?"

Winston's face revealed that he did not know; young Casey Hedrich's face showed troubled surprise. But as Keith Winston sank down upon a couch, he said: "Listen, Carson, this here isn't any of my business. I think the world of Lisa, but with one wife, I wouldn't be able to afford another one." Winston forced up a weak smile to accompany his weak joke.

Casey finally moved; he had been intently studying Jared and it was not difficult for Carson to appreciate that young Hedrich's new interest in him was based entirely upon the so abruptly revealed acquaintanceship between Jared and Lisa. But when Casey dropped down into a chair, he did not speak about this at all. He said instead: "I guess maybe we all owe you some thanks."

Jared looked rueful. "Thanks," he said, "I don't need. Tell me something, boys. What were you two talking about until after midnight tonight?"

Winston threw the word: "Rustling."

Jared swung his attention and his interest. "What about it?"

Keith looked over at Casey. Young Hedrich shrugged. "Go ahead, we agreed he had to know."

Winston said: "I was in the hills the last couple of days. I ran across a cow camp up there. I also ran across a big bunch of cows and heifers." Winston stopped speaking, leaned forward to dig in his pockets for a pencil and a shred of paper.

"Never mind," said Jared. "You're going to draw me a diagram of a wagon wheel. Right?"

Winston hung there upon the edge of his chair. "You knew?" he said.

"I knew. So does Sheriff Putnam. In fact, that's

where he is now . . . running down the registry for the name of someone down here around Cinnebar who owns a freshly recorded wagon wheel brand."

"Who else knows?" demanded Winston.

"Lisa. I told her today when those drygulchers of Brogan's came up."

Casey Hedrich sat forward in his chair, staring across at Carson. He slowly wagged his head back and forth. "You sure work fast," he said. "Carson . . . you sure work fast."

Jared neither smiled nor spoke. He could read doubt and wonderment in the younger man's eyes. Whatever he said would be interpreted by those two according to their convictions regarding him personally. He knew that and he therefore said nothing to Casey. He looked back over at big Keith Winston.

"Anyone up there at that cow camp?"

"No. There hadn't been anyone up there from the looks of things for several days." Winston fished in a rear pocket, brought forth a broken hatband, and held it in his fist, his eyes turning hard and thoughtful. "Do you know a man down in Cinnebar named Will Amber?" Jared woodenly nodded.

Winston held out that broken hatband without saying anything. Jared took it, read the name burned into the sweat-softened leather, and handed the thing back. "Forget him," he said, and explained about running Amber out of the country. He also explained why, told them about Amber's attempt at assassination.

Winston shoved the broken hatband back into a hip pocket, slapped his knee, and looked around at Casey Hedrich. "You said Carson works fast. Pardner, that was the understatement of all time."

Young Casey nodded, watching Jared. His face gradually cleared, became almost cheerful. Whatever it was that had been troubling him up to now seemed resolved in his mind. He said: "Yeah."

"Will Amber worked for Harry Brogan, at his livery barn in town," explained Jared. "If he was in on this rustling, then Brogan had to know about it, too."

Jared suddenly stopped speaking. He remembered something an elderly man in a bakery shop down in Cinnebar had said to him about Brogan, about Brogan being a big man hereabouts, about him owning a big slice of Cinnebar, and about his branching out into the cattle business. He said nothing to Winston or Hedrich about this, but he got up, took up his hat, and gazed downward.

"I reckon it's about time some of us rode on into town and had a little talk with Brogan. You fellers want to come along?"

Keith Winston stood up. "I do," he said.

Young Hedrich also arose. "Let's take my

men," he said. "Brogan's got some pretty rough men working for him."

They were at the door when Mrs. Hedrich and Lisa re-entered the parlor, one with a large coffee pot, the other with cups and saucers.

Casey said evasively: "We've got to ride out. Keep it hot, though. We'll need it when we come back."

Something solid and revealing passed back and forth between the women and the men at the door. Casey's mother put aside the coffee pot, straightened up, and, looking straight at her son, said: "Be careful."

Casey nodded.

Lisa put down the cups and saucers, crossed over to Jared, halted close to him, and smiled. Then she leaned forward on her tiptoes and kissed him gently and squarely upon the mouth.

Casey and Casey's mother looked stunned. Keith Winston crushed on his hat, eased the door open, and stepped out into the paling night where he could blow off a big, ragged breath, then go stumping on over the yard toward the bunkhouse where lamplight shone, and bawl out for the Circle Dot riders to get dressed and armed and ready to ride.

Later, when Jared and Casey came along, walking silently together, Keith turned, looked into those two solemn faces, and said to Casey without once taking his stare off Jared: "Carson

319

and I'll need fresh horses. All right to snare out a pair of yours, Case?"

"Sure," mumbled young Hedrich. "Sure, help yourself."

XVI

They took the pair of defunct renegades with them. This was Jared's idea. He did not count on that unnerving sight to cow Brogan or Pete Aleo, but he did count upon it to shake up Brogan's other hirelings. There were seven of them astride, in that party, and two tied belly-down over their saddles. In the chill of pre-dawn they did not have much to say to one another. For all of them except Jared there were a lot of questions that needed answering, but it was cold, they were not entirely awake yet, and, as they went along eastward, their thoughts were submerged.

Jared said he'd like to pick up his carbine at Five Pointed Star, so they angled a little southward. When they ultimately rode into the yard there, those corralled horses nickered at them. Jared stepped down and hiked across to the house. The others remained astride. As the moment passed with nothing to do but wait, they finally began asking questions. Casey and Keith Winston explained to Casey's riders as much as they knew, or had figured out, about the rustled cattle and the shoot-out behind the Circle Dot's barn.

Frank Silvius thought over all this for a while before saying: "This Carson feller . . . he's hell on wheels, ain't he? Man, I'd hate to meet every newcomer to the country the way we met him tonight . . . with a smokin' gun in his fist an' bodies sprawled all over the place."

One of the other Circle Dot riders piped up, saying he wasn't at all clear about this rustling. Winston patiently explained. Again balding Frank Silvius spoke.

"Casey," he said, "I told you a week or so back it didn't appear to me all them replacement heifers was on the range."

Young Hedrich nodded but said nothing. Jared was returning from the house with his Winchester in its boot. Casey watched him all the way across to Jared's horse. Then he said, speaking out so Jared would hear him: "I think there's going to be trouble in town, and without Al Putnam being there . . ." He let it trail off, waiting for Jared to take it up and perhaps complete the sentence for him.

Jared finished securing his saddle boot under the right fender, turned his horse, stepped up over leather, and looked across.

"There'll be trouble, all right," he stated. "You don't accuse a man of attempted murder, rustling, and being a no-good son- . . ."

"Hey, there's a rider comin' on from the south,"

broke in Frank Silvius, gesturing with an upflung arm, his face tightening with apprehension.

They all turned and plumbed the steely pre-dawn for that horseman. He was a long way out but discernible because, in all that otherwise hush and stillness, he alone was moving.

"Who'll it be?" someone muttered.

No one answered. Jared, watching that horseman closely and thinking of Amber and Amber's previous attempt to bushwhack him, said sharply: "Casey, take 'em around behind the barn. Don't any of you show yourselves until I give the word . . . or until the gunsmoke settles."

Keith Winston reined over. "I'll stay with you," he said, but Jared declined. "Go on with the others. If this is who I think it might be, I want him all to myself."

Casey led his men and Keith Winston on around a corner of the barn. The lot of them halted back there, being quiet.

Jared swung down, unshipped his Winchester, and kept judging the distance as that approaching man kept coming. When he was well in view, and in carbine range, Jared moved clear of the darkly backgrounding barn where that rider could see him.

Still the horseman came on. If he had seen Jared yet, he gave no indication of it. He swung in toward the house, slowed his horse, and bawled out: "Hey, Carson!"

Jared lifted the Winchester. "Over here," he said, and waited for the surprise he knew would come. It came; that rider twisted around and peered rearward.

"What the hell you doing over there this time of night?" he inquired, swung his horse, and came on over. Jared lowered his carbine, ruefully wagged his head, and ran a long look over Sheriff Al Putnam.

"You almost got a surprise, Sheriff. Casey, come on out."

As the mounted men appeared around the barn's side, Putnam looked in purest astonishment at them. "What's going on here?" he demanded.

Jared explained about the two dead men over at the Circle Dot, about his intention of riding into Cinnebar after Harry Brogan. Putnam listened, leaned back in his saddle, and said a tart word. "You fellers got all the answers but one," he stated. "What about stolen cattle?"

Keith Winston spoke up. "We know all about that, Al. In fact Carson told us you'd gone upcountry to check the brand registry."

Putnam put a downward glance upon Jared. "Looks like I didn't have to go. Looks like you boys got it all doped out."

Winston also explained about the rustler camp back in the hills, about Will Amber's hatband, and about the cattle he'd seen, obviously stolen from Circle Dot as well as Five Pointed Star, and worked over into wagon-wheel critters.

Putnam made a slow smile. "And you figure, because Amber was Brogan's man, that Brogan's behind the rustling . . . right?"

"Right," said Jared.

"Wrong," barked Al Putnam. "The wagon-wheel iron is registered to Pete Aleo."

No one said anything for as long as it took for this announcement to soak in, then Casey mumbled a little hesitantly: "Well, Aleo's Brogan's man, too, just like Amber was, Sheriff."

"Sure, Casey, I know that. But unless Aleo implicates Brogan, all I can do is go after Pete."

Jared holstered his Winchester, mounted, and said wryly: "We'll ride along on the strength of that, Sheriff. We'll roust Aleo out first. All right?"

Putnam nodded, looking glum. "Hell, I didn't get off the lousy stage more'n two hours ago, jumped right on my horse, and dusted it out here because I had big news . . . and it wasn't big news at all." He turned his horse, made a brusque motion with his left hand, and started back the way he'd come. Jared happened to look over at the same time Keith Winston looked up. Keith was grinning; he dropped an eyelid in a slow wink, then eased out behind the lawman.

No one said anything to Sheriff Putnam for a long time. He was disgruntled, weary, and hungry, and he showed it. Eventually he said to

Jared: "I owe somebody a punch in the nose. The trouble is, I'm not sure who he is."

Frank Silvius chuckled. Even Casey Hedrich grinned a little. Jared looped his reins, rummaged for his tobacco sack, and said—"As long as it's not me I don't care."—and went to work making a smoke.

"How many danged rustled animals were up in the hills?" Putnam asked Winston.

Keith shrugged. "I can't say. I saw maybe two hundred head, but according to Casey there's got to be more'n that, if the rustlers made off with most of his replacement stock."

Putnam looked over at Jared, where Carson was thoughtfully riding along, smoking his cigarette. "How'd your tallies come out?"

"I'm shy a hundred head. I think Hedrich's shy at least three times that many."

All the other men looked over at Jared wonderingly. Putnam saw those looks and explained. "Before I went north, Jared and I worked out a plan. He was to make rough tallies of his cattle and Circle Dot's cattle."

Casey Hedrich shook his head. "Be damned," he muttered. "When I said Carson works fast, I didn't know how fast."

Keith Winston puckered his mouth and quietly whistled. He was thinking how fast Jared worked, too, but it had nothing to do with tallying cattle.

They went along quietly for a long time. The

sky was steadily brightening toward dawn. Visibility was good but there was as yet no dimensional depth to this new day.

They were within sight of Cinnebar, before them on the south-westward horizon, when Jared said: "Amber worked at the livery barn for Brogan. Those two renegades I tangled with out behind Hedrich's barn also put their time in at the livery barn." He paused to look over at Keith Winston. "You said that cow camp in the hills looked deserted. Well, I'm thinkin' that it's likely Amber and those other two were probably the rustlers."

"All right," assented Sheriff Putnam. "It's possible."

"If it's so," went on Jared, "we're never going to get any first-hand confessions. Two of those men are dead and Amber's gone out of the country."

"Saves us hangin' 'em," growled a Circle Dot rider from far back.

"What I was thinking," went on Jared, "is that without any of those three to tell us . . . how're we going to know how many of those animals are Hedrich's and how many are mine?"

Young Hedrich turned this over in his mind briefly, then made a slight wave of indifference. "Don't worry about it, Carson. I'm supposed to have four hundred and fifty replacement heifers. I think Clem had something like four hundred cows. Maybe twenty more or twenty less. You take what you think is your cut and I'll take the rest. If there's half a hundred or so we're doubtful about, you take 'em."

Jared looked at young Hedrich. Casey smiled over at him. All that earlier doubt was gone now. "I need fifty more head of cattle like I need a bullet hole in the brisket."

Al Putnam was watching Jared. He saw Carson's lingering look at Casey, tried to define it, couldn't, and swung forward to gaze out where the town of Cinnebar was firming up dead ahead.

"Hate to fling cold water on all this generosity," he growled, "but we're a long way from dividing up those cattle yet. There's a man named Brogan down in town, and a man named Aleo. They just might have some unreasonable objection to what we got in mind."

Again the men dropped down into silence. Each one of them studied Cinnebar in its setting of gray murkiness. If there were lights burning, they cast no warming glow. A dog barked somewhere, evidently scenting strange riders. Other dogs took it up, throwing their voices back and forth. A rooster crowed and a man walked heavily out of the livery barn to look up and down the roadway, expectorate, scratch tousled hair, and turn to go back inside. He saw that bunched-up quiet body of riders emerging from the northward gloom, stood a long time watching them, then evidently saw something that caused him to whip upright, remain that way for a second or two, then go darting back into the barn.

Al Putnam was speaking. The others were looking over at him and listening; they did not see that liveryman. "I think we can do this without a lot of hoorawing," Putnam was saying. "Aleo sleeps up over the Palace. Brogan's got an apartment up there, too. They'll be dead to the world about now. Look yonder, look at the town. Quiet as a church."

"Or a tomb," muttered a Circle Dot cowboy.

Putnam ignored this. "Carson, you and Keith go around behind the Palace. The rest of us'll split up, half in front and half over at the livery barn. That way, I figure, we'll either catch 'em abed, or, if not, at least they won't be able to get to their horses at the barn. One way or the other, we've got 'em boxed up in town here."

Winston reined over beside Jared. "Aleo'll fight, Carson. If you spy him, don't give him a chance. He's deadlier'n a snake and ten times as fast."

Jared nodded; he hadn't needed that advice; he'd made up his mind long ago that when he and Pete Aleo met, he'd start shooting.

XVII

They took the horses bearing those two dead renegades to the rack in front of Brogan's Palace Saloon, tied them there in plain sight, then split up. Cinnebar was as hushed as any town would be at 4:00 a.m.

Jared and Keith Winston reined around, rode northward to an alleyway entrance, swung eastward, then cut southward down through a lot of débris, broken bottles, and cast-off broken chairs, boxes, and general litter, bound for the back of Brogan's place. Unexpectedly somewhere around the front a man's high cry rang out. Jared yanked back, swung a quizzical look at Winston, and waited for whatever came next. It was not a very long wait. Overhead, up above the Palace Saloon, a window being flung upward made its abrasive sound.

"Duck!" cried Jared, throwing himself sideways out of the saddle.

A gun exploded from up there. Jared, his horse between himself and whoever was firing downward, rolled clear, then looked for Winston. All he could make out in the little time he had for looking was that Keith's saddle was empty and his horse was fidgeting.

"You hit?" he called softly. "Winston, you hit?"

There was no answer to this, but against the Palace's rear wall a six-gun blasted, a lashing of crimson flame lanced upward toward that opened window, and Jared had his answer anyway. Winston had not been hit but he had been badly shaken and fiercely angered.

No other shot came down into the alleyway. Jared's horse, following the initiative of Winston's animal, began moving off southward. This left Jared exposed, so he got up and darted over where he'd seen that muzzle blast.

Around front somewhere, someone opened up with a shotgun. That weapon made a roar all of its own; no one who'd ever opposed a shotgun in a fight ever forgot its awful bellow or what it did to men at close range. At once three Winchesters made their more distinct, vicious cracks in reply to the shotgun. Someone also opened up with a six-gun, throwing three fast shots. Jared distinctly heard the impact of those big slugs where wooden siding was shattered.

From behind a mound of saloon refuse Winston called back: "Carson, you all right?"

"Yeah."

"Something went wrong."

Jared had no comment. He craned outward a little to see along the saloon's upper rear wall. Daylight was still a long way off but the watery grayness with its accompanying little early morning chill limned several windows up there.

It took a while to determine which of those windows was open because no light reflected off glass.

"Carson?"

"Yeah."

"Come up here. I got an idea."

Jared went, but cautiously. Whoever had fired at them was very likely waiting for a sound to tell him where Winston and Carson now were. This alleyway was strewn with broken bottles, tin cans, any number of objects which, if a man bumped them or stepped upon them, would make a telltale noise.

"You coming?" called Winston softly.

Jared hissed at him. "Hold your horses, will you? I'm coming."

Around front someone yelled loudly: "Hey, Amber, poke your head out again."

Jared, ten feet behind Keith Winston, slowly straightened up, slowly assumed a look of total surprise. Amber? That man in front called out once more.

"You shouldn't have done it, Amber. You shouldn't have come back."

A gunshot erupted from out of the building and a man's defiant roar accompanied it. Evidently, though, that bantering rider was not endangered for his sardonic voice came right back through gunshot echoes.

"He'll kill you for sure this time, Amber. Ol'

Carson's goin' to slit your ear an' pull your gun arm through it sure this time." That prodding voice broke over into loud laughter. Three savage gunshots drowned it out.

Jared came up and dropped down where Winston was pressing up to the back wall behind a shielding mound of rubbish. He and Winston exchanged a look.

Keith said: "Looks like you didn't scare Amber as bad as you figured."

Jared had nothing to say about this. He pointed with his six-gun over where a door loomed up in the rear wall less than fifty feet away. "Never mind Amber," he growled. "Is that door what you're thinking about?"

"Yeah. You reckon we stand a chance?"

Jared leaned out to study that door. It would probably be locked but that presented no great obstacle. A .44 slug would blow it open, but he'd never been in the Palace Saloon but that one time, the night Clem Forsythe was killed, and had no idea how the building was laid out. There'd be a backroom, no doubt a storeroom of some kind beyond that door, but beyond that he had no idea what they'd encounter. He eased back.

"You ever been in the rear of the saloon?" he asked Winston, and got back a head shake.

"No. But what I'm thinking is that we've got to get inside sooner or later. We'll never smoke 'em out from the alley or from around front."

This was true enough. Jared leaned outward for another look. While he was like that, a fierce gun duel broke out around front again. For almost a full minute this savage exchange rocked the town. Then it stopped as abruptly as it had commenced. Al Putnam's recognizable voice bawled forth in high anger.

"Brogan, you and those men up there with you come out! You're under arrest!"

At once a voice Jared had heard only once or twice before, but which he recognized unmistakably now as belonging to the big, hook-nosed, and arrogant Harry Brogan came right back. "You're not going to arrest anyone, Putnam, you old fool. But even if you could, you wouldn't have a charge that'd stick."

"No?" Putnam called back. "How about rustling, to start with?"

Brogan's booming, derisive laugh fluted outward from up over his saloon. "I never rustled anything in my life. You couldn't prove that in a million years."

"An accessory to rustling!" roared Putnam, correcting his earlier, angrier statement. "And an accessory to Forsythe's deliberate killing. Also an accessory to Amber's attempt on Carson's life."

"Anything else?" called Harry Brogan. "Putnam, you simpleton, you make me laugh."

"Resisting arrest. Defying an officer of the law

in performance of his duty. I can name 'em off until sunup," said Putnam, his voice turning sharp again. He had been stung by Brogan's derision. Jared could hear it in his voice.

Brogan laughed again, a nasty, contemptuous sound that rang clearly out over town. Beside Jared, Keith Winston, also listening, growled a bitter word and called Brogan a fighting name in a low voice. He squirmed to start circulation back into his cramped big legs and swiveled his eyes over to Jared.

"I'd give fifty good cows to be able to face Brogan alone right now."

Jared was unimpressed. He said shortly: "Keep your cows. You'll get the chance."

That unidentified, bantering voice took up the catcalling next. Jared thought that must be Frank Silvius. The voice was reedy and irritating to hear. "Hey, Amber!" that voice called out. "Where's your two rustlin' friends . . . that big feller with the floppy hat and his stupid-actin' friend?"

No answer was forthcoming to this question. A moment later the prodding voice went on again, saying: "It's light enough now, Amber. Look out a window down at the saloon hitch rack."

It was light enough now, Jared saw, for those overhead men to make out those two renegades stiffening upon their saddles. In fact it looked to Jared as though within a few minutes now, the sun would jump up out of the glowing, pale east. He raised his gun, concentrated upon checking its loads, growled at Winston to do the same, then, not heeding an anguished roar from upstairs, he jerked his head.

"Come on, let's go see about that door."

As Winston stood up, he cocked his head to hear that roar and its afterward echoes. "I guess Amber looked out an' saw his friends down there. I guess there'll be some queasy bellies up there among Brogan's friends now."

Jared nodded, only half hearing this. He was picking each foot up high and bringing it down very gently in order to approach the door without making a sound. He made it. So did Keith Winston.

Keith pushed his gun up to within two inches of the latch and cocked it. Jared shook his head at him. "Wait until the shooting starts around front again."

They waited, standing there quite exposed and with a rushing, quick warmth sweeping outward and downward from the far-away east where the sun finally swept up over the earth's distant curving.

Whoever had that shotgun, let off a blast again. This time, Jared and Keith heard glass tinkle. Winchesters furiously replied, making a roar of gun thunder. Jared nodded and Winston splintered the door's molding with one shot.

They jumped inside half crouched, half expecting blinding gunfire where they stood in a gloomy, stale-smelling room with laden shelves, but the only gunfire came from onward out in the yonder roadway, and overhead where reverberations like shock waves made the floor and walls quiver.

Jared moved out. He crossed this storeroom, peered around a second door, this one hanging ajar, saw the saloon's main room, empty now with its front windows smashed and one of its batwing doors hanging askew, riddled and nearly shot loose from its hinges, drew back, and looked around for Winston. Keith was pushing in a cartridge to replace the one he'd shot the door latch off with. A man in the predicament of those two never permitted a lull to pass without making certain his gun was at all times fully loaded and ready. Jared beckoned Winston forward. They passed on out into the saloon proper. There, Winston, acting on the spur of the moment, ducked over behind the bar, scooped up a sawed-off shotgun kept under the bar for emergencies, checked both barrels, snapped the weapon closed, and, satisfied, returned to Jared, his face twisted into a bitter, ugly grin.

That tumult out front dwindled again. Jared swung toward a battered stairway leading upstairs, went over by it, and stepped away from view. Winston crossed over to halt opposite Jared at the base of those scarred steps. Overhead, they could both hear men's voices and their solid footfalls. One man, either injured or badly frightened, said loudly to the others up there: "We got to get out of here. Listen, they might fire the place. There's a couple of 'em out back. They might . . ."

"Shut up," snarled a low, vibrant voice that Jared thought probably belonged to Pete Aleo. "Will, you took your chances when you came back, so dammit all stop whinin' and get back to that window."

A second voice spoke up now, this one matter-of-fact, crisp, and unafraid. At first Jared did not recognize it. "Leave him alone, Pete. He's right anyway. We got to get out of here. They won't fire the buildin'. The whole damned town'd go if they tried that. But they'll keep us bottled up here until we're finished."

Aleo's reply to this was so low neither Jared nor Keith could make out the words. Then that crisp voice answered and Jared finally recognized it. That voice belonged to Harry Brogan.

"I don't know how they got everythin' figured out an' right now I don't care about that. They did it, Pete, that's what counts. . . . All right, we should've had someone watchin' that damned Carson, but we didn't, so he and those others caught us like this. Pete, that's water under the bridge. I'm not concerned with today any more. I'm thinkin' about tomorrow. How we're goin' to get out of here with our hides all in one piece."

Aleo's low mumble did not reply to this. For a while nothing more was said. That hidden attacker across the road somewhere who Jared thought was probably Frank Silvius of the Circle Dot started his insults again, all of them directed to Will Amber. Jared thought that Silvius must know Amber quite well, must be particularly antagonistic toward him.

"Good thing you returned the shoein' nippers you borrowed!" called Silvius to Will Amber. "Even if you did nick hell out of the cuttin' edges. I'd hate like hell to have to sue your estate to get 'em back now, Will."

Amber roared a foul curse at Silvius, got back a hooting laugh, and emptied a six-gun downward into the roadway, evidently trying in this way to flush Circle Dot's range boss out where he could see him.

Aleo's snarl came louder, when Amber's last shell had been fired. "You stupid damned fool. That's what they want you to do, fire yourself out." Aleo paused. Jared heard his spurred boots moving, then he said, still in the same fierce tone: "Harry, make a trade with Putnam. Offer him Amber for two saddled horses for us and an hour's start."

Brogan's dour reply to this was short, final, and indistinguishable to either Jared or Keith, but they got the drift of it. Brogan wasn't going to lose Amber's gun if he could help it.

XVIII

Jared had no intention of going up those stairs. Across from him Keith Winston, with that ugly little sawed-off shotgun balancing in his two big hands, stood still and wary, looking up where he could hear men moving. Once, he turned, looked straight at Jared, and inquiringly lifted his eyebrows. Jared shook his head; he didn't know what Keith had in mind but whatever it was, it possibly involved going upstairs, and Jared had no intention at all of doing that.

They stood there, waiting. If Harry Brogan meant to get clear of his Palace Saloon, short of leaping out a window, there was only the stairway. He would, Jared felt confident, sooner or later, come down from up there.

Sheriff Putnam again called upon Brogan to surrender, and Brogan answered about like he had the first time Putnam had made that demand, only this time Brogan's refusal was not derisive; it was simply contemptuous and adamant.

Brogan, Jared thought, was beginning to realize fully his hopelessness up there. He looked over at Keith Winston and away from him. Winston was ready and waiting; he seemed also to realize that Brogan would have to come down, and soon.

Jared twisted to gaze out across the beautifully

sunlit road where morning's freshness was not entirely spoiled by gunsmoke. He could see the livery barn, southward a short distance and on across the way. He could even make out that little bakery below the barn. But he could not see a single man anywhere he looked, and during the lulls, like now, if one overlooked raw bullet scars upon wooden siding, broken windows, and the total absence of traffic outside, Cinnebar seemed as pleasantly basking in good springtime warmth as any little cow town could be.

Winston hissed, drawing Jared back around in a hurry. Winston gestured up the stairs. Jared pressed over close to the left-hand baluster, faded out from an overhead sighting, and listened. A man's spurred boots were stepping forward toward that upstairs landing. Jared nodded at Winston, and Keith also faded out.

For the space of a long-held breath there was not another sound. A man's foot stepped out; it settled downward making the first stair plank groan under weight. Jared had no way of knowing who that was up there, but thought it might be Will Amber. He was right. Amber took another descending step and said over one shoulder: "Come on, Harry. The place's a wreck down here."

"Never mind that," came Brogan's sharp tone. "Is it all clear?"

"Sure," said Amber, making his voice sound

just a little patronizing. Jared thought he was doing this to strike back at Aleo for practically calling Amber a coward. "Sure it's all clear. It's even safe for Pete."

That time two sets of booted feet sidled across the ceiling above. Jared heard the low, sneering voice say: "Safe for me, is it, you stupid simpleton. Go all the way down if you got so much guts, and look out into the alleyway."

That was Aleo speaking; Jared knew him now. He peered around under the stairway's boarded-up back for Winston, saw Keith crouching opposite him, trying to make his considerable size and bulk smaller.

Amber's long legs appeared. He was descending now with almost complete confidence. Three more steps and his right hand came into view. Amber had a cocked six-gun fisted, but he was carrying it almost carelessly. Suddenly a flurry of shots erupted from on across the road and Amber gave a big start. But so did Jared start. He had not realized how tightly wound up he'd been, watching that slow, inexorable descent.

Brogan roared something to Aleo and those two evidently ran across to the roadside windows to return that inexplicable gunfire. Less than fifteen feet from where Winston crouched with his cocked shotgun, and from where Jared stood like a stone with his cocked six-gun trained upon Will Amber's partially visible body, Amber kneeled upon the stairs and threw a number of shots out across the roadway, firing past shattered glass windows. He had no inkling at all that death was less than twenty feet away, not even when he twisted around, sat down upon the steps, and began reloading.

Keith gently raised his shotgun. Jared caught his attention, violently shook his head, and stepped out around the banister, pushed his six-gun up to within five feet of the completely dumbfounded man on the steps, and placed one finger over his lips signaling for Keith to be absolutely silent.

Keith Winston stepped out upon Amber's other side, brushed the rustler's back with those two unmistakably joined, big-bore barrels, and Amber got white to the hairline. He had his gun in his lap; he was helpless and he knew it.

Jared backed off, still covering Amber, made a brusque gesture for the rustler to get up, to come on down from the stairs. Amber obeyed, moving like a man in a trance. Once, at the baseboard, he twisted to see who had the shotgun. Winston's flinty, wire-tight face looked very deadly. Amber moved on over toward Jared, held out his gun, and seemed on the verge of fainting.

Jared pushed his captive around under the stairwell. Keith came up behind Amber and the three of them waited out the furious exchange going on elsewhere. When this ultimately dwindled, Jared raised his gun, placed its cold snout just below Amber's right ear, and spoke in a low but audible whisper: "Your friends out there tied across their horses said they wouldn't come back, either. They're dead, Amber."

The rustler wilted. Saliva formed at the outer corners of his mouth. "I . . . I had to come back an' get my bedroll over at the barn. Honest to God that's all I come . . ."

"You saw us ride in, didn't you?"

"Yes, but . . ."

"And ran over here to warn Brogan."

Amber's tongue darted around his lips and back into his mouth again. Jared pressed his gun barrel a little harder. "Call up to Brogan and Aleo," he ordered. "Tell them it's clear out back."

"You won't shoot, Carson?"

"Not if they come down."

Amber hesitated no longer. He raised his voice and sang out, making it believable, making it loud and clear.

"Hey, Harry, it's all clear out back! Them fellers who was out there are gone. I think we can make it."

For a long moment no answer came from upstairs, then Brogan moved over to the landing, looked down, and called out: "Will, don't do anything to draw their fire down there or it'll come through the damned front windows."

Amber didn't wait to be prompted for his reply

to this. He said: "Sure not. Hey, one of you fetch along my shotgun."

Jared and Keith Winston exchanged a look. Amber might be terrified, but he was putting his whole heart in this bit of treachery, was making it entirely believable to those men up there.

Someone started down. Jared pressed that reminding gun barrel harder. Amber braced into this pressure, his breathing uneven, his eyes rolling with pure fear.

"Hey, Will!" Brogan called. "Where are you?"

Amber could not reply without giving away the hiding place under the stairwell of his captors, and bringing upon all three of them a volley of wild shots, so he hung there, saying nothing at all, his glazing eyes fixed upon the back boards of the stairway directly in front of him.

"Hey, Will, dammit . . . !"

Jared moved now. He lowered his six-gun, stepped sideways where he could see upstairs, and this blurred movement made Harry Brogan whirl toward him.

Brogan had a shotgun in his left hand, a six-gun in his right hand. He recognized Jared Carson in the smallest fraction of a second. His eyes widened; his lips curled brutally downward. He gave a great leap forward and downward throwing up his right hand and firing as he did this.

Jared did not move, not even when that bullet

plowed a red welt along his left side over his ribs, tugging at him. He pulled the trigger, lifted the hammer, and pulled it again. Brogan's arrogant, hawk-like face was in mid-air when those slugs struck him; it smoothed out in an expression of astonishment. Then Brogan came down upon the last step, lurched, fell, and dropped his pistol. Jared lifted the hammer for a third shot.

Brogan's crooked fingers scrabbled desperately at the sawdusted floor. He gasped and fought to raise himself, using Amber's shotgun for that purpose, but he couldn't do it. He sagged, fell face down, and let off a long, bubbly sigh.

Overhead a six-gun exploded; a piece of railing splintered from impact, and Jared instinctively flinched. Aleo was up there, standing, wide-legged and defiant. He took one step downward, roared out a challenge, and took another downward step. That time he fired again. This second slug splintered back boards. Aleo had figured out where his enemies were. Keith Winston was showered with splinters from that second shot. He bawled a ripped-out curse, jumped sideways, raised his shotgun, and at a range of less than ten feet fired up through the stairs.

Jared could see Aleo. He saw that lethal charge lift the gunman off his feet, hurl him back up three steps, and leave him staggering there. Jared raised his weapon to end it, but there was no need. Aleo's gun clattered downward. He pawed at air, found no support, and pitched headlong. He struck soddenly, rolled, and came all the way down to land, broken and dead, within five feet of Harry Brogan.

Not until that last shot was fired did Will Amber come out from behind the stairwell. He stood, gazing at Aleo and Brogan. He turned his back on those two and waited for either Winston or Carson to say something, to do something.

Jared ignored Amber, jerked his head at Winston, and said: "Go holler out the window to Putnam that it's all over."

Winston was moving off. Jared was grimly, distastefully staring at Will Amber while he punched out spent casings and plugged in fresh loads, when a thunderous roar rocked the room.

Jared dropped flat, rolled, and stared over where Harry Brogan was gaspingly fighting to hold himself up off the floor. In Brogan's right hand was that six-gun. Six feet away Will Amber fell with a loud, rustling sound, shot through from back to front, and killed.

Brogan and Carson exchanged a long stare. Jared could have fired but he didn't. Brogan's gun arm fell, his glazing eyes lost their ability to focus, and finally the big, hook-nosed man's head nodded as though he were overcome with an irresistible tiredness, and gently fell forward into the sawdust. Harry Brogan had repaid Will Amber's treachery.

Jared got up, struck at adhering sawdust, and saw Keith Winston standing over by the window with his mouth hanging open.

"Call out," said Jared. "That really ended it."

Winston yelled for Casey Hedrich, for Sheriff Putnam, and the Circle Dot riders. He afterward seated himself upon the window sill, crooked his shotgun in his arms, and solemnly stared over where Brogan lay.

Al Putnam was the first one inside the Palace. He looked at Jared, at Keith, saw that they were both unhurt, then went over and stood above Brogan, gazing gravely upon the dead man.

The others came trooping in. Circle Dot's range boss smiled flintily at dead Will Amber, crossed on over behind the bar, poured himself a stiff drink, and turned to salute with that upraised glass.

"Good bye, Amber," Silvius said. "You rotten excuse for a man. You couldn't win at poker, you couldn't win at rustlin', and now . . . you couldn't win at this."

Casey Hedrich went over to stand where Jared was. "We thought you two were inside. That's why we didn't throw any lead downstairs."

Jared put up his reloaded gun, ran a grimy hand over his face, and said nothing. He felt drained dry and empty.

"There was a hostler at the livery barn wanted to come over here and get inside with you," continued young Hedrich. "Said he worked for you, said his name was Hank Phelps. You know him?"

"Yeah, I know him. I know something else, too, Hedrich. I know I've had all the excitement these past couple of weeks I'll need to last me a long, long time, and I'd like to get out of this lousy town for a while. I'm worn down to a frazzle."

Hedrich put a quiet gaze upon Jared without saying anything for a while. Around those two, other men were moving, mumbling back and forth, and eventually ending up over at Brogan's bar where Frank Silvius was setting up the drinks.

"Maybe you'd ought to ride on out to my place, Jared. You know, tell my mother I'm all right. She'll want to know."

Jared looked into the youthful, tired face, read the consent he thought he'd heard in young Hedrich's voice, and said: "Thanks, Casey. I appreciate that. I made a bad start with you and Keith. I'm downright sorry about that. It won't ever happen again."

Jared pushed out his hand. Casey shook it, dropped it, and said: "Maybe you'd ought to have a drink before you go."

"Naw, thanks just the same, but right now all I want is some good, clean creek water. I'll get that out at Five Pointed Star where I'll wash and clean up before riding on over to the Circle Dot. *Adiós*, Casey."

"*Adiós*, Jared."

Sunlight struck down hard, outside the wrecked Palace Saloon. Here and there a man or two showed himself as Cinnebar became totally and lastingly silent. Jared saw these things without heeding them. Across the road Hank Phelps, with a long-barreled rifle in one hand, was watching Jared cross through the dust toward him. Hank leaned the rifle upon a wall and waited.

When he was close, Jared said: "You got a fresh horse for me?"

Phelps nodded. "Sure." He didn't move though he said: "Brogan . . . ?"

"Dead."

"Aleo . . . ?"

"Dead."

"Then come along. We'll give you the best horse in the place."

Ten minutes later Jared went loping out of Cinnebar westerly, a big, powerful horse under him, a warm sun on his back, and a new start dead ahead.

ABOUT THE AUTHOR

Lauran Paine who, under his own name and various pseudonyms has written over a thousand books, was born in Duluth, Minnesota. His family moved to California when he was at a young age and his apprenticeship as a Western writer came about through the years he spent in the livestock trade, rodeos, and even motion pictures where he served as an extra because of his expert horsemanship in several films starring movie cowboy Johnny Mack Brown. In the late 1930s, Paine trapped wild horses in northern Arizona and even, for a time, worked as a professional farrier. Paine came to know the Old West through the eyes of many who had been born in the previous century, and he learned that Western life had been very different from the way it was portrayed on the screen. "I knew men who had killed other men," he later recalled. "But they were the exceptions. Prior to and during the Depression, people were just too busy eking out an existence to indulge in Saturday-night brawls." He served in the U.S. Navy in the Second World War and began writing for Western pulp magazines following his discharge. It is interesting to note that all of his earliest novels (written under his own name and the pseudonym Mark Carrel) were published in the British market and he soon had as strong a following in that country as in the United States. Paine's Western fiction is characterized by strong plots, authenticity, an apparently effortless ability to construct situation and character, and a preference for building his stories upon a solid foundation of historical fact. *Adobe Empire* (1956), one of his best early novels, is a fictionalized account of the last twenty years in the life of trader William Bent and, in an off-trail way, has a melancholy, bittersweet texture that is not easily forgotten. In later novels like *Cache Cañon* (Five Star Westerns, 1998) and *Halfmoon Ranch* (Five Star Westerns, 2007), he showed that the special magic and power of his stories and characters had only matured along with his basic themes of changing times, changing attitudes, learning from experience, respecting Nature, and the yearning for a simpler, more moderate way of life.

Books are produced in the United States using U.S.-based materials

Books are printed using a revolutionary new process called THINKtech™ that lowers energy usage by 70% and increases overall quality

Books are durable and flexible because of smythe-sewing

Paper is sourced using environmentally responsible foresting methods and the paper is acid-free

Center Point Large Print
600 Brooks Road / PO Box 1
Thorndike, ME 04986-0001 USA

(207) 568-3717

US & Canada:
1 800 929-9108
www.centerpointlargeprint.com